Those Who Can't

**CALUMET
EDITIONS**

Minneapolis

First Edition May 2023
Those Who Can't. Copyright © 2023 by Wade Laughlin.
All rights reserved.

This is a work of fiction. All of the characters, names, incidents, organizations, and dialogue are either the products of the author's imagination or are used fictitiously.

10 9 8 7 6 5 4 3 2 1

ISBN: 978-1-960250-84-1

Cover and book design by Gary Lindberg

Those Who Can't

Wade Laughlin

**CALUMET
EDITIONS**

Minneapolis

"I am but mad north-north-west.
When the wind is southerly, I know a hawk from a handsaw."

Hamlet, II.ii.

To Emily Christensen (Weitz) and Parker Young, who both told me at very different points in my life that if I ever wrote a book, they would read it. Challenge accepted.

Prologue

Maria Clefthorne drew in a breath that reached the bottom of her lungs, hoping it would give her a moment to calm down and convey to this insolent young jock-stain that he had upset the fourth-most powerful person in the United States Central Security Service.

"Your report," she said, "says that the agent was sent into the wrong building."

"Yeah," he smirked.

She stood over him like a slow-moving thunderstorm and spread her hands out on the mahogany desk as if power could radiate down from her steel-colored jacket through her runner's sinewy wrists and out from ten perfectly dark, gleaming fingernails. Her eyes, as gray as her jacket, bored into his stupid face. No "Yes, Director Clefthorne?" from this cub? Not even a "Yes, ma'am?" Good God, she could easily seize her ornate pen and ram the tip through the rubbery but ultimately vulnerable sheath of his carotid artery—

"I'm sorry," he said, his mirth more an uneasy breath now. "Yes, *ma'am*."

"Don't do that."

"Sorry, ma'am. I was trained well."

In her head, she hollered, *Spend less time ascertaining my thoughts from my micro-expressions, and* more *time* not *screwing up every single facet of this mission*. Instead, she took another lung-stretching breath. Not a strand of her perfectly straight auburn hair fell out of level.

"Clearly," she exhaled. "And clearly not. Why am I only hearing about this now? You and I both work—at least, for now—for the CSS and, by extension, the NSA. 'It, um, got lost in the spam filter!' does not pass muster here."

Again, came the chuckle. Cooper Baird was twenty-five, with a few successful missions and one of those stupid short beards, and he thought he could chuckle while being dressed down. By *her*.

"Funny story, our agent was supposed to go into the target school as a teacher, and some rando—sorry, a civilian—with the exact same name applies for a teaching job there, and so all my checklists are solid green up and down. Cray-zee, right?"

If he added "Wocka wocka!" she would actually have him killed.

"Do you see the giant insignia behind my head?" One perfect fingernail pointed to the insignia on the wall—the giant eagle holding a skeleton key—but her eyes did not leave his. "Do you see the word 'Intelligence' on it?"

"You have to admit, boss—I mean, ma'am..."

She took another deep breath, trying not to grit her teeth. "The dossier has the alias name on it. It's the weirdest goddamn name I've ever seen on an identity sheet."

"Yeah, the name—" The gears in the boy's head turned almost audibly. "L-E-G-something-something-B-B? Did an umlaut sneak in there? I think it's Polish. Wait, is Poland a country? Still? Of course, it is—not..." Baird's face betrayed a moment of genuine self-doubt, possibly for the first time in his short professional career.

She would have his corpse wrapped in a map of Europe before it was dumped in the Potomac. Where did they get these kids? Another deep breath.

"And someone with the *same name* shows up looking for the cover job?"

He made his fingers into a tent in front of his face and leaned back. "Yeah, what are the odds, right?"

"We don't play the odds. There are no odds. Because we have to control everything, or your co-workers die. So where is our agent?"

Now he looked a bit sheepish. "So, the different building I mentioned in the report? He got hired there. He's knee-deep in it."

"*What?!*"

"These schools," he shot out—at least now there was some remorseful panic— "these suburban school names are, like, interchangeable. Oak Grove? Aspen Heights? Maple Valley? It's all the same. By the time I realized he was in the wrong school… and, ma'am, how does a physical asset like this end up in a *school* if you don't—"

"I do mind you asking," Clefthorne growled. The permutations spun out in her head. She would get a hold on this—she hadn't gotten this far up, as a woman, by letting male idiocy derail her. "But I'll tell you, it's not a normal school. It's a sort of vocational program—run by the HRB."

"The…?

She sat down, and he finally exhaled. Was that a small bead of sweat on his forehead? "The HRB is the Human Resources division of the FBI, and they've been piloting programs in which trainers, posing as teachers—"

"Oh, oh," he said, eyes widening.

"Oh, *what?*"

"My one report said that this guy with the same ridiculous name was, ah, handled a bit after his interview, so it makes sense that there's some future, or current, operatives in this school." He paused. "Ma'am, this HRB—they're not friendly enough to where we could, you know, have them take care of our case of mistaken identity and, ah, kindly be persuaded to hand over this asset of yours?"

This is the first thing you've been right about, junior, Clefthorne thought. *It is mine.*

"Agent Baird, we just tried to plant our clandestine CSS operative in Maple Valley High School, which is run by the HRB. And we have CSS people on the inside of the school to make sure our guy got 'the job.' So the civilian will get hired at Maple Valley." She straightened even further in her chair and became all right angles; young Agent Baird tried not to shrink a little in his chair and failed. "To contact the HRB and say, 'Hey, looks like one of your child prodigies may have developed a pocket neutrino bomb, or a universal de-encryption key, or something of the sort, so we recently tried to steal it, even though we're all on the same team—USA! USA!, etc.—but we screwed up, and can you hand it over to us?' would be a sure way to get us all fired."

Cooper Baird studied her face without even trying to hide it. "'Us?' You mean me, right?"

"Absolutely." She didn't quite articulate it in her head because he actually had a bit of skill at reading her face, but he wouldn't be fired—he would disappear.

Did the little boy with his chest permanently puffed out just—gulp? Maria Clefthorne, the Iron Lady of the Central Security Service, hoped so.

"What do I do, Director?"

She spread her fingers across the desk again. "This—civilian—who is now working at the HRB school. What do we know about him?"

Part I

1 – The Interview

Dave Legnagyszerübb backed carefully into the parking space, despite the lot being completely empty. A red-and-white MAPLE VALLEY HIGH SCHOOL sign squatted over the searing blacktop, reminding parents of 2017 Spring Registration Conferences in yellow text that scrolled under today's date: JULY 23RD, 2019.

Dave stopped when he caught his reflection in the rearview mirror. His car was now an oven. Damp strands of dirty-blond hair were plastered against his too-wide forehead, and red blossoms threatened to take over his face. Despite the heat, he closed his eyes and imagined a stuff-sack for a sleeping bag, drawstrings and nylon held in his hands.

"Put everything from the past away," he said. In his mind, he shoved everything he didn't need right now so far down into the stuff-sack as to be inaccessible—even to himself. He exhaled and regarded himself in the crooked mirror, his eyes completely locked on his reflection. The car was a sauna.

Before entering for this interview, he needed a clean soul—the soul of a new teacher. He imagined all the work he'd done before as filthy socks and sweaty shirts all shoved down in the bottom of a stuff-sack where they couldn't be seen or even smelled.

"It's stowed away," he said in a low voice. "What am I doing here? I'm here to become a real classroom teacher." Finally, after a spell, he wiped away the sweat on his forehead with his sleeve.

He reached over and pulled the manila folder—scrounged from his last sub job in Oak Heights—from the worn but clean passenger seat, quickly making sure his resumé and cover letter were there, but just as quickly leaving sweaty thumbprints on the folder. Frantically, he checked the armpits on his best shirt, saw the stains forming, and nearly leaped out of the car, dashing absurdly across the cracked asphalt and into the yawning open doors of yet another faceless suburban high school, from which later in the day would issue a thanks-for-your-interest phone call, and then, a month later, a we-need-subs-and-even-you-will-suffice phone call from someone farther down the food chain.

"No, be *confident*, you worthless idiot, and stop thinking like that," he whispered to himself as he followed the inspiring white-on-brown signs to the main office. The signs were glued to cinder block walls painted white, illuminated only by recessed yellow lights and, perhaps, a stray beam of natural light that had, like so many secondary students, become lost on its way to the office. At some point, a logo had been hung on the interminable cinder-block wall, and only the glue remained—he thought he could make out "Fidelity" in the outline. The only glass panes outside of what could have been the counselors' office contained wired mesh. Although people often likened schools to prisons, Dave thought psychiatric facilities were probably a more apt comparison.

Since all signs only led to either the main office or a gym, he wondered if the terrible teachers who sometimes were hired as head coaches simply showed up in the gym and started playing 21 or something while the non-athletic teaching candidates just walked past the interview, out to the loading dock, and out of education forever.

The main office had the classic high school summer front desk staff of two: secretary and oscillating fan. Dave knew that while the teachers were away, this secretary was probably balancing class sizes and ordering building materials through her lunch break, as well as handling any and all asinine parent summer queries on the phone. She looked up from her computer and over her reading glasses; the pink and blue frames matched both her earrings and the broach on her blouse. Sharp gray eyes looked out over smartly applied lipstick that complemented everything else, and she smiled at Dave. "May I help you?"

"Yes, my name is Davi—I mean, Dave, and I'm here for an interview. For the English teaching job. I mean, position." He was trying to smile, but it simply felt as though the corners of his lips were being forced backward by some invisible orthodontal torture device.

"David, did you say your name was, young man?" she asked, eyes cross-referencing a tapestry of loose paper on her desk.

He paused, perhaps because the "young man" caught him off guard. She couldn't be more than forty, with no dyes or gray streaks in her hair. "It's Dave, actually. Even on my birth certificate. Guess my mom didn't know better."

Now it was her turn to pause, her eyes locking on his face as if she were trying to determine if he was an immediate threat to student safety. Dave remembered a story involving a tech ed student who'd cut his thumb off, screamed, and run from the classroom, the flannel-clad teacher on his heels. Another student had picked the thumb out of the dust collector, walked it into the office, and set it gently on the office lady's desk before collapsing. She'd packed the digit in ice and calmly called EMS. This type of woman did not flinch.

"Sure thing," the secretary replied. "They'll call you in a minute." She gestured to a set of old chairs with a hand that held three Post-its and two pens of different colors in its fingers.

Before he could plaster on another smile and say thanks, her overburdened hand hit a cat-eared coffee mug on the edge of the desk, sending it teetering toward oblivion. Dave's reserve of twitchy adrenaline kicked in, and he snagged the mug handle between his index and middle finger as the secretary gave an involuntary "Oh—" Hot tea splashed on the back of his hand.

"Got it," he said, now able to smile more naturally since his hand had been scalded.

"Oh, *thank* you, Mr. Davis!" she exclaimed. "Are you okay?" She was quickly wiping up the desk with one hand while holding bunches of paper in binder clips with another, but she regarded him with kind eyes. "Silly me for drinking such hot tea on a hot day, too."

"No problem, just glad to help. You know, the ancient Chinese drank hot beverages to cool themselves," he said stupidly. Now that his momentary success was gone, he was back to his old self. "I'm Dave, by the way."

"So nice to meet you, Mr. Davies," she said. "I'm Ellen. And thank you again so much. It looks like they're ready for you in the conference room through there."

"Thanks," he said, pulling his lips back again. He hit his hip on the desk as he made his way back into the conference room, stamping the tea's remnants into a damp arc on his cheap khakis.

Eight minutes later, he entered the conference room, which featured the lighting and decor of a gulag interrogation chamber: beige metal cabinets, dying fluorescent bulbs straining in cracked plastic, and the scents of various mold varietals. Someone introduced him to the interview committee around the table, but the nervous stew of his brain seemed unable to process them as individuals in the low, yellow light. There was a matronly woman with too-red cheeks and purplish lipstick; a small, square man with small, square glasses; a man whose ballooning frame had been stuffed into a purple tracksuit monogrammed with MAPLE VALLEY VOLLEYBALL; a lady with crossed arms who acknowledged Dave with a frown. In Dave's clouded mind, however, they all leaned back in their olive-green office chairs in unison and glared, like Easter Island statues, past him.

The young woman to his right, though, offered him a bright, if not predatory, smile and introduced herself as the assistant principal. She wore complementary earrings, bracelets, rings, and hairpins in her dark, wavy hair. She seemed—

"Young," she said, smiling with bright hygienist's teeth. "I'm Courtney Young, and I work with the English department here." She made a sweeping gesture over the table at the statues, and her bracelets clanged in accompaniment. "Thanks for coming in today." She pulled the top sheet of paper off what appeared to be a three-foot stack of resumés, and he reflexively crinkled his manila folder between sweaty finger pads. Frowning, she regarded it as if for the first time. Was that a pondering frown or a disquieted one? He couldn't tell. Her necklaces hung suspended from her neck as she evaluated his run-of-the-mill career objectives, paltry experience, and bush-league font.

"Yes... thanks for coming in today, Mr. Lay... Laydell..."

"It's Legnagyszerübb," he said, sweaty finger now rearranging the ink of his resumé. "Kids usually call me Mr. L."

Ah, "kids." As if he had been teaching nonstop and changing lives since getting his license. As if he'd distinguished himself as anything but a body in a room.

She plowed on anyway, her brow furrowing as the necklace parts swayed in midair. "Mr. Laganagga…"

"Just 'L' is okay, Mrs. Young. The rest of the letters are silent."

One of the statues let out a guffaw of displeasure—it was more like gas escaping a sewer pipe.

He *almost* added, "that was a joke." Somewhere, in the ceiling, a blower kicked on.

She looked up from his resumé with a determined smile, teeth blasting blue-ice light at him. For a moment, he thought she might just send him home. Despite Mrs. Young's age and winning smile, she did not have time to mince words, Dave thought, yet she insisted that she say his name correctly.

Eventually—thankfully!—she got to the standard interview questions. Yes, he was able to use education technology effectively. Yes, parent involvement is paramount to a child's education, even though it's the eight-hours-of-gaming-per-weeknight *kid*, not the second shift, working *parent*, sitting in class, drawing rocketlike genitalia that propels themselves into John Proctor's angry, open mouth on page 576 of the text. Yes, he answered, strangely enough, it was better to pull a student aside for a private, non-threatening conversation about problem behavior rather than chastise them in front of the class like it was 1972, and teachers actually still did that.

The statues responded to his responses with bored nods of assent, and Mrs. Young smiled hard. At the end, she asked if Dave ("Mr. Leelzelbub") had any questions about the school.

"No, Mrs. Young," he said, even though he knew he should have at least one question—did he not *specifically* think of some questions to ask on the car ride over? What was wrong with him? "Unless it's about us playing a basketball game in the gym to help me get this job!"

The statues didn't move, but Ms. Young's face contorted into a hybrid of wince and shrug.

Why? *Why* did his mouth insist on losing thoughts that his brain had not properly assembled or vetted?

However, Ms. Young did not let the silence last long. "Okay. It was very nice to meet you, Dave," she said, extending a hand that was on the verge of bony. Some of her bracelet features got caught under his grip. She seemed not to notice.

He shook hands with the Easter Island statues. The man who appeared to have been painted into the purple tracksuit said, "It was nice ta meet ya, bud." He didn't release Dave's hand, and though a tobacco-stained smile hung on his face, the small eyes behind the square glasses were hard. "I guess we'll be, ah, lookin' at yer resumé here inna minute." With a crinkle of tracksuit fabric, he released Dave's hand.

Was that a parting shot from the guy he'd already begun to think of as "Coach Rotundo?" Did it mean his well-crafted resumé was now catching gum in the recycle bin? Or was he being paranoid since his comment might be a glimmer of hope in this cave-collapse of an interview? Should he say something—okay, attempt to say something—back to Coach Rotundo? A "You, too, bud?"

In the dimly lit interview room, Dave only smiled, turned and left, and proceeded to thoughtlessly take several random turns in the small back-office hallways before he spotted the secretary—Ellen—behind her front desk. He gave a sweaty wave and told her to have a great afternoon.

"Oh, and you too, Mr. Legnagyszerübb! It was nice meeting you!"

Ellen went back to sorting, marking, and referencing attendance boundaries on the computer. All the work to run a school while, he imagined, Mrs. Young was balling up his resumé and banking it into the recycling bin in the back room while she allowed Rotundo to keep on desecrating children and the institution of education.

2 - The Exit

He exited the office and looked up at the brown and white sign in the hallway. But after several strides in the direction of the exit, he found the fire doors for that hallway closed. He squinted at his now creased and sweat-stained folder as if it contained some secret path out of this dull labyrinth. Maybe this was hell: trying to leave the interview you just blew, stuck in a building that did not want you there in any way, shape or form. Except the secretary *did* say his name right—unless she had, for some reason, practiced saying his name before the interview? Yet this was after calling him Davies earlier, even after he insisted—as he always did—that it was Dave, not David.

Weird. Well, he had given Ellen a chance to show she had a linguist's tongue after all, and he'd given Rotundo a chance to throw a jab. Everyone had been served. He needed to get out of here. Now.

He followed the signs towards the gymnasium, hoping there'd be a side exit. Instead, the hallway led directly to more brown doors: the basketball court, dimly lit, in the way that only old high school gyms can be dimly lit as if they're concealing missed free throws and sprained ankles in the shadows. He let out an audible "Huh," and nearly turned around. But would he wander back into the office to ask someone for directions, someone who would not be able to rein in their laughter after the return of the day's worst interviewee? Nope. He peered into that total darkness underneath old backboards at the periphery of the gym—among what was probably piles of old gymnastics mats and deflated rubber balls— and wondered at the number of class-skipping teens who had been lured into that darkness over the years. Except on this summer day, when the facilities seemed abandoned and the darkness threatening, it didn't seem alluring. Not at all.

Where was the exit? His heart beat audibly in his throat, and he was not above pushing open an alarmed door just to get out of there.

His "interview shoes" rapped loudly on the wood floor. He swallowed and contemplated a sprint-walk through the darkness to an exit—surely, he could walk right out of one of these anonymous gym doors in the dark perimeter and leave this school forever. His shoes made too much noise as he turned to look—

With almost no sound, a basketball rolled out of the darkness at him. He could not look up or look away from it, and since he could not move, he stood and stared. It rolled up his foot like a small dog, its tiny rubber *pat-pat* dribbles echoing throughout the otherwise silent gym.

His heart made the sound of the ocean in his ears, beating at full speed as he stood, completely frozen, somehow looking only now at the glare off the only illuminated part of the gym floor. The ball rolled off his toe.

Breathe. He had to breathe, and he had to fight the urge to sprint in any direction. Because running would mean panic, and there was clearly no reason at all to panic.

He pivoted, feeling the blood rush to his head, and as he faced the yellow square of light around where he had entered, he heard a *whoosh* behind his left ear. Before he could even think, his arms were pulled back behind him, and a tight, smooth cloth was pulled over his head and face.

At this moment, he remembered the young man he'd seen staring back at him in the rearview mirror as he sat in the parking lot before the interview. The image in his mind was clear. The young man's body had gone limp as if paralyzed with fear.

The sweat-stained folder fell from his hands to the gym floor, and then he had no time to cry out or protest before he was flat on his chest, the air forced out like a bellows. Suddenly blindfolded and restrained, he felt himself being dragged across the floor.

Several sets of footsteps pattered on the hardwood around him, but he heard no conferring or interrogating voices. Probing fingers dove in and out of his pockets, under his armpits, in his socks, as he heard a heavy steel door wrench open, and then the smooth gym floor rubbing against his exposed flesh changed to concrete. Through the cloth over his face, he sensed the light of the outdoors. Hands on his shoulders pushed him upright and sat him on something small and rough.

For a moment, nothing. His head was empty. Then, he craned his neck down far enough to rub the cloth covering his face against his shoulder, and after three tries, it slipped off. The heat from the parking lot hit his forehead and the summer afternoon light shimmered against the dry grass.

Looking down, he saw that his poor-teacher-interview shirt had been pulled down past his hands to restrain him. His poor-teacher-interview tie had bound his feet together, and the cloth pulled over his head had been the stretched collar of the poor-teacher-interview shirt.

Dave stood up, felt inside the pockets of his poor-teacher-interview khakis, and swore. No keys. No wallet.

He turned to look behind him just as one of those metal exterior gym doors closed with a slam.

The possibilities, each more unlikely than the next, flashed through his mind as he tried to stand up—some kids were playing a prank on him and were now uploading the video to Instagram. Some old friends thought this would be funny and would buy him a beer later. The guy in the volleyball jumpsuit hated his guts and decided to beat him up, or at least make sure he never came back. None of it made sense.

"What am I doing here?" he asked himself out loud.

For a moment, he thought about… no. That was best pushed back down into the stuff-sack of memories, crushed and stowed away.

He wriggled free enough to run—at first resembling a kid in a three-legged race, until the loop of his tie slipped free—and then jogged around the suburban brick perimeter of Maple Valley High School, towards where he figured he might have gone into the building for the interview.

But when he got back in, what would he tell them? "Yes, Ellen, I got lost on my way out of the interview, and believe it or not, I was robbed—or something like it—in your gymnasium. Call me about that job!"

He slowed his jog as he approached the front entrance.

It was locked, with the lights out. He peered inside, trying to see if the office light was on. Nothing but darkness. No doors open. If he had been the last interview of the day… and he was pretty sure he hadn't…

He turned around and saw his car right where he'd parked it. Except—

It was no longer backed into the spot. It was 180 degrees from where he'd left it. He walked slowly towards the driver's side and saw that the windows were down. Too shocked to think, he noticed his keys and wallet placed neatly on the driver's side door seat. Just on top of his sweat-stained manila folder.

3 – The Offer

"Well, the good news is," said Erik as he cleaned a pint glass with his towel, "is that you didn't lose a kidney. And you got your wallet and keys back, if not your dignity. And, kind of on a technicality, you don't have to pay double for this beer."

Dave, staring at the bar, snapped out of his reverie. "Wait, what? You're not still doing that, are you? It seems… wrong."

Erik laughed, his belly heaving under his plaid shirt. Dave couldn't remember. Did Erik ever wear plaid when he was teaching? Did he have a beer belly? Was he ever this happy? Probably no on all counts. Erik had shepherded Dave through the student teaching experience a year and a half ago, but Dave's memory of it was impressionistic at best: Post-Its covered in indecipherable lesson ideas, Erik's arms crossed over his burly chest as he listened to Dave's curriculum, shouts of distracted teens casually eating a student teacher alive, day after day. He imagined, briefly, the stuff-sack of memory, crammed with all sorts of laundry.

"It's all semantics, my man," Erik proclaimed. "What we tell people is that teachers get half-off taps during the school year." He shook his head, grinning, as he picked up another glass. "We don't tell them the beer costs twice as much during the summer."

Dave looked around. Large ceiling fans pushed air between square, wooden tables filled with patrons leaning over mugs, intent on being heard over the din. Between the colors of beer swirling around in glasses and the variety of wood paneling in Erik's brewery, the scene could have been a watercolor in various shades of tan, brown and amber. And for a hot July day, this brewery's strange approach to pricing didn't seem to be dissuading anyone from coming. "Seems to be working okay."

"Oh, man. The sheer—" he waved his hands in the air, attempting to articulate the precise word as only a former history teacher could, "*euphoria* of summer makes teachers just laugh about it. No visits from the Better Business Bureau yet. Hey, and of course, since you're sittin' here waiting for a thanks-for-trying call, first one's on me, anyway. What would you like?"

Clearly, Dave would end up getting the Staff Meeting Pilsner ("Everyone's Forced to Drink It!" said the beer listing), but he, of course, hemmed and hawed. Late Start Coffee-Infused Ale? IEP Stout ("Gets to Take Its Time")? Is this why no one hired him? Did he exude decision weakness?

For an instant, Dave was back in the sweltering parking lot, looking at himself in the rearview mirror. Then he was shoving filthy socks in the bottom of a stuff-sack—

Erik waited, both hands on the bar, with a coach's face that had coerced thousands of high schoolers to hurry up and say something. After waiting another beat, he asked, "The Pilsner?"

Dave didn't look up. "Yes, please."

He waited, not wanting to admit another small triumph of Erik's will over his own. After all, Erik had been a staff all-star at Oak Valley High when Dave had student-taught under him. Dave would watch him go around the classroom, getting every single kid to work on an essay about Rome or a speech about a Chinese dynasty, cajoling and manipulating them with his uncanny connection to every kid. He was the expert waitstaff, filling and carrying thirty-five cups of water at a time without ever spilling a drop.

Then, after well-wishing each student at the door, Erik would sit down in the nearest available desk-chair combo and put his forehead against the bacteria-ridden desktop. In the first few days of the student-teaching experience, Dave would try to pester him about his pedagogical choices and expert differentiation—the art of teaching a mob of kids, one at a time, as individuals. Erik's responses were less than enlightening. Or, to take the long view of education, more than enlightening, given that shortly after shepherding Dave into the teaching profession, Erik left it to start a brewery.

"It's killing me, kid," said Erik more than once.

"If I could teach, like, one-twentieth as well as you—" Dave sat, notepad at the ready.

Erik stared off in the distance, looking every bit the lumberjack that his ancestors probably were. "It's taking years off my life, Dave. You're the future. I need to find another line of work."

"My Secondary Pedagogical instructor says," and Dave knew it was a dumb, naive thing to say even as it slipped out of his mouth, "the day you wake up and don't want to teach is the day you should quit."

Silence. Erik kept his head on his desk.

Dave tried to walk it back, "I mean—"

"Second day of school, kid," said Erik. "Every teacher would quit on the second day, and the inmates would be running the asylum."

In the end, Dave completed his student teaching, graduated, and shuffled through various—it was best to think of them simply as unfulfilling—sub jobs. Erik, who could teach ballet to a class of manatees and who probably had to change his number to stop the flood of full-time offers, had quit to start his brewery, The Co-Curricular. And here they were.

"One Staff Meeting, on the house."

Dave took a long drink. It was a great pilsner: clean, with no tinny aftertaste. Not strange that Erik was good at brewing beer, too. If Dave tried to brew a beer, it would probably only be useful as a smelling salt for Olympic weightlifters.

"Do administrators ever come in for a beer? Are they offended by 'Everyone's Forced to Drink It?'"

"Ah, see, that's the beauty," said Erik. "I never have to worry about pissing off a principal. Ever. Again."

As if on cue, Dave's phone began to vibrate and ring. A 763 number—it must be Maple Valley. He scooted quickly off the barstool and made for outside, driven by a brief bit of hope. What if they actually offered him a job? Part of him knew they wouldn't. He had been God-awful in the interview, and then there was the incident afterward—he wouldn't even allow himself to think about it.

But now, at this moment, as he angled his way through the door and pushed the green button with his thumb, it was like those Christmas mornings all those years ago when the boxes under the tree could hold—anything. Mechanical dinosaurs, *Spider-Man* comics, Star Wars Lego sets—before you got to them, in that instant, your mind contemplated playing with these impossible toys every single day—until you opened up the box and surveyed the digital alarm clock radio. Then, Mom said from her chair through a puff of cigarette smoke, "Well, you're always talking about how you love music, so now... you can listen to any station you want. Merry Christmas, and don't thank me *too* much."

He paused for an instant, standing in the sun, taking in the moment, and then sighed as he held the phone to his ear.

After a few minutes, he came back in, eyes on his shoes as he approached his pilsner at the bar. Erik quickly shoved a few pint glasses down at the end of the bar and made his way back over, leaning both arms on the bar in the way powerful men do.

"Well, d'ya get it?"

Dave looked up, unable to contain his smile. "They offered me the job, Erik. I'm a teacher! Full time! A full-time Maple Valley Mammoth!"

"Hey!" exclaimed Erik, grabbing Dave's shoulders with both hands and giving a hearty shake. "Congratulations!" Then he paused—strangely so, had anyone been watching in the July heat. "You sure had me fooled for a second with that 'aw-shucks' face, kid. You could be an actor."

All smiles, Dave picked up his beer, fully intending to swallow the whole thing down in three gulps. After the first one, though, he coughed up beer all over his old Minnesota Twins T-shirt. Erik reached over the bar and gave him a hearty slap on the back.

"Hey, Mr. L," he said, "don't spit up that beer. You're paying full price for it now—those are the summer pricing rules for real teachers!" He paused, as natural speakers are wont to do, before uncorking a heady mix of inspiration and reality. "Remember that a teacher is nothing if society does not continually take a dump on him."

Dave tried to smile, but his eyes just watered. He grabbed the beer for another sip and managed to croak out, "Then consider me the outhouse of the world." After another drink and some happy not-uncomfortable silence, he added, "I was starting to think I'd never get hired. Like, *ever*, Erik."

"Yeah," said Erik.

Dave didn't want him to mention it, but Erik did. The teacher-turned-barkeep looked to the side, as he often did when trying to broach a strange or touchy subject. "Does it give you pause at all that the last time you were there, you tried to leave the school after the interview and got the third-world militia treatment from…"

"From a group of invisible people in a spooky, dark gym?"

Dave did not sip now but stared at the light-yellow column of pilsner. "Yeah. But here's the thing, if I don't take this job because of that… incident, then on every terrible day of this upcoming year when I'm subbing, I'll have to realize that I got offered a real job at Maple Valley and didn't take it—regardless of the reason why." He forced a laugh and took a deep breath. "I just need to remember not to sub in gym class during power outages."

He finished the pilsner in one long swallow.

"Hey," Erik said, catching his eye.

Dave looked up at his mentor and briefly wondered what parts of the human brain were dedicated to capturing the attention of other human brains. If there were some anatomical structure, he thought, it must be naturally developed in great teachers like Erik, people from whom you always felt like you were being imparted a critical secret.

"Yeah?"

"Just remember, when you're getting on your high horse about education, those who can, *do*. Those who can't, *teach*." He grabbed another glass to wipe and smiled. "Mr. Legnagyszerübb, the fresh-faced new guy! I hope you get what you're after, my man."

4 – The Workshop

The clouds hung low in the late August sky and seemed to radiate chill directly onto the Maple Valley parking lot. "New Teacher Workshop Week Itinerary" topped the pile of papers on the passenger seat, and Dave's mind flashed to that moment it had been trying to suppress for the last month: bound, dragged, bewildered, sitting beside this same car in the same parking lot. But he was quite good at shoving the past down in the stuff-sack of his brain. Sitting in his idling car, he closed his eyes and willed the memory away.

"What am I doing here?" he whispered. "I'm here to get ready to teach."

Dave noticed other cars in the lot, and had a fresh moment of much more pedestrian, first-job panic: did they start already? Did good teachers show up more than forty-five minutes early to a workshop? He pulled a bit closer, into a parking space three spaces from the Home of the Mammoths sign and about one hundred yards from the end of the school. He didn't want any early reprimands about parking too close to the building, so it was best to play it safe.

Dave had to shove the memory down in the bag again—he closed his eyes, hearing the murmur of passing cars and the electric hum of the old Mammoths sign. He opened his eyes, memory safely stowed away once more. The sign faintly buzzed as it switched to announce a happy and safe prom and to remind students that registration was due online Friday, February 12, by midnight.

He had no idea what to bring—but he should bring something, right? So he hoisted a bag over his shoulder with blank paper, colored pencils and a few novels he had pulled out of a box in his apartment. Mr. Legnagyszerübb, it seemed, was ready to teach—who, exactly? Handfuls of itinerant kindergartners, or, perhaps, a group of commercial fiction enthusiasts, right here on the street. He was twenty-five, with his first full-time high school job ahead of him, and if his course load somehow involved teaching the beauty of tacky, popular paperbacks, then, by God, after a week, his colored-pencil-wielding students would all be gainfully employed as readers for Random House, fully clothed and well-fed because of the power of education, cross-pollinated with random knowledge of the universe. He smiled at the thought.

This heady aspiration, of course, stood as "yin" to the new teacher's "yang" of not having a single concrete clue of how he would design and implement instruction. He had one thought only a new teacher could have: "I have no clue what I'm doing today, but by the time I go to bed tonight, I will be confident that I know exactly what I'm doing." Erik would have told him that such a thought would eventually take permanent root, even though only the first half would ever be true.

His mind raced around these same tracks—until he stopped in front of the drop-off lane at the building's entrance. To his left, Dave could see the anonymous brown metal gym door, completely unremarkable save for the fact that he had been shoved, or maybe dragged, out of that door by invisible assailants the previous month before finding his personal possessions inside his locked car. As he stood there, the horrible memory popped out of the stuff-sack unbidden, and he had a thought: was this an inside-teacher joke? Did every full-time instructor get the Secret Police treatment after an interview? Surely, not. Mrs. Pflaum, his sweet-and-soft-as-a-peach third-grade teacher, would have died. His eyes closed, and adrenaline-laced sweat dampened his armpits as he willed the memory back into the stuff-sack.

As he stood there, another new hire walked past him, leaning slightly forward like an action hero who's stopped her sprint at the building's edge. She paused and regarded him for a moment, holding a box of what appeared to be oboe parts as the chill wind blew her long, poppy-yellow skirt about her athletic ankles. One hazel-green eye looked at him with a hint of amusement, the other covered by a bob of light hair.

He realized he should stop and say, "Are you here for the workshop, too?" But she had already crossed the drop-off lane and was entering through the main doors—the ones that had been inexplicably closed, locked and otherwise drawn when he had run around to the building's entrance to try and find out what in the world had happened to him. Once again, he shoved the memory down and entered the school.

Ellen, the Super Secretary, greeted him at a fold-out table, where the young woman with the box of oboe parts was filling out some paperwork.

"Ah! Hello!" Ellen said, smiling directly at him while grabbing five different colored pieces of paper from seemingly random piles. Today, it was the same pink-and-blue glasses frames for the quixotic Ellen, and same keen gray eyes, but a different shade of precise lipstick. "Mr. Legnagyszerübb," she nearly sang, the name perfectly pronounced, "our new English teacher this year!"

Dave recalled how, at the interview, she couldn't seem to remember his first name.

"I'll try!" he said. Trying to solve the mystery of Ellen, the Ageless Secretary, apparently overrode the power of his brain to make small talk.

She paused but kept smiling. "Sure, hon."

He thought that Oboe Box, frowning, was looking at him sideways from the end of the fold-out table.

The colored pages were dense with text. His excitement about being a real teacher, combined with his trauma while entering the building, had suddenly robbed him of his ability to read. He could make out MAPLE VALLEY HUMAN RESOURCES DEPARTMENT at the top of a green sheet and EMPLOYEE CODE OF CONDUCT atop another. Other than that, it was a wall of dense, impenetrable text. Maybe this confusion mirrored how struggling students felt. How English students felt. How *his* English students felt. Yes!

"Ellie, I mean Ellen, do you need these back right now?" He felt sweat wicking from his fingertips into the paper.

She tilted her head sideways and smiled in the way that office ladies did when they felt bad that they were forced to correct you because you're an idiot, but they're too kind to say it. "Yes, Dave. If I could get these back now, that'd be great."

He quickly scanned the sheets. Signature, date; signature, date; print name, signature, date. He handed her back the paper in five different orientations, and in a nearly sleight-of-hand movement, she straightened them and put them in an organizer.

"Just follow Ms. Lehner, sweetie, and the principal and APs will join you in a minute. Have a great day!" Another school secretary trick: Dave felt she did completely wish for his day to be great.

He followed Oboe Box—nope, Ms. Lehner—down the hall and across the way from a staircase. Mrs. Young, still accessorized with bright pastel necklaces and bracelets but wavy black hair now pulled straight back, was shuffling folders at a desk near the front of the room. A mustachioed man with round black glasses, whose blue dress shirt strained at his biceps and shoulders, passed Mrs. Young stacks of folders that she reorganized and passed back. One folder had his name on it.

The man in the blue shirt directed a million watts of teeth at Ms. Lehner, formerly Oboe Box. "Sarah!" he said, in the sonorous, deep voice Dave expected him to have, "glad to have you on board!" He extended Sarah a hand that looked as if it could crush steel.

Sarah deftly switched the box to her other hand and hip and returned the smile and handshake. With her razor-straight blonde bangs and smooth cheeks, Sarah Lehner looked the part of the Swedish model, though Dave thought her smile looked… unhinged, perhaps. "I'm excited to get started, Mr. Carter. Very excited."

Their hands were still clasped in an iron handshake, and their faces seemed unable to stop smiling.

"Sarah, you gave a great interview, and we could not be more excited to have you on board." As he watched these two *Avengers* body doubles continue to shake hands and beam at each other, he wondered what Sarah Lehner's interview had been like. Something moved in his spine, but he stuffed it back down.

"In fact, on behalf of the administration—Ms. Cathy Young, the AP, and me, Don Carter, principal—we're glad to have you five new hires here this year."

Dave glanced around. In fold-out chairs around the table, sure enough, there were three other hires besides him and Sarah. He had not noticed them come in. Had they been here the whole time? Again, his brain refused to keep the assault in the gym out of his memory. Had these other new hires undergone the same experience?

"We're not the biggest southwest metro high school," continued Principal Carter, "but we're the fastest growing, so if you stick with us, we can build a future together."

Dave knew instantly that Don Carter was the type of man who could list clichès, and people would believe them. In fact, he imagined quite the future here: going from a humble start as a small-time English teacher to an award-winning, say, yearbook advisor; maybe a head basketball coach or a drama director for whom kids would work long hours; he would speak at graduation, and fathers would weep; he would attend the naming ceremony of the new wing of the building that would be named after him before he even retired; and at the church service for his funeral, the weight of the mourners would collapse the building, so he and his legions of dedicated students would be buried together, pharaoh-style, because the town's educational system could not go on without him. Don Carter—and Don Carter's expensive eyeglass frames, perfectly trimmed mustache, and bulging delts—made him believe it.

Ms. Young passed Dave a folder and paused for a fraction of a moment, wrist jewelry suspended in midair.

"Dave," she said and hesitated. "Le—Legardium—"

"Legnagyszerübb, Ms. Young. Thank you for offering me this gig. I appreciate it." Why did he say "gig?" Still, that was the most sensible thing to come out of his mouth today.

"We are so lucky to have you, David," she said, pencil-thin eyebrows widening in welcome beneath the dark ringlets that had escaped her ponytail.

As he opened his folder, he noticed Ms. Young pull Mr. Carter out into the hallway, the two of them speaking in a low tone. Dave opened his folder to see his teaching assignment. A few ninth-grade Englishes, a few American Literatures. *His* classes. *His.* He looked down the schedule and saw he had a box labeled VAULT: SURVEILLANCE. What was that? "Surveillance" must mean "nontenured"—that's what he told himself.

The threat-attuned part of his brain threatened to release the stuffed memories again. Surely there was some straightforward explanation.

Ms. Young was suddenly in front of the teachers. Everyone went around and introduced themselves: it was Dave; Sarah, box of music parts still perched next to her on the table; Nassir and Julia, both of whom taught science; and Derrick, a phy ed teacher. Nassir had a thin frame, black hair that stood up lightly from above his acne-scarred forehead, and a long nose; he sat impassively with his arms and legs crossed. Julia was a plump woman in a long teal dress, matching earrings (what female teacher didn't have some kind of matching earrings?) and a perma-smile. Derrick was the kind of hugely muscular individual who, no matter what kind of car he was driving, would make you wonder how he crammed himself into it—a Mr. Incredible with dark hair and heavy brows. His voice was loud in the way that a phy ed voice needs to be, honed by years of letting everyone in the fieldhouse know that it was time to put the badminton racquets away.

Though it seemed the kind of smile that could turn into a wince quickly, Ms. Young smiled broadly at each of their introductions. She then went on to introduce the staff mentors. Due to budget cuts (what Ms. Young labeled "budgetary—you know—moving things from left to right, and here to there"), several new staff would share mentor teachers. One of the mentor teachers was Rotundo—real name, Larry Yearson—inflated into a slightly different volleyball coach tracksuit. Remembering his interview, Dave's teeth ground together a bit at the sight of him. Yearson, it turns out, was a science teacher. "I'll be workin' wit you, Nassier and, ah, Julia, but I got a volleyball practice this morning, so, ah, Mr. Carter will take carah ya." Yearson readjusted his waistband between every sentence of his pronouncement. He then got up and left.

Would it have been worse, thought Dave, if Yearson had farted loudly on his way out? Carter's face was inscrutable. Dave tried to imagine a situation in which he would simply leave a meeting his principal was leading. He couldn't.

Dave's mentor was a genial-looking woman named Nicole Saunders, who only looked up from her phone when she was introduced but reached over and shook Dave's hand right away. Mrs. Young clapped her hands together, and the charms on her bracelets swung and jangled accordingly. The smile now seemed to be a struggle to breathe, married somehow to a genuine "beaming" plastered poorly over a wince. "We could not be happier to start the year with each and every one of you," she said. "Let's go over some procedures."

Dave took notes on the bottom of his teaching assignment: there were lunch schedules, hall passes, counselor roles, field trip requests, grade book and online course updating—all the thankless bureaucracy of a teaching job. Dave was not bored at all; he could see himself following through thoroughly and properly on each discipline referral and Student of the Month nomination. He was no longer a sub. He was a Real Teacher.

Nicole leaned over, took a look at his schedule, and beamed. She gave him the thumbs-up.

"Now, as for the schedule," Ms. Young went on, and everyone turned to a new page in their folder, "Authentic Learning is a key part of what we do here at Maple Valley. Kids need a chance to apply what they've learned. Your students won't have to ask, 'When are we ever going to use this?' because on odd-numbered block days—that's every other Monday or Thursday, on days one and three—we have time built into our schedule to accommodate real student learning. *Genuine*—" she leaned forward at each of them, necklaces leaning in time—"learning. You were hired over other candidates precisely because we believe that you will fit into our Maple Valley Authentic Unstructured Learning Time, or M-VAULT, though we just call it VAULT, so extraordinarily well. And although we'll need to be flexible to give our kids their best opportunities, we sincerely believe in your commitment to this authentic learning, especially as it pertains to the area of specialization outlined in your hiring contract."

Dave looked down at his sheet again: SURVEILLANCE. He tried to cast a sideways glance at Derrick's sheet, but a shoulder the size of the Rock of Gibraltar was in his way. His Dri-Fit T-shirt struggled to cover the tattoo on his arm—all Dave could see was an eagle talon with the letters F-I-D stenciled in each claw.

"Let's remember that authentic learning—" here, her shoulders shrugged upwards violently, and she clutched her fists in front of her face, "is a chance for all of our students to get out of the classic bookwork and actually apply what they know to real life. And we know that in the careers our students will be in, they'll have the space to follow their passions and experiment. Think of the folks who work at the big tech companies, riding around on one-wheeled scooters and working twenty hours on a coding project that's going to... to—" her hands balled up tighter, and her cheeks seemed twisted by her smile, "to change the world. We like to say that we're unlocking the VAULT to student learning!"

There was silence. The administrators and mentors raised their eyebrows. Dave could almost hear the other teachers thinking, "So... what exactly do you want us to do? Let kids have the run of the school and 'experiment' for a while?"

He thought of some of the students he had encountered while subbing who asked him to tell them the time because they "never really understood" old-fashioned clocks. Or students who got their fingers caught in the napkin dispensers at lunch. Perhaps Maple Valley served a different caliber of average suburban kid, but he could not imagine any kids he'd encountered ending up working for Google's Project X. Though maybe, now that he was a Real Teacher, he simply had to believe in the kids harder.

Mr. Carter cleared his throat. "Your job is to be a supervisor, and, hopefully, a mentor as these kids get their hands dirty. But we need to keep them safe. You don't need to prep for each week's two staggered fifty-six minutes of Authentic Learning Enrichment, but you can't be in your rooms working. You'll have to be present in the halls, the lab spaces, the gyms, where kids are working on their projects."

No hanging silence this time. Conversation, apparently, over. Mr. Carter's bearing did not seem to indicate that he fielded many questions after an explanation or decree. Therefore, Dave would have to worry about Authentic Learning Time when it occurred. Until then, he would focus on the rest of this meeting and then work out exactly what he would be teaching during the first few days of the year. "PREPARATION," he wrote in his notes, underlining thrice. "= KEY TO STUDENT ENGAGEMENT." When he looked up at Young for another cue to annotate, he was instead blocked by Derrick's shifting pack of shoulder muscle. Almost absently, he jotted down the letters F-I-D. When he bent his face back over his notepad, he could sense Derrick looking back at him, eyebrows arched.

5 – The Short Lesson

"Mr. L, I need some help," said JB, whose real name was Oscar Real.

From the first day, when Oscar had said, inexplicably, that Dave could just call him "JB," that's how Dave had addressed him. Because he cared about kids. Because he was that kind of teacher. Their parents might let them down, might forget to pick them up at Walmart or neglect to buy them a graphing calculator, but Dave would not disappoint them.

He expertly wove his way through the desks to help JB. "So, I was looking at this," said JB, holding up the green Gatsby worksheet, "and I'm not sure what it means by 'sillaou,'" I mean, 'sillyho—'"

"Silhouette?" offered Dave, kneeling next to JB's desk and straddling the young man's backpack, portable speaker and thirty-two-ounce Gatorade.

JB, whose braces still gave his mouth a pursed, overstuffed look, offered up an index finger in agreement. "Like, that, and the 'dock.' I'm not sure what I'm supposed to write for that." He looked up at Dave expectantly.

Dave leaned across and grabbed his copy of *Gatsby*. "Do you remember the part the question is asking about? Let's find that spot in the book."

Mr. L—Dave, to his friends—did not mention that the part of the worksheet JB referred to was the one they had done together, as a class, two days ago when Dave had handed out the worksheet. The drawing of a silhouette, done as an example as he read the text out loud to the class, was in Dave's field of vision as he bent over to help JB, as were

31

the notes on the board that directly answered the question. In fact, as Dave regarded it coolly out of the corner of his eye, he noted that he had written the question on the board, too. At the time, JB had been drawing a barfing emoji face on the back of his hand using a black felt-tip pen that he had borrowed from Dave last week but never returned.

JB nodded, more of a slight head bob than anything. "Yeah yeah. It's just that I haven't read that chapter. You know? I mean, I *kind* of read it. Like, I *saw* it."

Dave tried not to frown but failed. On the second day of school, after the notes were on the board, Dave had read and reread portions of the text aloud to the class; then Dave had given them about half of the hour to plow through more of their own *Gatsby*, Chapter I. He didn't get the impression that many of their lives had changed because of it. Yet.

Dave bent his head to catch JB's eyes. "What were you up to when we had the reading day yesterday?"

JB stopped the head bob and regarded Dave from beneath his curly black hair. "Yo, L, I got a lot going on right now, with work and stuff. And I have this project that's due during the homeroom time today, or whatever—"

Ah, crap! The Authentic Unstructured Learning Time! When was that supposed to start? He looked up at the clock, but his view was blocked by several hands in the air. How much time did he have? He had just begun class time to work on the sheet, and the JBs of the class were threatening to compose an answer to one of the ten questions on it. He looked up from JB's desk and noticed several hands were now up.

"Yes… Cam. What's your question?"

Cam dropped his head back to reveal his blue eyes. "Uh, what time do we get outta here?"

The class buzzed. Gatbsy's shadow, for any high school English teacher, represented the fundamental human longing for an object of desire that ultimately turns out to be a hollow dream, fading away across the bay separating East and West Egg. Fitting, he thought. Sucks to be the only one in a room who understands the metaphor just laid on your head by the universe.

He clapped. "Okay, sophomores, day three of school is almost over, and lucky for you, Maple Valley's got some enrichment time, I think, planned for this afternoon. Before we go, make sure you—"

The bell rang. A whirlwind of sophomores moved past desks and out the door, and Mr. L's precious literary analysis sheets were strewn, incomplete but for a first name or two, on the mottled carpet floor. The class was empty, and the school's constant background noise had switched to hallway mode.

"That went well," he said to himself as he picked up the worksheets.

Dave set the pile on a desk, took a swig of his green tea and headed out to the hallway. No student looked puzzled or confused; all slammed their lockers and shared snacks and jokes with the confidence of kids who knew exactly what's going on. He wondered what kind of projects they would be working on, or where, or what kind of supervision they would need.

The bell rang twice, and the halls quieted somewhat. Mr. Carter's voice cleared its throat over the PA. "Maple Valley High School, this is Principal Carter. The time is now 1:54 p.m. It is time to open the M-VAULT. Good luck with your projects, Mammoths!"

He did not realize it, but Dave had been looking at the speaker in the ceiling during the announcement. When the PA clicked off, he looked down and around the hallway.

No one. Anywhere.

No kids gathered around lockers, sharing worksheet answers. No groups of girls huddled together watching dance videos. No teachers drank coffee outside their rooms. The lights were on, and in far-off hallways, there seemed to be the clashing metal sounds of locker doors opening and maybe the familiar hallway sounds of shoes and sandals being dragged listlessly from class to class. But that could easily be the school's decades-old HVAC system kicking in.

He swallowed, trying to keep the stuff-sack of memory from releasing its contents and trying not to think about what had happened to him in the dark gymnasium after the interview.

6 – Bathroom Check

What now?

He felt a twinge of panic in his legs. Down the hallway, he told himself. Walk calmly down the hallway, find an adult, and follow them to whatever magical assembly the school's students had suddenly teleported. But he felt frozen to the ground as if he were having some kind of hallucination that would only worsen if he became unstuck and tried to figure out what was going on. The hallway had been filled with the usual teenage flotsam and jetsam just moments before.

Okay, he said to himself. With that strange numb chill that occurs as confusion starts to slip into fear, Mr. Legnagyszerübb, rookie teacher, ordered himself to walk down a hallway that had become deserted in the middle of the day. Room lights were on, but he heard no movement. Right now, he would be relieved to see any other faculty, staff, lunch lady, custodian—or even Student with Earbuds In, wandering in dark teenage solitude down the hallway, ignorant of the Chernobyl that Maple Valley had suddenly become during this unstructured, authentic learning time.

He was several feet from the stairwell, which was always a little bit darker than the surrounding hallways, given its place in the interior of the building. The numbness crept up to his ears, and his steps became stiffer as he approached the stairs. It was almost as if he were scared of the sounds his cheap dress shoes would make on the wrapper-and-gum-covered risers.

A sound—the smallest of shuffles—made him pull his hand back from the railing. He moved just his head, trying to pinpoint the source,

34

but the blowers kicked back on, and the sound was lost. Yet he was almost sure it had come from the bathroom, just a few feet to his left. For some reason, every detail of the school seemed to register to him: the beige, damp-smelling carpet punctuated by random rectangles of linoleum. The white walls with pen slashes at about waist height. The muted purple lockers. The smell of body spray applied after gym class. There were sounds, too, that usually only were audible during the quiet summer: passing cars on 10th Avenue in front, the old humming blowers that seemed to be cycling at intervals designed to make the whole situation spookier, and the wood-paneled boys' bathroom door, which bounced softly open a fraction of an inch with the change in air pressure—

He saw some shift in light in the bathroom. Again, his brain seemed to pull gears wildly back to full cognition.

It was M-VAULT time. Kids were supposed to be working on some kind of independent project, as Young had gushed about during the workshop and as he had heard Carter announce at the end of the hour. Was the whole student body in the gym or in a hidden basement? Were they all in the tech ed labs? He realized he really didn't know, but any time spent in a high school made one thing clear: kids were experts at not going where they were supposed to go.

He supposed that at least a few teachers had scurried away to secret supply closets to get work done, but he was That Dedicated New Teacher. There were rules designed to give kids a chance to do some hands-on learning of their own, and he would give every kid that chance. If they'd rather hang out in the bathroom, he would coax them from the urinals of ignorance down into the labs of independent learning. Plus, he'd better make sure no one was vaping.

He took a deep breath and walked towards the bathroom door, reaching out toward the metal rectangle to push it open. There were two more shifts of light from under the door. He wondered: That bathroom's tiled. Why can't I hear them walk across the floor?

"What am I doing here?" he whispered to himself. With his fingertips, he pushed the door open.

Only the low, yellow emergency light was on in the bathroom. The odor of cheap cleaner and urine was heavy in the humid bathroom air, and long triangles of light hit the stall walls and the white urinals from the open door. He stepped as quietly as possible into the bathroom and kept his body still as his eyes and ears scanned the room. Nothing on the floor, or the walls, or the—

An acoustic ceiling tile was set crooked on the metal hanger, leaving a thin black triangle of darkness above the toilet. Dave had seen enough movies to know what this meant. What kind of *Ocean's 11* authentic learning were these kids up to? He thought of Erik back at the brewery. Whatever was up there, it would make a good story later. But right now, it felt like he could hear his heartbeat reverberating off the bathroom stall walls.

He took a deep breath—the mixture of feces, smeared-on cologne and cherry vape smoke reminded him that no matter what kind of weirdo stuff was going on right now, he was still just a teacher in a high school bathroom. The low yellow light was just bright enough for him to read above the toilet paper holder an etched-in familiar boys' bathroom lament about the narrator's inability to produce something substantial in his brief time in the stall; the meter was noteworthy in its expert rhyming of "broken hearted" and "only farted." Grounded enough to slow his heart rate down, he put one clearance-shelf dress shoe on the toilet paper holder and the other on the lid.

He put his hands out to steady himself and peered up at the tile ceiling. Unfortunately, it was too dark to see, so he removed his sweaty hand from the top of the stall divider and reached into the triangular void.

As soon as he raised his foot from the toilet seat, both feet left their holds, and he was weightless. Instantly, his right elbow struck the inside of the toilet bowl, his arm was wet, and his left leg was bent unnaturally underneath him. He heard a grunt escape his throat, and all the while, his brain tried and failed to put these disparate sensory details together into a cohesive structure of what had just happened—

A shadow cut over the yellow generator light glow. Dave's face was covered by cloth, and he felt a hand grabbing at his school keys, now twisted in his khaki pocket and wet with toilet water. The keys wouldn't budge, even though the assailant had a hold of his staff lanyard. Dave's mind popped back into gear: This kid, or whoever, kicked my legs out and is now trying to get my keys. But I can fight back.

He twisted his body on the stall floor to pin the keys held by the offending hand to the ground. Some part of him wanted to bark out, "Ha!" but his hand was wrenched behind his back, and his forehead slammed into the bottom lip of the toilet bowl. The assailant's hand began to pull the keys from the twisted, wet wad of his pocket again, and he let out another grunt. Dave's initial blank surprise gave way to white-hot, indignant anger.

And here he was again, on the bathroom floor of a high school. His previous blind assault—in the gym in this very high school, though he'd tried to keep the memory stuffed away—had caught him so off-guard he hadn't even thought how he could have actually defended himself. Not so this time.

The low emergency light cut in and out as the stall door bounced off the frame and his assailant re-positioned himself to better grasp the keys. Pure outrage prevented Dave from wondering why this bathroom ninja wanted the keys or if their loud tussling was echoing down a serene, empty hallway outside the bathroom. He grabbed the wrist of the hand that tore at his keys. When it pulled back, Dave twisted his entire body and drove the would-be thief into the stall wall, head and shoulder first. The assailant grunted, and Dave knew that he had stunned the key thief. The stall seemed to pull away from the floor with the force of the impact.

Dave yelled as he pounced on his enemy. The two twisted back and forth, Dave in a frothy rage, grunting and yanking on the arm he held with both of his hands, and his opponent making no noise but keeping a hold on the keys' lanyard. Finally, Dave pushed himself up on his assailant as they gripped each other, jammed between the toilet and the wall.

The hand lock between the two held the ninja's legs open in the closed space. Dave rammed his foot in the fighter's crotch: one, two, three, four, with no attempt to escape or do anything but *hurt* him. His white-and-red anger seemed to merge with the color of the emergency light as the strikes compounded: ten, eleven, twelve, thirteen. He heard the person grunt from under his face covering, and Dave shouted near-nonsense with each knee strike, blinding anger leading to strike after strike.

"WHAT… THE… *ME?*… VAULT TIME… INSUBORDINATE… SNEAKY SON OF A…"

The victim of the crotch strikes let out a higher-pitched whimper than Dave expected. The timbre of the whimper made him pause for a fraction of a second.

"JB?" he asked, hoarse.

The assailant took advantage of the break in Dave's crotch attack, let go of the keys and rolled underneath the stall divider. Dave reached a hand under to grab him but had his fingers stepped on and immediately yanked them back under the stall. He heard a pained moan and saw the outline of black shoes shuffling away, and then, inexplicably, he heard the blowers turn back on. Then the bathroom door opened and closed.

He pulled himself up by the toilet bowl and ran his fingers over his face to check for blood. No cuts, but he did speak out loud, and it came out in a hoarse croak.

"What was *that?*"

7 – The Rescue

He pushed the stall door open, limping slightly as his knee protested. He repeated his questions but only received the background blower sound as a reply.

"Did I just kick a kid—repeatedly—in the nuts?" His question echoed slightly in the bathroom's silence. Was it JB? Did Oscar Real just try to assault—

No, it wasn't an assault, at least in the typical ambush sense. Dave had some understanding of real violence, not just the film conceit of it. He caught a look at himself in the mirror and did not feel strange about addressing himself—although several memories threatened to punch their way out of the stuff-sack in tandem.

"It was a trap."

He tilted his head back at himself, wondering, if this was a movie, would this be the time the audience realizes the main character is mentally disturbed? Sure, thirty-five minutes ago, he was teaching canonical literature in a civilized society. Three minutes ago, he had battered a student's testicles to prevent his keys from being taken. So, again—sure, why not? Now, he would walk back out to the empty hallway—and avoid investigating any mysterious bathroom/locker room noises.

As he went to push the bathroom door open, he paused. Something made him freeze, a change of light, perhaps, on the other side of the door. He sensed that someone out there in the brightly lit hallway was holding his breath, too. He wondered if he should try to hide—

The door opened slowly, but the fist that grazed Dave's right temple was quick, like a single frame of a film. He went to push the door closed and heard a grunt from the other side—but it was followed by the noise of another shoulder hitting the door and then another. *How many?* he wondered. At least three?

No matter the number, they were coming in, and when they got in, their knees and feet might return the favor on him. His shoulder cracked as he shoved the door, and his "teacher-nice" loafers struggled to find friction against the pockmarked tiles. But the three interlopers on the other side of the door out-shoved him and entered the bathroom.

Their faces were obscured by black masks of some kind, and again, there was no cursing or shouted oaths. They came for him, but no one made a move on his vulnerable anatomy. With an almost-clinical detachment, a taller one seized his right wrist and pinned his arm back against the toilet stall, and the second held his body back with a knee to the left side of his chest. He struggled, but it was hopeless. He braced himself.

The one he thought was JB, who had shown no self-restraint in search of long-term educational goals, yet had seemingly been able to take a series of horse kicks to the fruit basket, now hobbled towards him. There were no shouted curses about Dave's mother or any cocked fists. Instead, he pulled the keys from Dave's writhing hip and turned. The two henchmen proceeded to guide Dave down to the floor at the edge of the stall so coolly that Dave wondered if he would escape without more injury.

He didn't have time to wonder. The kid he thought was JB came flying at him—back-first, jarring the left assailant into the bathroom wall. The other figure took off in the direction of the doorway—and from where Dave lay, he could only hear a thump before the silhouette hit the floor.

Whoever was standing in the doorway did not take up much space or waste much time. The two masked men attacked him, but both were immediately struck by whatever whirling weapon had felled the first individual. Again, no words were exchanged. The kid who'd been the first to go down sprang back up and sprinted across the tile bathroom floor back at the person in the doorway.

The lithe figure in the bathroom entrance allowed the second masked assailant to fall but caught the first in what appeared to be a wrist hold. In the low light, Dave saw the weapon again appear as a blur—was it some kind of baton?—and crack down on the arm that still held Dave's lanyard and keys. JB, if it was him, emitted a small yelp as he was thrown against a bathroom sink. All three figures were incapacitated but conscious—just lying or sprawling on the floor, silent. Dave simply stared with his jaw open.

Instantly, it seemed, he was being pulled up by his hand and guided out of the bathroom. In the bright, still-empty hallway, he blinked at his savior, who brushed the hair out of her eyes and held her "weapon"—a flute, it looked like—parallel to her forearm.

"Sarah?" he said. "Ms. Lehner?" He paused. "Oboe Box?" he whispered, trailing off so that there was no way she could possibly hear him.

She was breathing faster than normal, and her dirty blond hair looked only mildly "off"—several strands were out of line with the rest that landed perfectly above her shoulder. And was she standing straighter, like a soldier or a black belt, than she had before? He hadn't really noticed when they'd met at New Teacher Workshop.

She looked at him directly in the eyes, and her eyebrows wrinkled almost imperceptibly as if she'd smelled something slightly unpleasant, perhaps the saliva of an assailant she'd struck in the mouth. Dave's mind whirred, considering the possibilities of his future—would he be interviewed by the police?—to the past five minutes—had he just beaten the testicles of a costumed student?—to a swirling combination of the two—would he be reprimanded, fired or squirreled off to a secret prison?

But of *all* the things he thought a co-worker might say to him at that time, in that empty hallway—"nothing at all" didn't seem like a possibility. After all, had she just dropped three guys with the greatest of ease in order to prevent his beating?

Or... no. They had been after his *keys*.

Sarah maintained that stare. Her eyes were a gentle brown, made ironic by the hardness of her stare. Or was it a glare?

"Hey, that was crazy, right?" he offered. Was it crazy to her, though? She certainly wasn't acting as though an assault and then a counterassault had just taken place. What the hell was happening?

They had been introduced several times during the new teacher workshop, but he still added, "I'm Dave, by the way."

"I know," she said.

Was that a smile? A pitying smile or a knowing smirk?

"Thanks for... for that." He tucked in the back of his shirt and tried not to wince as the tips of his fingers grazed several abrasions. "Thanks a ton."

Another smirk. "Sure," she said. "So you have your keys, correct?"

"I do." His lips moved momentarily, but nothing came out. He finally managed, "What was that? What is happening right now?"

She nodded. He wished his face could just become a question mark followed by an exclamation point. Had he wandered into some sophomore's half-baked plots from second-period Creative Writing? Finally, he let it out.

"What is happening? I was just attacked in the bathroom. By undercover students. Or student-ninjas. Whatever. Do I call Mrs. Young? Or Don Carter?"

Sarah's response was to spin her weapon-jazz instrument between her fingers. The smirk was back. He now wanted to be loud, but then she answered, a composed teacher making an unextraordinary behavior report.

"Three of my students were in the bathroom during M-VAULT time without sufficient self-defense equipment." The way she said it was as matter-of-factly as a "Most of my first hour didn't have the assignment done."

She brushed more hair off her face. It looked as if she wore hardly any makeup and as if her cheeks were chiseled out of marble or designed by a French automobile engineer.

"And you..." There it was, the check-you-out-and-you're-dismissed look. "You've got your keys, Dave. We've got only a few minutes before fifth period starts, so I'm going to head back to the band room."

With a swish of her yellow skirt, she was gone, stylish Vans tapping their way down the stairs as he stood there.

She hadn't answered his question, but he knew she was right. Of course, he would not go to Carter or Young. What would he say? How would he even lead into it? "Hey, during unstructured time, the whole floor of students disappeared, and I fought a kid who then came back with two of his buddies, but I was saved by the young, limber new band teacher. So, do I open a Behavior Referral tab in School Hub from the Attendance Tab? Or do I enroll in a community ed Krav Maga class on Tuesday nights?"

They might hear it as, "Hey, boss, I was worried about how best to approach M-VAULT time today, so I consumed some hallucinogens and was attacked by a group of Faceless Men in the bathroom. No, I'm okay, because the music teacher is a Faceless Man, er, Woman, and she saved me. Yeah, I think we're going to PLC about it next week."

So—no. No one was going to know. Even pettier was this concept: he was a new teacher trying to do a good job. If it turned out he was supposed to be supervising a hallway while he was busy reenacting a scene from *Cars 2*, then he did not want that on his boss's radar. It was embarrassing to shirk your duty, so he would not volunteer any information to anyone. Deal? Deal.

He shook out his hands and feet and patted himself down a bit. No major sprains or bleeding injuries, though his hip felt sore—and he recalled the ball-crushing he'd administered to someone who, you know, might be a student.

Okay, so one more reason not to share this with anyone.

Principal Carter's voice went over the loudspeaker: "Alright, Mammoths! We saw great things during our M-VAULT today, so we will build on this success next week. Please report to your fifth hour, and have a fantastic day!"

Dave looked behind him. In six minutes, he would be Mr. Legnagyszerübb again, and he'd forget about the bathroom in the unstoppable ocean current of the school day. But first—

He opened the boys' bathroom and looked in.

The emergency lights were off, the ceiling tile was on straight, and— yes, the floor had been wiped clean. Even the Maple Valley custodial staff, it seemed, operated silently, under cover of darkness.

8 – New Teacher Check-In

Dave Legnagyszerübb looked around the brown-and-white decor of the back office. So far, the only teachers at this before-school meeting under the dull fluorescent lights and among the brown metal filing cabinets were he, Nassir and Julia. Neither Principal Carter nor Assistant Principal Young was there yet. Nassir was vigorously grading a stack of tests with a lime-green fountain pen, writing a small treatise on every free-response answer. He appeared to be one-hundredth of the way through the pile, and judging by the paragraphs of feedback he was writing on each essay question, students could count on receiving their essay tests during the graduation ceremony.

Julia, another science teacher, sat with her head tilted at about ten degrees, her eyes staring off at some point far, far away. Dave wanted to stare to see if she was blinking or catatonic. But who was he to judge other rookies? Any mirror these days would reveal him for what he was: a nervous, fastidious wreck, with lesson planning books filled out to the margins and sweat stains already growing under his arms. At what point did one *not* sweat through a school day? A part of him realized that over-perspiration was more commonplace than being attacked in a bathroom stall and having his keys stolen. But that was just more material to stuff down into the memory sack.

Julia blinked and looked up. "Hey, Dave," she said with a tired but pleasant smile. Her dimples formed small crescents on her face. She would make a good elementary teacher, thought Dave, if this job spared her life. "How's the world of English? Any kids using, like, a semicolon lately?"

This was a phenomenon he had noticed recently in his dealings with colleagues: the stereotype of the English teacher who, forsaking all forms of art and self-expression, made a religion of the seemingly arbitrary rules of the language. For the first time, it gnawed at him, and he regarded Julia with an unguarded moment of disdain. Dave wondered why someone like Julia, if they were so great at testing hypotheses and other existential crap, didn't get a job building a smallpox bomb to drop on North Korea. Or curing cancer.

"Yep," he said and forced a smile. He didn't ask her if she was trying to create life in a beaker in her room or if she planned on dying nobly from radiation exposure.

Nassir did not look up from his grading. Both of them broke off as the room darkened. A shadow the size of Jupiter filled the room as Derrick, the new phy ed teacher, entered the room. Before realizing it was clearly Derrick's bulk blocking out the light, Dave thought it might be someone else—a haughty assassin in a yellow skirt, perhaps—and his heart slowed just an imperceptible grace note before returning to normal speed.

"Mornin'," Derrick said with a voice low enough to shake the floor. He added a hip-high wave and did not so much as "sit on" but "gluteally enveloped" the stool. He shifted his enormous feet, and the four of them waited in fatigued silence until the principal showed up. And when he did, how would Dave ask if a normal part of M-VAULT time involved students ambushing teachers in the bathr—

Mr. Carter deftly moved past the door and Derrick in a quick lateral movement that immediately made Dave think that he must have carried the ball quite well on his high school football team. At that moment, light from an ancient high window hit Principal Carter right in the upper chest and face, and Dave saw that he was, indeed, a closet Adonis. Every small detail of Don Carter—the faint hint of expensive aftershave, the way his eyes seemed to take in everything behind his blue-rimmed glasses, even the clipped, succinct way he managed to say the phrase "Maple High Mammoths"—suggested that it probably wasn't just football he was good at. Most likely, while other guys were trying to make varsity, he was putting in the minimum amount of time learning the playbook so he could go home and practice writing his AP test questions. Or polish up his All-State audition trumpet solo. Yes, Dave thought, it must be difficult for the Don Carters of the world to relate to those who cannot accomplish every task within eyesight. Including running a high school.

"Good morning, rookie all-stars," he said, not looking up from his clipboard as he pressed his perfectly perfect mustache with his thumb and forefinger. Had he heard Dave thinking about the sports stuff? Probably. He was probably a mentalist, too, which he'd learned by watching a couple of YouTube videos while his soufflés baked.

"Morning," replied all the teachers, sitting up a bit straighter. Dave did notice that Nassir was a bit slower than the others to put his grading away for the boss man. Had he, Dave, been grading when Carter cut into the room, Dave would have gladly thrown the stack of papers into the recycling to make it seem he had simply been waiting idly, not distracted from his principal's impending visit.

"Does any—" began Carter when pandemonium erupted.

Dave thought the room was cramped with four people in it (though he lamented that it wasn't five). Somehow, in the instants that followed, the space seemed to expand to accommodate several interlopers.

A man in a dark blue outfit, wearing a bulletproof vest and holding an automatic pistol in front of him, banged through the door with enough force to slam it against Derrick, who appeared to take no notice of the door or the gun-wielding man directly behind him.

"GET DOWN!" the man shouted, his eyes obscured by his hat brim.

Four other strangers in dark suits surrounded him, and he threw himself on the floor, noting that they were now all brandishing some kind of government badge in one hand, weapon in the other.

Dave's mind shut off, with only partial drips of thought surfacing through his shock. Was this a drill? Was there a shooter in the building? Was this a joke of some kind?

It did not seem like a joke. He saw Julia crouch on the ground, hands over her head, fingers shaking and clenched behind her tight brown ponytail. Dimly, Dave realized he was following suit, lowering himself onto his knees. The three strangers—one man, three women—

were shouting, pointing, pushing the chairs the teachers had been sitting on out of the way. He could see Carter kneel quickly on the ground but slightly slower than the instant-down panic of Julia.

Nassir, however—Dave could still see his feet dangling off the stool in front of him. In case the scene of the required first-year-teacher morning meeting wasn't surreal enough, it appeared to Dave that Nassir was still grading tests. He could only see Nassir's feet, still crossed and dangling, hanging from the stool—his white shoelaces standing out like a sheet of unblemished snow, tied with a tidy ribbon and dangling down in four arches, each appearing to be about an inch and a half, and matching the snazzy white leather arc on the bottom half of his brown leather shoes. These details seemed to stand out to Dave in high resolution, yet others were strangely indistinct, like the barked orders of the intruders who, guns drawn, had them pinned (and weeping, in Julia's case) against the ground.

Yet Nassir finished writing his feedback on the essay, leaving a lime-green paragraph that would undoubtedly go unread. Then he clicked the silver binder clip on the pile and set it on the ground. The brief shot of Nassir's acne-scarred face that Dave glimpsed showed... nothing. His face was a mask. No fear, no indignancy, no confusion as he got to his knees, capping his green pen carefully and placing it in his pock—no, he was sliding it up the sleeve of his Izod checkered blue shirt sleeve. And Dave Legnagyszerübb then knew that it was Nassir, the harmless skinny science teacher, whom the intruders—with their vests and guns and boots—were here for.

He heard Carter say something, but again it was indistinct as if heard through several piles of blankets. Dave's sight seemed to be in high-resolution mode: the busted gray rubber cap of the stool Nassir had been sitting on, the pitted brown tile, the file drawer that took up the east half of the room, with its bottom drawer labeled GRADUATION RECORDS 07-10 in neat capital handwriting. Yet as his mind registered these things, his brain was producing conclusions—it was Nassir. He had attacked Dave after his interview. He had sent emissaries to get his keys from the bathroom. He was the one being dragged away by armed interlopers with bulletproof vests.

In his mind, Dave pushed the clothes back down into the stuff sack.

Dave's vision was flooded with boots. They swarmed Nassir and picked him up. Suddenly there was less shouting—just the thunder of boots as they took him away. The science teacher's pile of papers was still on the floor when the herd left, silver binder clip still intact.

Dave had seen movies where law enforcement agents surrounded a character and dragged him away. But the camera always followed the arrestee afterward, after he had his head pushed down into a squad car, after making either a pithy or patently evil remark. What happened to the poor folks present at the scene of the violent arrest? Did they have to crouch indefinitely? Were *they* taken into custody as well, under some obscure Supreme Court interpretation of the Fourth Amendment?

He was still clutching the back of his own head so hard that two hand-sized areas of his skull had started to hurt. On the tile below his mouth, a thin dribble of spit had pooled into a small, shiny slick. Out in the hallway, the boot noises of the—were they police?—had faded away and were replaced by a different sound.

It took Dave a few seconds to realize the hallway, rather than being full of yells and screams, as it was during a fight or a seizure or some other major disruption, was simply noisy like it was every morning at this time. Occasionally, the shout of one student to check if a buddy got his text, or the squeal of two upper-echelon girls greeting each other, would rise above the din, but otherwise—it sure sounded normal from here on the ground where Dave lay, just inside the side office entrance. Dave's eyes, inches from the floor, blinked.

He finally looked all the way up.

Carter was already sifting through the notes on his clipboard, adjusting his glasses slightly. Derrick was setting up his stool and perching his enormous frame on it in one easy movement. Only Julia looked a little hollowed, but she was steadying herself on her chair, getting back up.

"And you're on the floor," came his own gentle teacher voice in his head, that adult register who simply pointed out existing situations in the hopes that a dim student would see, without too much embarrassment, that there was a situation to be rectified, like bringing a tissue over to

48

the kid who sniffled all hour, instead of saying, "Will you just blow your freaking nose, Thomas?"

He was sitting up, too, and then back on the stool. He looked around at his fellow new teachers. He looked at Nassir's pile of papers on the floor. He heard, again, the incongruously run-of-the-mill student noise from out in the hall. He smelled his own spit on his upper lip. He heard Mr. Carter clear his throat.

"So," the principal said, making an okay-let's-move-on gesture with his pen-holding hand, "what questions can I help you with now that you've dipped your toe in the teaching pool at Maple Valley?"

Somewhere in Dave's brain, a laugh rose up, but the laugh was stopped because the other two new teachers left here by the interlopers seemed to think he was serious.

"Actually," said Julia, smoothing her dress over her knee as if she had just sat down for a normal-ass meeting, "I was wondering, Mr. Carter—"

"Don," said Carter, smiling.

"Yes, Mr.—Don. If we need to make colored copies, do those have to go through our department, or can we just send them down to Duplicating by ourselves?"

Dave wondered, as he had at several junctures since first walking into the darkened Maple Valley High School gym, if he was losing his mind. He stared at Julia, the woman who taught hard science and not fluffy humanities, and therefore must have the most stone-cold scientific calculator of a heart—or be suffering from post-traumatic stress disorder.

"I've been running my own colored paper sets through the staff copier in order to make stoichiometry worksheets because the kids seem to hang onto those more when they're lemon yellow..." She trailed off, apparently satisfied that her administrator knew that she'd been spending her own money on lemon-yellow paper. For chemistry class.

What Mr. Carter should have said at this juncture, Dave thought, was this, "Miss Julia. Several seconds ago, your colleague was arrested, or abducted, or extraordinarily rendered, by a group of armed intruders with guns. Right now, they may be making him watch as they lower his parents into boiling vats of acid. Or perhaps they're currently exchanging him for a prisoner in a Kamchatka gulag. Or maybe he's lucky, and he'll end up getting a jury by trial and not some secret court tribunal in Pakistani tribal lands. Put the worksheets online for the kids because you're going to be giving a deposition to a US marshal while a yoga instructor, cum-substitute-teacher, cum-lunch-lady watches your class. Now, let's get our stories straight."

Instead, Carter smiled. smoothed his razor-straight mustache between a perfectly trimmed thumb and forefinger and said, "The Duplicating Center at the district office can make paper copies—in yellow, if it helps—but you've got to use the new Duplicating Request Form since the old ones don't have any colored paper options under 'Special Instructions.'" He looked up as if remembering something truly important. "And I'll have Ellen try to just get rid of the old forms. They don't have stapling options either." He made himself a note, with his architect's handwriting, on his clipboard notepad.

Dave felt he should say something.

"That's good to know, boss," said Derrick in a low rumble that reflected his massive stature. "Forgot to get my anatomy copies stapled last week and spent ten minutes handing out the papers sheet-by-sheet! Rookie mistake, right, Mr. Carter?"

He laughed, Carter laughed, Julia laughed. Nassir did not laugh because he'd been abducted, and it seemed that everyone was cool with it. Dave tried to laugh, but it was as if only a puff of smoke escaped his lips.

Mr. Carter smiled with his whole face, and the effect was glorious. "I understand the struggles of you poor, beleaguered new teachers," the smile said, "and you have no greater hero than me."

Unless you repeatedly smash a student's genitals in the bathroom during unstructured time while trying to defend your school keys—then, perhaps the government agents are coming for you next, thought Dave.

"Mr. Trumbull," Don Carter said, still smiling at Derrick, "you are fighting the good fight as a new teacher. Mistakes will happen—that's the only way you'll grow. In fact, that's the only way your students will grow, too." He punctuated this mini-pep-talk by pointing his pen and making eye contact with each of them. "You're all *good* teachers, and that's why we've hired you—to make mistakes on your way to becoming *great* Maple Valley High teachers."

He was now leveling his pen at Sarah Lehner, who... when, exactly, had she shown up? Dave felt his hands grasp the edges of his chair. Surely, he would have noticed had she squeezed into this dingy back office recently. After all, the room would have brightened up. In fact, that rectangle of light that had shot through the ancient ground-level window and hit Derrick's right pec earlier now illuminated her cheeks and hair. Her eyes lit up—an almost aquamarine green soaked in brown—as the morning light flooded them. And could Dave smell her shampoo?

"So sorry, I'm late, Mr. Carter," she said, blushing in that singular frame of light. Dave thought his heart, which had stopped for a moment, must be audibly hammering the inside of his ribcage—and then he was instantly embarrassed by his own infatuation. He remembered how she looked after she'd easily smoked his would-be muggers when they stood outside the boys' bathroom. She hadn't even been breathing hard. And now, after materializing into this tiny office, she also seemed completely nonplussed, except for the lovely embarrassment of being late. "I had an IEP and could find the room the meeting was taking place in, and then Mom didn't show up—"

Carter smiled the smile again. "You were trying to help our special education colleagues and our special education students, Ms. Lehner," he said.

She smiled, and Dave's fingers clenched even tighter.

"There is no apology needed," continued Carter. "I'm sure your fellow new teachers will tell you all the critical information about using Duplicating Central."

Again, laughs all around.

"Make sure to staple your handouts, Sarah," said Derrick, wagging a bratwurst of a finger at her mockingly. "Otherwise, kids'll think you're a phy ed teacher."

More laughs—but the room darkened for a moment. The square of light was partially eclipsed by something outside. Dave's first thought was that someone had decided to dig and plant an early autumn perennial this morning. Everyone else looked up at the window, too, and saw the handle squeak as the rusty catch moved against the latch.

The light shifted again, and the new teachers, as well as Mr. Carter, looked up at the window, which appeared to open, slanting down towards the office. Dave thought he heard a "Hmmm" escape Julia's lips, but otherwise, the room was silent. The smell of outside dirt blew in, focusing Dave's attention further on the old window and its tilted pane. Then, a small clump of dirt actually did fall through the pane, landing with a soft *pat* on a dented gray filing cabinet.

Dave looked up and stopped breathing for a moment. He looked away and saw everyone else in the room staring at what was coming through the windowpane as well—well, almost everyone. Mr. Donald Carter kept writing on his clipboard.

A dirty boot lowered itself through the windowpane and into relief against the worn, off-white foundation block wall of this inner office. It was followed by another boot; the two twisted around and dipped their respective toes downward at an angle, clearly looking for some kind of purchase. The right rubber toe touched the gray filing cabinet, and then the left foot found a surface, too. Both legs were now inside the building, followed by gray slacks, which evidently had also been in the planter bed dirt just outside. Dave thought to himself that, say, Derrick Trumbull or Rotundo the Volleyball Coach would have never been able to fit through this battered old exterior window. But this person was able to without looking as if they were some kind of yogi.

Now the upper half of the person who was busy turning windows into doors revealed itself: an FBI jacket and high-hip gun holster. The jacket and corresponding shirt were lifted up for a moment to reveal a light brown underbelly as the clothes caught the windowpane. Soon, however, the FBI agent used a quick finger to release himself and crouched down into the office, where he knelt on the top of the cabinet and smoothed his hair over his acne-scarred forehead.

It was Nassir. He held a slow exhale in his cheeks as he looked around at the meeting's attendees, raising his eyebrows as if embarrassed. Dave stole a glance around the small room. Carter was still not even looking up at his science teacher. Derrick and Sarah gave a small grin and nodded as if to say, "Well done." Only Julia, the scientist and chief enquirer of all things banal, stared with her mouth open as Dave himself was doing.

Nassir hopped down from the cabinet with one hand and walked, still not making eye contact and looking a bit sheepish, over to his pile of tests. He put the lime-green pen in his pocket and set the stack on his lap, silver binder clip facing forward.

Carter still had not looked up but finally deigned to say, "The jacket, Mr. Salhi."

Nassir's head seemed to bow even lower. "Oh, yes, Mr. Carter, I'm sorry." In one motion, he removed the jacket and the gun holster, setting them on the floor—and then he was in the exact same attire he had been in when he entered the meeting.

"And sorry to be trying to get a bit of grading done during the meeting. It won't happen again. At least until I give another test." Polite laughter bounced around the room, though Dave and Julia made no noise.

"We're all learning, as I said, Mr. Salhi," said the principal, finally looking up. "So—don't forget that we've got homecoming next week, folks. Do you have any questions before I let you go?"

The rest of the new teachers shrugged.

"Well, then," smiled Mr. Carter, "have a productive day, Mammoths."

9 – The Homecoming Lesson

It was brilliant.

He knew, after teaching four days during Homecoming week, that the students would be more than a little distracted. "Excitable," Ms. Young had said, both fists clenched in front of her shoulders, wrist jewelry reflecting her characterization of the student body's energy. This week Ms. Young seemed eager to discuss student behavior, but made zero mention of, say, the arrest and—was it an escape?—of any biology teachers. Nor any mention of student projects involving restroom ambushes. And since any first year of teaching is surreal enough on its own, the more remarkable phenomena occurred, the less Dave felt like asking for explanations.

"Our young men and women will be excitable this week—and would we want them any other way?" It had been a rhetorical question at the staff meeting. But then again, these were high school teachers, and though many of them had sat in the familiar Easter Island pose of implacability that Dave remembered from his job interview, there were exceptions.

A thin, wobbly hand went up from the front row above a halo of red-and-gray hair that looked a bit like a bird's nest.

"Yes, Michaela?" Ms. Young had asked. The face was a barely patient evaluator's smile, painfully maintained. Ms. Young was ready to make her point about homecoming being for the kids. Michaela Thompson, a twenty-year district veteran unable to distinguish between Reply and Reply All, was ready to ask some clarifying questions.

"As far as my understanding of homecoming goes, Ms. Young, it appears to be designed for everyone in, ah, our student body, especially those students on the, um, fringes, to have a chance, a vessel if you will, to participate, to, ah, be a Mammoth with the other Mammoths." Her pale, emaciated hand shook, still somehow aloft as though she'd been called on. Dave had wondered if Ms. Young, given the chance right now, would murder this woman. It was 7:35, and the meeting was supposed to end at 7:30.

"Yes, Ms. Thompson," winced Ms. Young.

Michaela, when pressed to actually ask a question, had suggested that the school, if it truly cared about every student, would pay for school buses to transport kids to homecoming activities. And when allowed to roam freely upon her own idea, she had spit-balled a plan to put together homecoming decoration stations on the buses, giving kids a chance to not only attend the homecoming activities but create the requisite "Mammoth-wear" for them. This would include, but not be limited to, paper-mache tusks, woolly jeans that kids make each year, etc.

Dave had been reminded—at the time of the surely apocryphal anecdote in teacher circles about the razor-sharp teacher who, when given a chance to ask a question of a successful businessman at a presentation, ensnares him with rhetoric that exposes the false equivalence between entrepreneurship and public education—that the business picks the freshest blueberries for its premium ice cream, but teachers have to take every mushy, stupid, poorly-cared-for blueberry and put it in the pie.

Whoever first observed and/or concocted that anecdote, Dave thought, had never seen Michaela Thompson in action at a Maple Valley staff meeting. Whatever the thrice-divorced Ms. Thompson did with these blueberries, it wasn't education.

But her point—in some roundabout way—was correct. Kids were concerned about their Mammoth costumes this week, not to mention the homecoming dance, the football game (Mammoths were 0–4 on the season), the girls' soccer game (11–0, locked-in conference champs, with an inability to draw more than twenty attendees to a game), and the pepfest. David Legnagyszerübb had little to no idea what a "pepfest" was, having never subbed at a school when this event occurred.

Actually, scratch that—at Oak Heights, he had subbed for a woman who was having her gallbladder removed. "Third gallbladder in five years," mentioned the wry, bespeckled farmer who was the math department head in that particular building. He had supervised the pep rally in the gym for about four minutes before being pulled to supervise in-school suspension.

But Dave was no longer a substitute teacher at Oak Heights. He was a full-time instructor and Savior of Young Souls at Maple Valley, Home of the Mammoths. And he had a brilliant plan to capture the students' homecoming energy and redirect it into a pure vortex of *Gatsby* analysis. Yes, the pepfest was this afternoon, and if every other teacher in the building was going to watch as the train derailed, *he* would drive a brand-new set of tracks into the ground, spike by brilliant pedagogical spike.

Five minutes into second period, the English 10 class sat and listened while he laid out the day's work.

"Are there *any* questions?" he asked. "Please. There are no stupid questions."

A hand went up. It was JB, whom Dave had carefully watched every time he got up to throw away a gum wrapper or recycle a chemistry worksheet. Had he been limping, or walking strangely, since the M-VAULT time a few weeks ago?

"If we gonna pick music for, like, this homecoming dance assignment," he asked, "can we take out our phones out for, you know... ah—"

"For reference," said Cam, blond hair threatening to leave its block-out-the-world duties in front of his eyes. The kid was wearing a bandana with MAMMOTH NATION written in puff paint on the front, and somehow his hair was still in front of his eyes. "Can we listen to music on our phones for... reference?"

"Aw yeah, *that's* what I was trying to say!" said JB, exchanging a handshake with Cam, the finger movements of which always looked somehow perverse to Dave.

Dave paused, which was a huge mistake.

His idol Erik would have definitely never given the class this kind of spacious, half-second emptiness into which blossomed every student protest, argument and request for leniency. Soon, even the good kids—Teikya with her attentive eyes and color-coded notes, Randall with his painstakingly polite sentences in his newfound English—were shouting about how they *needed* their phones to do this assignment.

Dave had conceptualized this assignment and its corresponding execution thus: Gatsby's hosting a homecoming party (of course!) and needs to plan out the DJ's set list, meaning one song for each character. Talk with your partner and write a rationale for each song choice. Students would unwittingly delve into true character analysis via debates over popular music, undoubtedly shouting, "Naw, Myrtle is not 'bad at love,' bro! She carries 'her flesh sumptuously!' She's not trying to find a man to 'fix her'! She's a begotten piece of proud female sensuality!" and find themselves ready for the essay exam next Monday. Yes, after this killer Friday lesson, students would be eager to take an essay test on Monday, ecstatic to set down the pom-poms of homecoming and embrace the critical thinking required of *Gatsby*.

But now students were reaching for phones. He decided to roll with it.

"Sure, you can use your phones to look up music," he said, smirking, as if he hadn't just made a colossal, new-teacher mistake. "But first," he said loudly, hearing his voice bounce off the back concrete wall, "does anyone have any questions?"

"Yeah," said Cam, whose hand was on his phone. "We just gotta pick some music?"

Dave could see his fantasy slipping away. Administrators and college education professors often blithely tossed out the "We've all had days when the lesson didn't go *quite* as planned, right, everybody? Like, you had the best lesson plan, and it all went down the tubes!" So cavalier when they all said that. In truth, it roiled his stomach to watch his class and the kids and the learning slip away like that, knowing he'd simply have to wait twenty-three-and-a-half hours to try and fix this thirty-five-car pile-up.

"Cam," he said, without sighing, "each character needs his or her own—"

He kept talking, but earbuds were being jammed frantically into ears, and kids were thrusting phones in each others' faces. Now kids were—no, they weren't thinking about Gatsby. Now Dave heard not a single character's name mentioned.

He almost shouted, but that would have been too rookie of a mistake, even for him. Instead, he just got loud enough. "These songs *have* to be for Gatsby characters!" Two girls in the back corner were taking selfies of their pouty Mammoth homecoming lips. "Think of a character, and then pick a song!"

"That's *fire*, bro!" shouted JB, hitting his homie on the shoulder repeatedly with the back of his hand. "Ay, my man can *spit fire*!"

Dave made a veteran move. Having lost control of the class, he glared at the kid he might have a bit of leverage with—JB—and said nothing.

"I mean—" JB barely paused. "This rapper represents Gatsby, you know!"

One kid, thought Dave. Maybe I can get one kid to do this, or possibly two, if I can get Evan. Evan was JB's huge, lacrosse-playing sycophant. In a cool YA novel, they'd call Evan Moby Dick because he was huge, white and seemingly bent on ruining things. In real life, Dave only referred to him that way in his mind and only at home while entering grades, in case it accidentally slipped out at school.

"Yeah," said Evan, thumbing through who-knows-what on his phone. His low register rumbled through the room. Then he looked up at Dave. "What are we supposed to do?"

Think, thought Dave. You're supposed to think for the first time in your life.

"Pick a character, dawg," said JB. The class was out of control. Dave thought he saw a paper airplane fly across the room in his peripheral vision. He looked out and wondered if it was that bad. He wouldn't have been surprised to see someone use the edge of his last *Gatsby* handout to light up a cigarette.

"The only guy I know in the book is Gatbsy," rumbled Evan. He turned away from his phone, seemingly with great effort, and asked, "Mr. Legnagyszerübb, can you help us out? Who's another, like, character?"

The room seemed to cool by a degree. Later, Dave would think that it appeared as if each molecule in the room slowed nearly to a stop, and suddenly he was reminded of the time he stood in an unfamiliar, dark, empty gym.

Stuff the memory back in the sack, he told himself. Shove it as far down as you can. Student conversation didn't stop, and the phones didn't disappear back into backpacks. But, oddly enough, it became quiet.

"Klipsringer," said Dave.

In an instant, the classroom was quiet—no, silent. Cam, JB, Evan, the girls in the corner—everyone was looking at him. The totality of the stares was unnerving. His eyes jutted back and forth, and he even looked behind himself in a move that could have been misinterpreted as an attempt at humor, but Dave was suddenly sure that there was something he wasn't picking up. Was there some sort of special schedule today—was he supposed to release them early? For lunch? He looked down at his shoes and saw them rotate and swirl. What was happening? To mention lunch now would throw the class into total pandemonium.

"It's late lunch," he said. Several seconds ago, no one would have heard him say that. Now everyone did. And now, since his kids had gone full *Children of the Corn* and stared through him like automatons, he was doing his regular Dave Legnagyszerübb move: verbalize any thought that piped its way through. And now, awkward silence.

In the front row, a kind and quiet girl—Nina dos Santos Pandlay, that was her name—sat staring at him, her hands laid out on her planner. Dave, now getting scared, could not look at her face. He looked down at her calendar and noticed her perfectly painted nails: bright yellow, no jagged edges like his own. As his panic rose, it seemed he could not look away from those nails.

"Lemon yellow," he mumbled to Nina. "Your nails are lemon yellow. Why is it so *quiet* in here?"

A student's voice broke through the silence. It was one of the two selfie girls in the back.

"Mr. Legnagyszerübb," she said.

The quiet was pervasive and very unlike anything in high school. The way they all held their phones out as if pulling up music for the assignment he had conceived to defeat the homecoming distraction but was now regretting for several reasons, including, but not limited to, the eerie silence it had somehow created, and the fact that of course, every sixteen-year-old with a phone was going to pull out the device to "research a song."

Every single thing was weird, including the way that the first selfie girl pronounced his name perfectly and correctly and then paused afterward, like a lawyer.

She continued. "So we can just pick an artist's songs to use? Like, say, Lil Yakov?"

Dave had an image of himself in the rearview mirror of a sweaty car. In his mind, he pulled the drawstrings on the memory sack hard enough to make his fingertips turn white.

"Yes," he said. He felt like he might be calling her bluff. He wasn't supposed to know who Lil Yakov was. "Like, *yes.*"

Three nights ago, he had been compiling a set of articles for his only non-English-10 class, which was College Prep Writing. "College Prep" Writing means "You are not—and probably never will be—prepared to write at a college level; otherwise, you would have taken an AP or College in the Schools course. However, we're happy enough to fool you into fooling a college admissions counselor into fooling your parents into paying for a four-year school, so let the con begin."

He was ecstatic to get some kind of upper-level writing class his first year, rather than simply sharing his enthusiasm for *Gatsby* every single hour of the day, so he planned out two months' worth of intense writing curriculum: personal essays, literature analysis, and the like. On his first day, he tried to get through attendance quickly in order to get to the writing, "because that's why you're all here, right?" He had been slowed down by no fewer than four students who had been so busy silently—but with ample hand and shoulder movements—reciting song lyrics to themselves. After class, he had asked one student, Tipuan (who went by Golf), what song had locked him in so hard that he might miss his own name at attendance, even with no earbuds in or backpack speaker blaring.

"Oh, just El P, Da Sheik, Flupf tha Spork Lord, all the coldest rappers, Mr. L," Golf said.

"How do you find out about these hip-hop artists?" Dave asked, slightly insinuating that it would be difficult to receive song recommendations from anyone if you were always in an imaginary soundproof recording studio that followed you around.

"Oh, Mr. L, you know. NoiseNimbus. I even have my own tracks on there," said Golf, whose arms crossed over his chest in a look that Dave immediately recognized from the b-boy days of hip-hop.

So that night, he'd looked up Golf on NoiseNimbus. It was lo-fi, poorly conceived, skill-less, terrible rap. Clearly, Tipuan—sorry, "Golf"—had an idea: Lay down the beat, and I'll freestyle. But every third bar, Golf could not end his line with a rhyming word, even discounting his attempt to rhyme "cheddar" with "Ferrari," so he would switch up the pattern. Dave suffered through a track or two before realizing there would not be a single syllable he could compliment Golf on at school to prove that he, as a caring and dedicated instructor, had put in time at home to support his students' "talents."

Golf, however, was not the only teenager with a poorly crafted regurgitation of the hip-hop lifestyle as portrayed by social and mainstream media. So, that night, Dave lost himself down the rabbit hole of "musicians" on the NoiseNimbus site: block-letter face tattoos, willingness to consume prescription drugs with the patient's name not even blurred out from the orange bottle, cheap gas-station sunglasses that surely must be worth hundreds, and, of course, marijuana-leaf necklaces of every size and gold/diamond combination. And somewhere in the town dump of online egalitarian rap, he had spotted a name whose references to security checkpoints and unexploded mortars seemed to Dave, at least, to be someone interesting. He was Lil Yakov, nee Judah Beran, of suburban Tel Aviv. He was hot. Or cold, Or whatever the word "hype" had evolved into. And so, Dave Legnagzerübb filed away Lil Yakov in his teacher memory banks to be deployed—now.

"So yes, yes to Lil Yakov and the rest of the Golan Hype crew," Dave said, almost smirking at his cutting-edge knowledge of "what the kids were listening to."

The class was still silent; in fact, it was as if some of the kids had sat up even straighter in their seats, eyes a bit bug-eyed. He had expected this activity to captivate them—just not because of this.

"So," said the girl, in a voice ridiculously clear for a high school student in a non-honors class, "*you* know who Lil Yakov is?"

"Like, *yes*," he said. The entirety of the classroom was locked on him. The silence seemed to ring, and then another blower turned on.

"Okay," said the girl, and the class immediately resumed its earlier decibel level.

Dave checked the clock and then the special schedule he had written on the board. Four minutes left. No student frantically wrote any phenomenally insightful connections about their chosen character and the song they had picked. He tried to make his way around the room, but no learning seemed to be happening. Rather, there were phones and videos on the phones, and TikTok was open, and all was lost. Except—

The bell rang, and the class streamed out into bonkers pepfest madness—and he noticed Nina, with nails of lemon yellow, writing the names of her chosen songs into Cornell notes as the last two kids flooded out past her. One of them knocked her binder with his hip and said no words of apology after looking back. She did not look up—rather, she erased the bump mark, finished her notes for the assignment, and looked up at Dave.

"Thank you, Nina," he said. "I appreciate your actually doing the assignment."

Nina's brows furrowed on her cherubic face, and she looked around the class, puzzled.

"Nina?" Dave asked.

For just a flicker of a moment, he thought he saw something pass over Nina's face. Something like seeing a set of slow-moving clouds revealing a waning moon against the black sky, knowing the gap in the silver clouds will obscure the crescent moon.

"Mr. Legnagyszerübb," she said, putting the caps on her variously colored pens without looking at them, "I know that not everyone is listening to you talk about Gatsby. Or—um—hip-hop music. But some of us are. And I'm paying *very* close attention."

Now it was his turn to feel his face change unwittingly. He felt like a molting rattlesnake, moving around inside a sleeve of dead skin. The homecoming din in the hallway seemed like it was in a different time zone.

"Nina, is there a question you want to ask me?" In his mind, the stuff sack bulged and shifted. He nearly added, "What am I doing here?"

The clouds moved again, covering the moon, and her face took a look of almost comic confusion. "Where is everyone?" she asked.

Dave opened his mouth to speak, but Nina blurted out, "Oh, there's a pepfest today!" and sprinted out of the class, loose paper streaming behind her as her black braids bounced out the doorway.

For a moment, he felt dizzy and closed his eyes. Images swirled before him: yellow fingernails, his own reflection in the rearview mirror of his car, the inside of the boys' bathroom in the dark, Nassir's lower body coming through the window, and—

He stuffed the memory jumble, like a poorly rolled-up sleeping bag, back down into the memory sack of his brain.

10 – New Teacher Observation

"Hey, Abdiaziz! Played any good FIFA games late—"

Abdiaziz looked past the battered door to Dave's classroom and ignored his brother, Abdihamid, trying to push him out of the white fluorescent hallway lights into the yellow fluorescent classroom lights.

"Is that the principal? Are you gonna get fired, Mr. L?"

The omnipresent roar of passing time was outside, but within Dave's class, it was several notes calmer. Mr. Carter sat in the back, writing notes on his clipboard, occasionally chatting with students. Dave stood at the doorway, trying to greet every student by name and trying not to sweat through a wrinkly shirt that suddenly felt thick enough to power a sailboat. So far, he'd called four kids by the wrong name and picked up the same green dry-erase marker seven times.

"If I do, Abdi," he fake-whispered, "essay's still due next Tuesday."

It was not lost on the rookie teacher that the last time the principal had been in the same room as Dave, one of his employees had been apprehended, only to have that employee reappear several minutes later wearing an FBI uniform and a wry smile, and his boss had... barely looked up from the same clipboard he was writing in now. Perhaps they were notes on Dave's probability of escaping a Super Max prison if *he* ever got dragged away by federal agents. "Likelihood of escaping custody by costume change: 2 percent. Likelihood of trying to start a Creative Writing class behind bars: 72 percent. Likelihood of being murdered by an inmate over criticism of narrative voice in memoir: 54 percent."

Regardless of what Mr. Carter might be writing about Dave at the moment, the cascade of teens continued to fill the room. Finally, the bell rang, and the first observation of Dave Legnagyszerübb's career began.

Some kids, less astute than Abdiaziz, dropped their bags on the ground in everyday first-world blasé fashion before noticing the inscrutable Principal Carter sitting over in the back row, shirt blazingly white, tie blazingly blue, mustache blazingly one-eight of an inch wide throughout. Suddenly, phones disappeared, slouchers stood up a bit in their seats, and casual conversation became almost scripted. "Homie," JB said, patting his friend on the shoulder, "I been studying for this bio test, little to no rest."

His friend Cam furrowed his brow, followed JB's gaze to where Carter sat, smoothing his brilliant blue tie, and instantly removed his stupid Dodgers hat. "Yeah, me too, yeah, yeah. I'm doing, like, all the bio homework. Like, every night."

JB lowered his voice a bit, though Dave was standing right there. Apparently, there was only one adult—the principal—who shouldn't hear this.

"Shut up, dummy. You don' even *have* bio this quarter!" he hissed.

Cam whispered back fiercely, "Stop whispering!!! He's gonna hear us!"

"Good morning, gentlemen," Mr. Carter said without looking up, his voice several octaves lower and several sandpaper-grit levels smoother than theirs. "Keep up the good work in Bio."

The "gentlemen" covered their mouths with their hands and mimed shock, but when Dave started the class off with some workshop-model reading time, the kids in the class—especially the males—paid attention a degree better than usual. Mr. Carter eventually looked up and asked a few questions while taking a few notes. And though Dave's voice sounded so nervous as to be hollow—with Carter sitting there, every gesture and engagement felt more than a little forced—he made it through. The last four people to leave the classroom, both chronologically and in order of importance, were Cam, JB, Abdiaziz and Mr. Carter.

"Good luck on your bio test, gentlemen," Dave offered on the way out.

"What bio test?" asked JB, and Cam flicked his ear with his finger as he and JB were absorbed into the passing body of students.

As he lifted his hand in farewell to the teens, he felt the sweat-soaked folds under his armpits pull apart. Was nervous sweat more disgusting during the stressful event or just after, when it began to cool?

Now came the real test—would Carter offer a "Good job" on the way out? Or just a curt nod? Or even worse: "See me in my office after school?"

Don Carter gathered all his papers and writing utensils, checked his phone, and simply smiled at the new teacher on the way out.

"Thanks for, uh, visiting!" Dave offered.

"Thank you for what you do, Mr. Legnagyszerübb," he said, smiled again, and cut into the mass of students.

Two smiles? Maybe he wouldn't get fired before Thanksgiving after all! He turned to go back into his room and collapse on the floor—but a clear voice cut through the hallway din, "Mr. Legnagyszerübb, are you busy at the moment?"

Turns out that although Carter's smile *could* have been correlated to Dave's excellent instruction, it was more likely related to the fact that Ellen, the secretary-really-in-charge-of-the-place, had been on her way down to get him to sub. She came into his room like a suburban Lutheran geisha, fans of attendance sheets, rosters and lesson plans splayed out in her hands. Dave had seen her opening a door once with her foot as she held two lunch trays—one still full of chicken patty remains—in one hand, and a school's worth of parent consent forms in the other, all color-coded by grade. And when he had gotten over his own awkwardness and rushed to open the door for her, she stopped and turned and thanked him as if what he'd done was the greatest display of magnanimity in history. "Why, *thaaaank* you, young man!" He'd wondered if any Larry Yearsons who worked here regularly let the door slam in this kind woman's face.

"No... of course!" he stumbled.

Ellen stopped in the same gray steel door frame that Abdiaziz had entered just one observation hour before. She had a retinue of balanced paper stacks that continued to move an instant after she halted, like an entourage. "Mr. Legnagyszerübb, proof that chivalry is not dead! Can I get you to cover a 3rd block, A-period gym class?"

He was new and needed every second of his prep—

"Of course, I can, Ellen," he'd said.

"Attendance and lesson plans are in your hands," she said, already moving towards the door. On top of the pile he was holding were his two subbing documents. "I know that it's team-taught, Dave, but I'll have another teacher covering Burkhardt's section. They'll take the kids to the other gym for volleyball, and you'll all reconvene at the end of the hour."

He looked up to ask Ellen how in the name of sweet Jericho, she put the plans in his possession using sleight-of-hand *and* remembered specific phy ed instructions for concurrent classes. But she was already maneuvering down the hallway, off to find another young, impressionable teacher on whom to David Blaine some sub plans.

He looked at the gum-flecked floor of his classroom. Flopping down on it in exhaustion would have to wait—he had to get down to the gym.

11 – The Sub Job

He knew that essentially every backboard and rim in every gym in America were the same. So why did the red-orange metal hoop here look a bit more faded? Why did the square on the backboard look a bit dingier? Why did all the basketball goals look like soldiers who hadn't been paid or fed in months?

Probably because they had spent decades observing American high school students attempt to play sports.

He did not begrudge Ellen for asking him to sub. But watching one more kid shoot the ball from their stomach over the blackboard might kill him. Subbing wasn't a bad way to recover from being evaluated during 2nd period today—had he actually had his prep period, he would have accomplished less than nothing. But watching this group of students attempt to play 21 was brutal. He looked around at the other clusters of students: mostly mixed-gender or all-girl clumps, shooting free throws or, if they were feeling particularly athletic, playing some lightning.

The one guys' group, and the one that had his attention, was attempting to play 21. As Dave watched, a young kid checked the ball in, dribbled twice, picked up the ball with both hands, ran around his friend, began dribbling again, ignored his friends' shouts of unfair play, bounced the ball off his foot, ran, picked it up, and shot it directly underneath the backboard, where it bounced straight back into his face and then out of bounds. Dave could tell the kids' commitment to terrible play by the fact that none of the other boys laughed. The heaviest kid simply chugged toward the bleachers to grab the ball, hopefully unaware that he looked like a kid in an anti-bullying ad.

Dave looked around again. The staff handbook said that students needed to be kept under direct supervision, especially when subbing in an unfamiliar class. But if he went and joined the game, he would still be supervising the gym, right?

He decided to do it. These kids needed to learn.

He slipped off his cheap black dress shoes and placed them on top of his backpack—better to play in almost-bare feet than try to do it in those shoes. It would heighten the impression of his athleticism. Meanwhile, the heavyset kid had made it back to the court with the ball. He had tried to check it to a boy in a green collared shirt—"boy" being a bit of a stretch, as the kid appeared to be about six-foot-four and still growing by the second—but the Man-Boy had also dribbled directly off his own foot as he reached down to try and dribble, or maybe eat, the ball. The ball was currently rolling away from the court into the always-dark recesses of the gymnasium, and none of the boys were making any effort to get it.

He opened his computer and went to save his attendance like an actual responsible adult and not someone who was trying to get into a basketball game against some unskilled teens when an email alert popped up: the district HR person had sent out her recent vacancy report.

One posting caught his eye before he had to run out and sock-slide through an educational game of 21. It was under the Athletic Department banner, Oak River School District. Apparently, Maple Valley, a Minnesota Star School of Excellence, had a posting for a Head Volleyball Coach. Was that Rotundo himself, Larry Yearson?

Somewhere in his brain, the stuff-sack of memory jostled, but it was shoved down fairly easily this time.

He raised one eyebrow, shrugged, and closed his computer. As he walked across the court towards the game, he paused to toss his keys back onto his bag—and then thought better of it. The shadowy edges of the otherwise flash-bulb-lit gym reminded him of his interview. And putting his hands on his keys reminded him of his time in the boys' bathroom during the last M-VAULT time.

He pushed his keys deeper into his pocket and approached the boys with a smile. Man-Boy picked up the ball and held it with both hands as they all stared at him: the Sub.

"Good morning! Or afternoon. Good something, gentlemen!" said Dave, his voice weaker than he had anticipated. Suddenly deprived of a clear teaching role, he felt the tightrope-nervousness of asking a group for acceptance.

"Hey, Mr. Lizardoglub," said the smallest kid, who wore a KISS shirt, glasses with no lenses, and what appeared to be dad-golf shorts. Was that cool now? Hey, at least the kid had tried to remember Dave's sub introduction at the beginning of the hour.

Again, in an out-of-body experience, Dave felt thirteen again. But he stifled it in his throat and asked in a voice still several steps above what he'd imagined, "Mind if I get in your game?"

The boys looked at each other. Given the high school maxims equating reaction with weakness, no one said anything.

"Well, Gene Simmons and I"—the small kid didn't blink, or look at his shirt, so was he wearing it, like, ironically?—"we'll be on D first." He moved his hands as if parting the Red Sea, indicating his own team on one side.

His month and a half of teaching experience told him that when they shrugged and didn't move, they agreed. Dave handed the ball to KISS kid to signal that the game of 21 was about to start. Peter Criss held the ball and looked down at Dave's feet.

"No shoes, Mr. L?" he asked, frowning.

"Yeah, I've got my professional clothes on today. Dress for the job you want, not the one you have, right?" Of course, no one smiled or moved. KISS still held the ball.

"Well?" asked Dave.

"What time do we get out of here, again?" asked KISS.

"Whenever the game's done." He motioned in the universal hurry-it-up gesture, spinning his index finger in a circle like a rolling ball. "Let's play."

KISS stood unmoved. "Don't we have M-VAULT time today?" The others murmured, seconding the question. "So, don't we—"

Dave pushed off one besocked foot and slapped the ball out of KISS's hand. He tried to stop in front of Man-Boy to cut to the side, but his socks kept him sliding, so he dribbled the ball under Goliath's legs and picked it up on the other side, popping up for an easy layup.

"Hey," said KISS, still standing at the top of the key, running his fingers through his hair to tousle it to the side.

"That was sweet, Mr. Leonardo," said the heavyset kid, who had not moved through the whole endeavor.

"Thanks," said Dave. "One-zero, me. I call make-it, take-it."

He felt something inside of him that had been stretching this whole first two months—it didn't rip apart, exactly, but it tore in a spot, and it felt good, like peeling part of a wrapper off a can it was stuck to. The odds were that he would see these kids again, but he felt no obligation to reach out and be kind to them or engage them as an emissary of the faculty. The tear in the fabric was big enough to stick a hand through, and right now, he didn't want to repair it in any way. Must he always be a Teacher who Cares? What if the fabric inside him tore first?

As he walked back to the top of the key, he felt a sneer spread across his face—not the sneer of a person who got jumped and hog-tied helplessly in the gym or of a teacher who'd been tricked into entering a bathroom and nearly robbed. It was the sneer of the assailant, of the aggressor. The fabric spread a bit wider.

He bounced the ball to KISS, who backed up to actually guard him. Instead, he pulled up for a jumper and nearly slipped over in his socks; the ball clanged off the rim. But he was already sliding towards the rebound, a step ahead of Man-Boy and right in front of the heavyset kid. He pump-faked Man-Boy, and the kid nearly jumped over his shoulder. He slipped inside for the layup.

"Two-zero."

"Hey, what position did you play in high school?" asked the heavyset kid, shaking his dreads back and forth. Dave had already decided not to go after this kid, but KISS, Man-Boy, and a few others were going to get their ankles broken by a teacher in socks and dress slacks.

"I actually didn't play in high school," said Dave, wheeling KISS back and forth across the top of the key.

KISS stopped, running his fingers through his hair. Having enough instinct about the cadences of unsupervised basketball, Dave slowed his cross-up dribbling.

"Is that why you wanna use a women's ball? To beat up on some of your high school kids?" KISS asked, trying to smile. Instead, his jaw just jutted out while his lungs visibly flailed and heaved for oxygen, sending Ace Frehley's painted head in and out, in and out.

"This was the ball *you* fellas were playing with, then *I* came over," said Dave, who knew right away that it was a women's ball but had assumed by the graceless ballhandling he'd witnessed from across the gym that these boys would not. Honestly, it'd be fun to torch these kids with a deflated rugby ball.

KISS's jaw was still stuck out. He gestured at Dave's pockets, where his lanyard was attached to his keys. "Let me into the PE closet," he wheezed, "and I'll get a legit ball, so this game will be—" He breathed deeply. "Official."

Instead of answering, Mr. Legnagyszerübb began to dribble and cut back and forth across the top of the key. He did not acknowledge that random students had tried to grab his keys a few weeks ago, not thinking about *any* of the Maple Valley-related anomalies he'd pushed deep into the stuff-sack of memory. More pertinently, Dave did not have faith that he could cut up the lane in his socks without falling. So, he pulled up, air-balled a jumper, sprinted in, grabbed it off the bounce in the air, and laid it easily off the glass.

"Three-zero." The fabric inside his chest, with the well-worn "Teacher Who Cares" logo on it, was stretching but comfortable He wasn't interested in ripping it further or sewing it back together. Man-Boy was bent over, mouth open, and the large kid didn't seem to have the energy to compliment Dave anymore or ask him any background questions. In a way, it was the ultimate compliment.

Seeing their aerobic distress, he checked the ball, pulled back and let fly a loooooong two-pointer. It hit the back of the rim so hard that neither metal nor rubber made any noise as it arced back through the air, right into the heavyset kid's hands. As he labored back past the arc, it gave Dave a chance to make sure the rest of the class hadn't wandered out into a different pasture. The small groups of gym students were still occupied—and here, the other half of the co-taught class was back. The other sub was holding the door—

It was Sarah ushering kids back in. She caught his eye and gave him a wave.

The heavyset kid threw the ball off the side of the backboard, and Dave returned Sarah's wave. They had worked together in the cohort of young teachers for the last month and a half, and this was her first time initiating contact with him, besides the time she had saved him from being eaten by three high schoolers for whom M-VAULT time might as well had been a chance to practice cannibalism. His face flushed, as he hoped, like a desperate sophomore, that she'd noticed his last two scores in this pickup game. Did regular adults with real jobs think like this too, or was this a consequence of working in a high school? If so—at the moment, feeling the sweat start to accumulate on his brow and squinting under the suddenly-bright gym lights, it felt like a shortcut to permanent youth.

He waved back, but she was holding the door open for the stream of entering students. This also meant that there could only be a few minutes of class left.

KISS, of course, was letting the heavy kid run down KISS's own out-of-bounds shot, even though Paul Stanley and friends were closer. The Starchild stood combing his hair over with his fingers, making inane hand gestures to his friends in the other half of the co-taught class, who were now streaming into the gym. Dave's teeth clenched.

"Hey, when I was in high school," said Dave, stepping closer to KISS, "you airball a shot that rolls to the other half of the gym, *you* go get it." The fabric of his bleeding teacher-heart stretched again.

The kid did not hear Dave and continued his finger comb, occasionally stopping to give his friends a finger twist and exaggerated smirk.

By now, the poor big kid was back with the ball. Dave's pituitary gland, firing at high-school levels, cut through his rage at KISS by noting that if he got the class gathered and the equipment put away, he could make a bit of small talk with Ms. Lehner before they both had to leave the gym.

"Okay, guys—sorry to cut our 21 game short, but it's time to get the balls put away," called Dave, making an aw-shucks gesture.

"Oh, is it M-VAULT time today? So when is class done?" asked Man-Boy, for whom the incoming stream of students combined with Dave's announcement that it was time to pack up was, apparently, not *quite* enough context to figure out what was happening.

"Okay, guys," said Dave again, "that's it. Actually," he began, glancing at Sarah, who was talking with a student and looked over at him right after the student did, "let's play. Next point wins."

The large kid checked the ball and had taken a single dribble when Dave slid in on his socks and knocked it away. He took the ball to the top of the key and waited, bouncing the ball slowly.

KISS approached him to play defense, and Dave waited one extra beat for KISS to put his foot forward. When he did with his left, Dave slipped by on his right and cut deftly to the basket. He took off for the layup and—

The backboard shook. Man Boy had leaped up and blocked his shot so hard that it shook the entire backboard apparatus. Dave, completely posterized and unable to process what had happened, had tumbled to the wooden gym floor. A second later, Man Boy's bulk smothered Dave's ribs as he lay on the ground. Dave saw the overhead lights momentarily dim as the air was forced out of his lungs, and the heavy sledge of the "kid's" elbow seemed to be intent on breaking his ribs.

Like some kind of spry, gigantic crocodile, Man Boy hopped up on all four sets of finger/toe-tips and bounced off Dave without so much as a word. Luckily, Dave did not lay on the ground—certainly not with the possibility that his co-substitute over on the half of the gym might have seen him play French Guy to Man Boy's Vince Carter—but scrambled off to the top of the key to steal the ball from KISS, who was trying to dribble past the three-point line.

Dave sprinted out to meet him; KISS greeted him with a grin. As KISS drove right with a clumsy batting of the ball and a slow step, Mr. Legnagyszerübb reached out to grab the ball—and KISS suddenly pivoted on said clumsy foot, effortlessly drawing the ball back underneath his leg. Dave, now frantic, lunged for the ball, but it was as if he was several film frames behind. KISS was already dribbling smoothly past Dave, and Dave hung there, suspended and, once again, posterized, before his face slammed into the heavy kid's stomach. The worst part of it was that he would at least have ended up on the ground instantly, but he was suspended in midair by the wavy bulk of the child's midsection. His "hmpfh!" was absorbed by the boy's wet gym shirt—Dave could smell the laundry detergent his mom used, and it was the best part of the whole experience—before he was down again, this time on his stomach. He opened his eyes to see KISS drop a lazy finger roll off the glass and into the net.

He got to his feet and looked over at KISS, who was shuffling off the court towards the locker rooms, Man Boy just behind him. Like a school of fish, every student had got the signal simultaneously to veer towards the north gym exit; Man Boy was right behind KISS, merging into the swarm of kids who were already thinking about their next class. Which was—

"M-VAULT time," said Sarah, who had materialized next to him. This was better, for he didn't have time to become petrified, but it was worse, too, for he knew that as soon as his brain started churning, his mouth would follow by allowing the nonsense in his head to have center stage.

"Yes, ma'am," said Dave. "Are you ready?" Wow. Nothing awkward had spouted out of his mouth. Had he sustained a concussion?

"Yeah, I think I've got it. A few kids are coming into do make-up band lessons, so that will be… well, it will be make-up band lessons." She smirked, and it was as if her cheeks were carved out of exquisite, malleable marble. "Though it looks as if I might have to give you some make-up basketball lessons first, Mr. Legnagyszerübb."

He swallowed. Quick, what was it? Was it a) an allusion to the fact that during the first unstructured time, she had rescued him from being robbed in the bathroom? b) A reference to his recent basketball "effort" here in gym class? c) An invitation to some sort of social…something? Yet again, somehow, miraculously, he was able to respond in a way that made syntactical sense:

"Yeah, basketball was never my forte," he said coolly, taking a swipe at the sweat behind his ears, hoping she wouldn't see. Or smell, for that matter. "How about you? Did you ever play?"

She shifted, gazing off momentarily at the hoop in the now nearly abandoned gym. It was funny how her wrist still rested on her hip as if she were still holding an oboe. Or a truncheon.

"I was a three-year starter, actually, in high school. *And* I played in the pep band at the guys' games." There was the smirk again.

Dave thought that he would replay this conversation in every detail—the way her bobbed blonde hair hung to the side, the bright blue nail polish on the invisible-nightstick-wielding hand, the unguarded wistfulness she exhibited at that moment—at the close of the school day, as he sat in his room surrounded by lower life forms who could not figure out how to write the *Gatsby* essay.

"Wow, you must have been some kind of star," responded Dave, leaning over adroitly (he hoped) to scoop up the ball. "Like New York Philharmonic meets WNB—"

He was standing by himself in the gym. Only the hum of the fluorescent lights and the ever-present but ineffective HVAC blowers accompanied Mr. Dave Legnagyszerübb, the Gym Sub, as he stood alone on the gym floor.

She had disappeared—and he was almost scared to look behind him. What if she were just standing right there? Say, with a group of other teachers, waiting to hog-tie him again just to remind him of the interview day?

Mechanically, he walked the basketball over to the phy ed storage closet. It was open, with no interior lights on.

His heart hammered faster, and his skin became clammier than during his embarrassing game of 21.

He rolled the ball on the floor, like a seven-year-old too scared to take his dirty laundry downstairs by himself into the concrete, dank, dark laundry room, who pitches the ball of clothes onto the basement floor and sprints back up the stairs.

The basketball bounced off of a rack of assorted, semi-inflated, vaguely round balls and rattled around into dark recesses David could not see. He took a deep breath; not putting something back where it was supposed to be was anathematic to the core principles of his existence. He took a step towards the dark mouth of the storage room, trying to let the numbness wash over him so he could robotically pick up the ball and put it up and get out of there—

He heard a noise: the scrape of a rubber footstep across the wood floor behind him.

"Sarah?" he called out, his voice much more normal than it felt. "Ms. Lehner?"

The blower turned off in the gym. There was the faraway sound of kids going to class, but otherwise, it was quiet. Shouldn't there be kids streaming in here right now?

Except it was M-VAULT time. He had to get the equipment put away.

Just take a deep breath, hold it, and stroll on into that room. That he could do. He reached into his pocket and knew immediately. His keys were gone. And it was M-VAULT time. And he'd just been hustled by a group of kids who had made a *lot* of physical contact once they'd revealed themselves to be capable basketball players. And Sarah had been here. Had she seen it happen? Given a few more minutes, might she have joined up in the game, saving Dave's dignity and physical well-being once again and helping him keep his keys?

The thought of how that would play out snapped him out of his frozen state, and he broke into a run toward the gym door. He pushed the battered, dark-brown metal door to the gym open and went to pivot to charge down the hall—but the door was stopped mid-swing. A well-maintained hand, with even cuticles and no trace of ink around the nails, grasped the door.

Dave hit the door with his shoulder, like a junior high kid trying to learn to tackle, and bounced to the side. He skidded to a stop on one foot and turned to face the door ju-jitsu practitioner.

"Mr. Legnagyszerübb," said Principal Carter, adjusting his glasses up his nose while referencing a clipboard, "I know your post-observation is scheduled for tomorrow.'

"Okay," said Dave, his mind blank.

"Let's talk in my office now, hmm?"

"Okay," replied Dave. A part of his mind that was trying to process everything noted that, in terms of employment, this wasn't good.

"There's a few things we need to discuss," said Don Carter, without looking back. His crisp, dry dress shoes clicked against the linoleum floor, in contrast to Dave's loose shoes, with feet and socks slick with sweat.

12 – The Evaluation

Dave followed Mr. Carter through the random brown-and-white hallways—though mostly labyrinthine corners where Dave felt like he might lose Carter at any second—of Maple Valley's offices. There was no small talk or even a head turn from Carter. Perhaps he didn't want to put a single wrinkle in his perfectly smooth shirt. The radiant blue shirt did provide a beacon for Dave to follow through the back offices. At one point, he noticed what seemed like an old eagle icon—definitely not a mammoth—on one of the beige hallways, but he had to keep up with Carter, so he didn't stop to look closer.

As he passed Ellen at the front desk, she smiled, looking up from a stack of papers about a foot high. Dave's anxious brain noted the various colors of each binder clip within the stack, regarding each glossy clip's place from top to bottom: red, orange, yellow, and all the way down to violet. If anyone owned an ultraviolet binder clip, invisible to the human eye but useful for the superhuman school clerk, it would be Ellen.

She almost always addressed him by his full last name, at least since he'd been hired. During the interview process, she'd called him all sorts of incorrect variants of Legnagyszerübb, but once he'd been hired, she casually enunciated her perfect pronunciation, like a gymnast who nonchalantly does a pike-tuck with a twist onto her couch. And suddenly, since he had just received a smile but no "hello" from her, he panicked a bit: what if his evaluation was not good? What if he was let go at the semester break?

His spirits were not buoyed when he saw Ms. Young already in Mr. Carter's office. Of course, it didn't mean anything; she was probably just checking in with her boss about something else. It didn't mean—

"Ms. Young," said Mr. Carter, "thanks for coming down." Well, never mind.

"Of course. Happy to help." Her head tilted to indicate her eagerness to aid anyone at any time, and her necklace and earrings chimed in agreement. She then gestured to Dave to sit, walked behind him, and closed the door. Dave swallowed. Suddenly, the office of the principal—mostly shelves with whatever educational leadership guides were popular during their five-year lifespan, a few succulent plants, the requisite diplomas, and, of course, large brown filing cabinets—seemed tiny.

"Mr. Legnagyszerübb," said Carter, leaning forward so that his elbows rested on his desk, "can you explain why you did it?"

Before he could think to regulate his brain, words streamed out of his mouth. "I know, it was foolish to let JB and Ricky sit next to each other. And I actually thought those boys—JB and Cam—might do the exit ticket activity, but I was clearly wrong, and I will be honest, I was nervous about being observed. I don't want to make excuses—"

Ms. Young leaned in, the patronizing smile widening. But then she squinted and shook her head as if unable to say anything.

Carter also narrowed his eyes. His immaculate eyebrows wrinkled in unison. "Dave, what are you talking about?"

"My..." He looked at both of them and frowned. "My observation. This morning."

"Your... *observation*?" Carter asked. "Wow, you are one smooth customer, Mr. Legnagyszerübb. I mean... to speak candidly, I... well, I—"

Young jumped in. Dave wondered if she was as flummoxed as he. It was kind of shocking to see the always-poised Don Carter search for words.

"We didn't think you'd be back at school. And when you did show up, we thought, 'Here's a guy who can keep his cover under any circumstance.'" She nodded to show her admiration.

"My cover?" It was hard to keep up the nearly-obsequious, new-employee, chipper-and-up-for-any-challenge attitude when he had no clue what was going on, though something about being in this office—no, not now. He shoved the memories back down into the stuff-sack.

He had also started to sweat. Again. And he knew that once he started, he would not stop.

Mr. Carter looked down at his desk and stirred a pencil in an empty Mammoths Homecoming 2015 coffee cup. He looked up with an "Are you going to make me say it?" arch in his still-perfect eyebrows.

With nothing to verbalize, Dave thought, not for the first time: "What am I doing here?"

Ms. Young opened her mouth and pushed her palms together, but nothing came out. What, exactly, were they waiting for? Again, memories threatened to come loose from the stuff-sack, but he held them down and said nothing. Finally, Ms. Young looked at Mr. Carter, and he gave her a hint of a nod, so she looked back at Dave.

"Mr. Legnagyszerübb, why did you assign Larry Yearson as an elimination target for student authentic learning?"

Dave had seen Ms. Young's mouth articulate the words, but they made no sense, in any sense, so he did what he always suggested his kids do when faced with a difficult sentence: latch onto the one thing you understand.

"Larry Yearson? The volleyball du—coach? I think he's a Social Studies teacher?"

"*Was* the volleyball coach," corrected Carter. And added, as an afterthought: "And Social Studies teacher. *Was* a Maple Valley social studies teacher."

"*Was?*"

Principal Carter laid it out like a teacher explaining to a student how he'd been caught plagiarizing an essay. "You ordered Mr. Yearson eliminated as an authentic learning project during M-VAULT time. Several students attempted the task, and eventually, one succeeded." He handed Dave a photograph.

Dave looked at the picture, but it didn't make sense, so he just kept looking at it. His hand did not shake, and he did not cry, move or grimace. Rather, he stared at the photo, which showed an overweight man in a tracksuit lying in the grass in what appeared to be a wooded area. The man looked as if he might have fallen asleep.

Mr. Carter's voice, as if from a very distant end of a tunnel, spoke normally, "Larry Yearson, a twenty-three-year employee of Maple Valley High and the district, was found dead this morning in a park about a mile from his house. It looked as if he'd been unsuccessfully stabbed several times, hit with a blunt object, burnt in several places—he even had several BBs lodged in his leg. The stab wounds were—they weren't what investigators would qualify as sequential. It seems they were done with multiple weapons at different times. This explains the copious amounts of blood at the scene, including dried blood found on the victim... on his monogrammed tracksuit."

Dave stared at the photo. He couldn't turn his head or ask for the information to be repeated. Different details of the photo held his eyes—the shrub that hid half of the body, the way two white stripes of the pants leg were now a dark brown, the asphalt walking path lined by weeds—and then he bounced elsewhere in the picture because not a single thing made sense.

"However, what eliminated the target—what *finally* eliminated the target—was a dose of strychnine administered that morning. And, when that failed, applied directly to the victim's mouth several hours later."

Again, Dave had no capacity to ask anything. This must be a dream, right? He would tell Sarah tomorrow at school that he was interrogated about a murder at school. It must be some kind of—stress or anxiety response? Had the whole day been a hoax played on him by his subconscious? Well, he would still try to follow along gamely.

Ms. Young was, for some absolutely inexplicable reason, still smiling as she lowered her head to try and make eye contact with him.

"Dave?" she asked.

He opened his mouth, but only a vacuum filled his lungs. No words. He closed his mouth and shut his throat against a wave of nausea. He finally produced some words, speaking in a voice that was not his own.

"I did... do you think I did this? That I would, or could, or have ever—" His throat clenched again, and his brain spun because Dave hated Larry Yearson. Had called him "Rotundo" in his mind, in fact.

Had Dave somehow murdered a colleague through the power of negative thinking? Did Ms. Young and Mr. Carter know about his feelings through some kind of employee mind-reading software? Did it scan Dave's banal emails offering updates on students with IEPs, using deep learning technology to ascertain that he loathed his popular, portly, ineffectual co-worker?

"I—I never liked the guy—I mean, Yearson. He's dead, and you honestly think I killed him?"

Carter and Young looked at each other. Why didn't they just say "no?"

"Mr. Legnagyszerübb. We're not sure where to go with this, so we'll level with you," said Young, bracelets jangling as she gesticulated. "You might be a very sophisticated outside agent with an extraordinarily deep cover going back years. Tomorrow you may vanish, and we here at Mammoth will consider ourselves—beatable, vulnerable to infiltration. Though you're obviously better at it than most."

She made eye contact with him and drew in a long breath, moving her matching necklaces slowly out and in. Carter made no noise. For a moment, a clock somewhere in this ancient building ticked like a final gasp.

Somewhere in the swirl of Dave's thoughts, he kept a foot pressed firmly on the stuff-sack of memory.

She smiled more broadly and continued. "But here's what I think, Dave. You were looking to give our students—our brightest, most precious resource!—a surprise bit of authentic learning! Learning by *doing!*" Her fists raised themselves in front of her face, and her smile widened.

It had a touch of insanity, he thought. This type of administrator did not have insanity as a main ingredient, but it was maybe just a garnish added during the final plating. "So you jumped the gun a little—out of *enthusiasm!*—and ordered your students to kill Mr. Yearson. As a real-world application of their skills!" She paused, then added—apparently, without joking!—a "Yay!"

Dave went to wipe the sweat from his forehead; his skin there felt rough. He pushed hard with his fingers and could hear the noise it made against his hairline: a papery, empty sound. Carter and Young did not speak, the "Yay!" hanging in the air. Dave's mouth dropped open, and out came, "I don't understand."

But then he did, just he had been sure a moment before that he had been dreaming. Of course, this was a joke. His mentor and beer-hall buddy Erik knew these two somehow and had set this up as an elaborate practical joke. He almost smiled, though he couldn't, and swabbed at his forehead again with his fingers, right below the hairline.

"Ah," he said, managing to say this out loud. His voice still sounded strangely musical, as if it had been raised or lowered an octave. "This is a joke."

At this point, his two bosses should have cracked. One should have started laughing, and then pulled up Erik on FaceTime, and then they all would have laughed, and then they would have gone down to the brewery for a beer, and after a few, Carter and Young would confess that they actually liked him and his work quite a bit, and just when the conversation lulled, Rotundo would walk in, and he'd be different and super-cool, and his actual name would be Cormac del Cristo instead of Larry Yearson, and they would all laugh together so hard that beer would slosh out over their wrists, and they wouldn't care.

Dave's whole chest cavity seemed to chill. No, he responded to himself here in the silence. No. Larry—Mr. Yearson to the students—was dead, and it wasn't an accident.

"Oh, Mr. Legnagyszerübb," began Ms. Young, "you're thinking, it's so *tough*. It's so tough trying to marry your excellent pedagogical practices with the curriculum you work so hard on, and so you might try to pass this off as a joke!" Ms. Young's hands clenched on either side of her face and then moved together, quickly miming "marry." "But—but you're not in trouble, Dave. These kinds of messy learning experiences are going to drive us to make better Mammoths."

Dave had heard Ms. Young go on like this for scores of minutes at staff meetings, but now that he was trying to process what was going on, his brain couldn't do much of anything else. She continued anyway, "But while we *do* have to say that contracting the death to a group of tenth graders was... unorthodox, we—"

"'Contracting the death?'" He rubbed his forehead.

"Yes," said Ms. Young. Her hands were still clenched, but she blinked her eyes particularly slowly. "On Friday, October 4—right before the Homecoming assembly—you ordered members of your fourth hour American Literature class to eliminate Larry Yearson, using a clear, albeit—" her cheeks seemed to squeeze as she searched for the word—"very *antiquated* cipher. Most of your students got the confirmation, the requisite re-confirmation, and even a redundant confirmation, so there was no doubt."

His fingers went at his forehead as if they were looking for food. "A cipher?"

"Yes. And again, Dave, I need to reiterate. You're a young teacher. You were trying to do the right thing and give kids an opportunity for some authentic learning. That's a good thing!" Her hands made inscrutable scooping motions, and the bracelets banged wildly. "It's a good thing, Mr. Legnagyszerübb!"

"We just want to make it clear, Dave," said Mr. Carter, "that this type of project explicitly requires administrative approval here. If you think about your work at the HRB, it's akin to needing several project leads to green-light the command."

Dave took his fingers from his forehead and looked up. His mouth opened and closed, wondering what question to ask. He started with the most recent: "My work at the—the what, exactly?"

In the movies, he would have laughed and spread his hands out in incredulity. This wasn't the movies, however, so he just stared at his bosses.

Ms. Young was the one who laughed first. "Again, Dave, your commitment to your cover is admirable, but everyone in this room works for the FBI's Human Resources Branch, so you can..." She smiled at Carter. "Do you remember being this—this *new*, this *idealistic?*"

"I suppose," answered Carter, though his face indicated that he did not, in fact, suppose.

"You think I work for the freaking FBI?"

"The Human Resources Branch—the HRB," said Ms. Young.

"Okay, okay. I work for the HR department of the FBI, and I used a secret code to instruct high school students to murder a colleague. That's literally what you're saying to me right now."

"In terms of what we can prove, Dave," said Mr. Carter, "at least two of those assertions are factually correct."

Dave shook his head as if trying to wake himself up.

"Wait," he said. "I used some kind of secret—cipher, you said?" His mind was in freefall right now. "If enough monkeys bang on enough typewriters, they'll eventually write the works of Shakespeare. So because I talked enough, I unleashed a bunch of *kids* to—"

"Is he wearing a wire?" interrupted Mr. Carter. His face had somehow become even flatter and more impenetrable.

"No," said Ms. Young curtly. Her face also went to stone. "The kids in phy ed checked him." She paused. "Right before they took his keys."

Dave threw his hands up in supplication. "Okay, then. How are these kids stealing keys and... and attacking teachers in the bathroom during unstructured time... and—"

Carter crossed his arms. In any other performance eval, that cross would have intensely worried someone like Dave, but at this point, he was too confused for worry.

Don Carter squared his shoulders at Young. "They got *his* keys? Without cheating?"

"Without cheating," she assented.

Carter cocked his head towards Dave. "Is it *possible*, Sarah, that he doesn't know? Or is he simply trying to get me to say it out loud?"

"Say *what* out loud?" exclaimed Dave.

13 – The Magnet School

Ms. Young looked at the ceiling, and then—he saw her do it—she looked at the door. Dave did not like that. Not one bit. She then looked back at Carter, and her face relaxed.

His face relaxed in turn, too, though it wasn't as obvious. "We run a high school that caters to a certain career path for many of our students. It's one reason we allow unstructured time—we need it for students to explore their newfound skill sets."

Dave raised his eyebrows.

"He's not wearing a wire, Don. You can just say it."

"You don't think he knows right now?"

"If he's involved in work to document legally admissible material, then we can beat it," she said, "or—" She looked at the door again.

"I'm sitting right here," Dave mumbled.

"Maple Valley is a vocational high school for state espionage, security penetration, assassination—the skill set of a government service operative," said Principal Carter. He paused, ostensibly so that if Dave made a motion to leave, or to transmit some recording to someone, they could murder him. "This is, obviously, not public knowledge. Not even to all the students."

"This… this is a school for spies and assassins?"

Carter gave a flat nod. The gesture might be funny under very different circumstances.

"But some kids here are just… normal high school kids?" Apparently, Nina dos Santos Pandlay, the nice girl from his 3rd hour, might have a

87

biology lab partner who would sell her to human traffickers in order to obtain the "skill set of a government operative," and she would have no idea. Maybe he'd do it for an A on a Criminal Org Infiltration lab.

That seemed unfair. Immediately, his mind raced through his rosters. "About what… what percentage of these kids are Jason Bournes or Lorraine Broughtons in the making?"

There was silence. For once, Young and Carter did not look at each other.

"You can't—you can't tell me?"

Carter rubbed his mustache. "No—it's supposed to be listed on the attendance sheet, but there's something wrong with the system. The kids on the operative career path are supposed to have an asterisk by their name in Course View."

As a new teacher, Dave spent many hours looking at Course View. And Student View. And Section Roster View. And every other view that was available in the attendance system. He pictured it in his head for a moment.

"They *all* have asterisks—astrices?—by their names. Every student. It doesn't indicate anything."

"Yes, they do," said Ms. Young. "So at this time, we are—" her fists clenched, as if everyone in the district office were working right now to solve this happy accident, and the work just made everyone so satisfied, "we are seeking to resolve this issue, but unfortunately, until then, it might be difficult, or even impossible, to determine which Mammoths are actually on the operative career path."

"Operative career path," repeated Dave. His fingertips had found his forehead again.

Operative career path. That explained a few things, like the gym after the interview. And the unstructured time in the bathroom. And the hustle he'd received subbing in gym.

Carter and Young weren't speaking. That gave him time to think—for instance, about what he would do next. Apparently, he had murdered a co-worker. Using students. And apparently (the photo they'd shown him of Rotundo's body), it had not gone smoothly. Because—

"Our students are exactly that," said Mr. Carter, as if reading Dave's mind. He sighed, which, given his mustache, was a classy gesture.

"Normal kids blow off chemistry tests in order to play video games with their friends. They make awkward proposals for prom dates and then immediately regret it and try to recompense by even more awkward proposals offered to the prospective date's best friend." He shrugged. "So whereas a normal Oak Heights High School teen might bungle an essay about the Renaissance, our students might—despite very good intentions—make a few mistakes in a targeted elimination."

A few mistakes. Stab thrusts that missed their mark, in the same way a student might forget to use MLA while writing a research paper. Ineffectual and tortuous doses of poison because kids sometimes forget to put the math answer in simplest form. Easy-to-understand mistakes.

"Again, we're so glad you extended the opportunity for true authentic learning to your students with the orders," said Ms. Young, smiling.

"Are—are you kidding?" Dave asked. He heard his voice falter, but the words poured out now. "Honestly, if this whole thing isn't some weird joke to play on a new young teacher, I'm not sure what to think right now. It doesn't bother you that I murdered the volleyball coach?" He faltered again. "What about his family? I mean, Jesus."

"Oh, Mr. Legnagyszerübb," began Ms. Young, "a family? In this profession? That would be irresponsible. Mr. Yearson, like you, was unmarried with no meaningful relationships. Of course, we don't want staff members lost to assassination. But it's part of the—the line of employment." She paused, and Dave sensed an earnestness that hadn't been there before. "Larry Yearson," she said, in a lowered voice, "won't be missed. Agents, operatives, embedded collectors who contract with the I IRB—their duty is to give their lives, if necessary. How *wonderful* [her voice went up in pitch, horribly] for us to be able to say that our sacrifices have been for *education*. For *students' education!*" Her bracelets tinkled like a Greek chorus.

"Did you ever get to know Larry?" asked Carter. Now it was a snideness that surprised Dave. "Was he loveable? In fact, do you get those kinds of relationship vibes from *any* of your co-workers?"

His mind went to one in particular. And he realized if this particular music teacher was targeted for death because of an English teacher's unintentional misstep, she would emerge without a scratch on her. But he quickly shoved that aside.

"No, I don't."

"We work hard to find the right people for this job," said Mr. Carter. "Larry Yearson spent many years as a field agent working for organizations far outside of the HRB's purview that I, frankly, am not allowed to talk about. He served his country—and a few well-paying, private organizations—well. But his cover, like many good covers, wasn't all subterfuge. He was more than a little nuts about his coaching job and more than a little negligent of his teaching work. And most importantly, at least where your conscience is concerned, he was a self-serving jerk."

And now, here he was, listening to his bosses convince him that Larry Yearson would not be missed. That's what spies, even teacher-spies (or spy-teachers?!) did, eventually—they died under mysterious circumstances. Or everyday circumstances, like a miscommunication between a teacher and a class of high school kids.

"So the kids on the—uh, 'operative path' won't collectively grieve for Mr. Yearson—but what about the normal kids here? However many there are?" Because the cut-rate web application used for attendance and grades couldn't work long enough to inform staff who were murder-ninjas in training and who were average kids worrying about friends and snacks and phones.

"That's the great thing," said Ms. Young earnestly. "It's one more truly authentic learning experience for these students. Information flow, information control—it's all right there." She paused, as a teacher will do when trying to determine if a student will grasp the concept they just "threw out there."

Dave was not so numb that he couldn't figure out what she meant by "information control." This was just another opportunity at Maple Valley High School for students to practice their real-world espionage skills. They would, as groups of students do, try to collaboratively accomplish a task, and in this case, the task would be to make sure that no one really found out what happened to Mr. Yearson.

Dave's mind quickly assembled the footage: Groups of four kids on the "pre-operative" track met in the library after school. They figured out how to effectively spread the word that Mr. Yearson had moved to Montana to be closer to the grandkids. Or, even better—they would add the accelerant of scandal to the fire. "Ay, you hear about Yearson? Some girls on the volleyball team said he got fired after screaming at the manager. Yeah, the special-ed kid who does the water and stuff. I guess Larry just went off on him, and it was too much, so they fired his ass. What you think he'll do with all those Maple Valley volleyball tracksuits?"

Authentic, real-world experience in information manipulation—or, as Young had said, information flow and information control.

She was still talking to him. "So, again, we're not upset at what you did. We would have just appreciated a simple heads-up."

Dave almost grinned. Instead, he blinked slowly, carefully handling the stuff-sack of memory and allowing one item through. Perhaps that's what his post-interview attack was about, "Hey, don't work here unless you've got the skill set—and callous attitude toward human life—of The Terminator."

"I'm upset at what I did," said Dave. The words landed on silence— he could hear the ticking of the tasteful quartz desk clock near Mr. Carter's left hand, which read "2009 Administrative Conference: Principal of the Year Semifinalist." Dave wondered if he had taken it as some kind of memento after a rival principal "fell" into the ocean during a stroll outside the conference hotel, or went down with a mysterious illness from which she never recovered. Now every thought that flashed through his mind, like a blur of a speeding car, made him feel more hollow inside. Was this why so many people, when murdered in horrible situations, never ran, hid or fought back? How could he even move now, with hollow legs that were welded to the floor? Later, would people wonder (not that any of them would find out) why he hadn't run out of Carter's office before he was "eliminated?"

If they could have seen the look Young just gave at the doorway, they'd understand.

However, words could still escape his dry mouth, so he repeated them. "I'm upset at what I did."

"Frankly, that surprises me," said Mr. Carter, now leveling his gaze at Dave, who immediately looked down at his worn teacher-business-casual shoes, "given your background. Don't forget that we looked at your resume during the hiring process, Dave."

"What *background?* Yeah, I got one stripe on my white belt in second grade. And I accidentally stole a Snickers bar that I was holding in my palm behind a bottle of Sprite from a gas station, but I returned it. I hardly think that makes me a Highly Qualified Teacher in the licensure area of Reconnaissance and Subversion, or whatever."

Mr. Carter sighed. The lid was back on for him; he wouldn't break his professional demeanor.

Ms. Young, though, frowned, her earrings giving a tandem, small wave. "We saw your resumé, Dave Legnagyszerübb. When you applied. Special Forces training, overseas enhanced surveillance training in the Koreas, cyberwarfare in Eastern Europe. That's why I can't see the sense in your trying to maintain your cover now, Dave. You had Yearson eliminated by covert order, but that's what we do at this school. There will be no extrajudicial prosecution or… any other consequences. We've got work to do. We've got to educate kids here. In fact, unstructured time ends here, soon."

It was true—kids would be heading to class soon, and there were few things in the universe that could usurp the need to put an adult in front of kids. But Young shifted off the edge of the desk on which she was sitting.

Maybe they were telling the truth; not that he had much contact with assassins (that he knew of!), but they sure looked like a school administrative team headed back to work rather than two people about to create a body disposal problem. But then why would they lie about—

"You mentioned that you saw my 'resumé.' Do you want to see my real resumé? The one that I brought to the interview? I have it with me, and I'm pretty sure it mentions nothing more 'FBI-ish' than bringing a group of at-risk boys to an archery range at a school last year." He reached for his backpack.

In the large compartment, under the stack of graded short-response essays, ungraded *Gatsby* reading quizzes, exit tickets from an activity yesterday, and a few Health Information sheets—here it was. The manila folder, with a few sweaty thumbprints still on the front. He recalled the parking lot that day and the feeling of hopelessness that there would be one more job he wouldn't get.

In his mind, he pressed his foot firmly on the memory-sack.

He handed the folder to Ms. Young—after all, she had been in the interview that day, along with a table full of teacher types whom Dave could not remember in any detail. She pursed her lips and looked at him with her head cocked to the side, but then she opened up the folder and glanced at it. Then, her well-maintained eyebrows furrowed, and her cheeks became just a shade redder. Dave could see it even in the poorly lit principal's office. Without saying anything, she passed his resumé to Don Carter. His eyebrows went from being arched in interest to pointed in—was it disappointment?

"I'll call Ellen," he told Ms. Young, but then Ellen herself came through the door, stacks of folders balanced on the crook of her left elbow, individual papers of some kind arranged in the organizer that was her right hand. She dipped her head down a bit to regard Carter since she clearly had no way to adjust her glasses otherwise. Dave, perhaps looking to add one more thing to the list of unraveling knowledge of his workplace, looked at Ellen to find she was already looking at him.

He looked down at his feet immediately but wondered again at her inscrutability. Mr. Carter calls, and Ellen's already there. Young woman's haircut—no, actually, young woman's *hair*—but clearly needs to wear some multifaceted corrective lens. And Dave was willing to bet that—

"I've got the interview papers right here," said Ellen. She somehow slid the third pile from the top of her left elbow with the softest of thuds onto Dave's desk. "Good afternoon, Dave," she said with a genuine smile. "And thank you again for subbing this afternoon! Hope the kids in phy ed treated you well." And she disappeared from the office.

He looked back at Carter and Young. They stared at him.

"Spell your last name for us, Dave," said Young evenly, though there was an unmistakable edge there, like a nail hiding behind a piece of soft wood.

"It's spelled just like it sounds." No laughter at that joke. He articulated the letters for her.

Ms. Young peered at a piece of paper midway down the stack she'd received from Ellen. "Yep, that's the spelling we have here. 'David Legnagyszerübb.'"

"Nope," Dave said reflexively. Ten minutes ago, he would have never said "Nope" to a boss, or a principal, or, God forbid, a combination of the two.

"Sorry?" said Ms. Young. In a surreal way, Dave wondered if a secret agent ever thought, "God, I could kill you right now!" when that was, in fact, true—such was Ms. Young's "sorry."

"My name's not 'David.' It's 'Dave,' with no middle name. It's on my birth certificate."

"Well, that's..." Ms. Young trailed off, showing the resumé to Carter while looking at him. She might be the boss of the FBI's Spy Academy, but she wasn't managing her visible consternation very well.

"You hired the wrong guy, didn't you?" said Dave. His mouth hung open, and his eyes darted back and forth between Carter and Ms. Young. "You would *never* hire a normal person to work here. Who did you think I was?"

"I'm not sure what—" Ms. Young began, but Carter interrupted her by handing her another resumé from the pile Ellen had dropped off. Her jaw went slack.

"Dave..." she began.

Carter picked it up. "Dave," he began, "is... have you... How common is your last name?"

Dave laughed like a volcano belching sulfur. "Um, it's not." Then it was his turn to let his mouth fall open. "*Another* Dave Legnagyszerübb interviewed for this job?!"

Neither of them answered immediately.

Ms. Young arched her eyebrows and looked up at the ceiling. She then leveled her gaze directly and uncomfortably at him. "Dave," she began very slowly, "have you ever heard of the CSS?"

He kept his foot pressed firmly on the memory sack. "Isn't that a computer script acronym of some kind?"

She kept her eyes locked on his. "The CIA has several branch—"

A concussion of sound energy blew through the office, shaking the metal cabinets and blowing several of the resumés off Carter's desk. Dave instinctively covered his ears. Carter and Young reached for their walkies as several distant shouts made their way down the back corridors of the office.

"Call Ellen," said Carter evenly. Dave felt instantly forgotten, and it was wonderful—but it only lasted half a second. The two administrators broke for the door, but Carter, who was first out, stopped short and looked back at Dave.

"Those kids in Phy Ed who you mentioned before," said Mr. Carter, his eyes drilling into Dave, though he was also peripherally addressing Ms. Young. "Dave, did those kids get your keys before M-VAULT time even started?"

Dave instinctively put his hands in his right-hand pocket. They weren't there, and in that second, he knew. A few weeks ago, the kids in the bathroom hadn't been able to accomplish the task—but today, there had been no Sarah to protect him when he was playing basketball an hour ago.

Carter bit his lip. "We've got a situation," he said in a low voice.

Two more sonic booms—at least that's what they felt like to Dave—tore through Maple Valley High School. A few more screams sounded, and then they blended into the general din of kids and adults running and yelling. The hallway became a blur of shadows going by, and by the time Dave's brain began thinking rationally, he realized he was the only one in the room.

He looked around. There was more noise from the hallway and the rest of the school, but Dave felt like it was far away and underwater, surreal and tangential. His head swept through the room, and some part of his disjointed consciousness realized three things. First, some kind of a catastrophe had been unleashed upon the school since students— apparently, students who were training to be covert agents—had taken his staff keys as an exercise.

Second, since he was responsible for the situation, when he inevitably died during the tumult, it would serve him right—and no one would grieve for him, apparently, because he and everyone who worked here was a sad soul removed from close relationships.

Third, Carter and Young were gone, off to defuse the bomb or whatever, and he was alone in this office. Again, his head slowly surveyed the room and landed on a walkie. He picked it up and switched it on.

"They got in," Carter's fuzzy voice announced, and then the line went dead as all the lights went out.

Part II

14 - The Field Trip

David Legnagyszerübb slid his motorcycle over the loose asphalt, braking hard on the front wheel at the last instant so that the lighter rear would skid into the parking spot without tossing him over the top like a rodeo rider. Late autumn leaves immediately flew into the wheel spokes, like a group of little kids haplessly trying to push over an adult. The spokes not immediately covered in leaves cast laser lines of yellow into the teacher parking lot at Elm Ridge High School, the sun's shift towards the redder end of the spectrum another indication of the shortening days as the school year turned a corner and headed quickly toward Thanksgiving.

But as he loosened his gloss-black helmet and planted his equally gloss-black shoes on the uneven parking lot surface, David was not yet thinking of Thanksgiving break. He was going over his to-do list for today's field trip, mentally parceling the day into chunks, with corresponding responsibilities in each time frame. He stopped, though, after locking his helmet in the holder and setting the gleaming 800 cc monster gently on its stand. The November air had no right to be this pleasant. Nor did it seem fair that he could escape the worn green, blue and white painted concrete interior of Elm Ridge High School for the day by taking a fortuitously timed field trip. Some things simply need to be stopped and enjoyed in the moment, he thought, appreciating those golden rays upon his spokes.

His reverie was interrupted by a shout from the bus. "Mr. L!" One window was suddenly down, and the head that stuck out had straight blond tresses that blew all the way across an adjacent bus window in the warm morning wind.

"Good morning, Miranda," he said, fixing his helmet hair. "Is everybody all loaded up and ready to go?"

Miranda did not answer but laughed as she tried to get her entire shoulders out of the window, in violation of several bus rules. "You are *so* late, Mr. L! I'm going to ask the bus driver to—" She stopped, mouth parting in awe. "You drive a—"

Several other windows were now down, and David could hear the loudest voices of chatter from the inside. "Dude," one male voice said, "that dude is such a badass. What teacher drives a motorcycle? To *school?*"

"I do, Brett," said David, who had swiftly mounted the bus steps and was now perched on his elbows overlooking the front seat. "And watch your language, doofus. We're still in school." He smiled and removed his sunglasses to soften the blow. Brett could be a little fragile, especially in regard to his relationship with a certain adored male teacher.

"Sorry, Mr. L," said Brett, whose voice was now low enough to almost be obscured by the diesel engine, which the driver had fired up. He could be loud, but Brett's slightly pudgy frame was completely eclipsed by the bus seat. As David walked down the row, he had to stand on his tiptoes to look down at Brett, alone in his seat.

Brett had hollered his school-inappropriate proclamation regarding David's status because Brett had no friends to address directly. But his cheeks rosied up a bit when David offered him a conciliatory fist bump, which the boy accepted with a sheepish grin.

"The bigger transgression," said David loudly—again, with the tempering smile—"is Caroline's entire upper body being out the window."

Again, the teacher's criticism was followed by the instant look of a chastised puppy from Caroline, who sat in the back with her retinue of friends. Like Brett, she offered a quiet apology in front of her giggling friends, so he walked it back to save her embarrassment, "Worse, Ms. Caroline, is your harassment of those of the motorcycle persuasion in our parking lot! Please do not attack your humble fellow citizens who know that loud pipes save lives!!"

It certainly wasn't that funny—but Caroline and her herd rocked back and forth in the torn green bus seats, laughing and slapping each others' shoulders—"He is so friggin' hilarious! My mom was even laughing at conferences!"

"Ms. Caroline," he added, shaking his head at his own wit, "make sure your window is up past halfway."

"Okay, sorry," she said, her blond hair obscuring her face as she struggled with the pincer clips on the window.

Normally, at this point, he would go back and snap the window up for her—a quick problem-solver *and* I'm-here-to-help-you move that would garner further goodwill. But as he stood up in the front of the bus, now seven minutes late to his own field trip, he had a different business in mind, so he made an equally affection-garnering move.

"Brett, can you get that window for Caroline?" In a few weeks, when he truly needed Brett to do something, he would address the boy as Mr. Larkin or possibly even Mr. Brett.

"Got it, Mr. L," said Brett, his voice now gaining volume again. Brett would gain proximity to a student out of his sphere, if only for a moment, and it would be David he owed for it.

Next, as he stood up front, was the bus driver. "Good morning, sir," he said. No big smile here—that wasn't the way in.

"Morning," responded the bus driver, whose bushy white mustache and Carhartt jacket did not move to meet David's eyes. "We headed to... it looks like, the InterCell building over on 160th?" "To" was "ta," and "on" was "ahn," and "InterCell" was "Innercell."

"Yes, sir," responded David, "and I apologize for the late start and for the kids and their windows."

The bus driver started the engine. "Oh, that's no problem. Hey, I was late anyways on account of tryin' to figure out the track equipment loaded under the seats back there."

"Track stuff? In November? The weather's not *that* nice!" said David, loud enough over the diesel rumble.

The bus driver laughed. "Ch'yeah, ain't that right? Anyways, I had to figure out what it was doing back there."

It was back there, David knew, because he had placed it in the bus yesterday. He had driven to the Schroeder Bus Company yard in the middle of the afternoon, opened the back door, went about his business of loading the pole-vault equipment container (really, just a long piece of drain tile with a cover over it) while the rear-door alarm blared throughout the yard. And then he left. The field trip permission form had the bus number printed on it when he'd picked it up last week—thanks, effective and efficient Schroeder Bus Company schedulers. No one had stopped him or asked, "Can I help you, sir?"

In his experience, most of America was left unguarded. Only in films did people need clever disguises and high-tech falsified IDs. Here, you only needed a bit of confidence.

"You know what," said David, biting his lower lip in a moment of falsified epiphany, "I have a coaches' key for the equipment storage at the high school. When we get back, me and the kids can unload it for you."

The driver's eyebrows raised above his circular-framed sunglasses. "Boy, I'd appreciate it."

David looked out the window. "That's why I'm here," he said, more to himself than to the bus driver. After a moment, he regarded the driver through the awkward angle of the rearview mirror. "I'll also ask the AD why, exactly, you had a bunch of track equipment on your bus in November," said David, moving to his seat.

"I would certainly appreciate that. Hey, I'm Carl," said the bus driver. He extended a hand over his shoulder, keeping his body square to the road as he drove the bus.

"I'm David." He shook Carl's hand firmly. "Thanks for driving us today, Carl. And again, sorry about the late start. Couldn't get that Yamaha back there to start with the battery—I had to kick-start it."

Carl laughed. "Hey, that's impressive that you kick-started that big engine. What's that about, Dave—about 850 cc's?"

David didn't correct him—but it was David, not Dave. And making the bus driver notice the bike was all part of this morning's machinations.

About six hours later, David stood outside the main entrance to InterCell, juggling a conversation between Dhip, the InterCell engineer who was David's contact in the company and also the main speaker today, and Carl, who had the bus parked in the drop-off lane about seventy yards away from the building's entrance.

Whereas the Elm Ridge High School parking lot was a Who's Who of concrete decay nestled in a valley of decrepit and ill-maintained mounds of grass and weeds, InterCell's was a liquid-smooth black set of rectangles, with parking spots crisply delineated by bright white lines. Carl's bus sat on the edge of the parking lot, right in front of the tree-lined walkway to the communications company's main entrance. The building itself was a gleaming exercise in glass that rose out of the ground, buffeted by beautiful shrubbery and tasteful potted plants. David and Dhip chatted about the students' reactions to the presentations and the tour. Carl mostly craned his neck to get a better look at the building.

"The kids were really into what you and the other engineers were saying about effective teamwork," said David, sipping on the company's coffee. It was ridiculously good, even better than the java David had had every morning when he'd been embedded with a humanitarian-organization-cum-warlord-support group in Borneo.

"Oh, excellent," replied Dhip, checking his phone. He was short, and under his crisp suit, appeared to have the physique of the closet bodybuilder. The sun gleamed off his perfectly shaved head. "I'm glad they reassigned some of my hours so I could set this up for your class. Bright kids—I'm sure some of them could work here someday. I wish my kids' school offered something like this, but all they seem to do over there is put out fires."

"Your kids go to school in the district?" asked Carl, still gazing up at the InterCell tower.

There was something funny, thought David, in the idea that Carl never looked down during the course of the conversation, and Dhip never looked up.

"Yes, at Maple Valley," answered Dhip. An awkward silence followed, but luckily, the mob of kids was making its way out the front doors. Most were holding InterCell drink cups to match David's coffee. Offer these kids a free fountain drink, thought David, and they would agree to work here in a stockroom for the rest of their lives with no retirement or health insurance.

"Well, what do we say to Mr. Lodha?" An amusical chorus of "thank yous" hung in the air as the kids filed past to get back on the bus. Their lives undoubtedly changed for the better by this real-world experience.

Brett stopped next to David on the walk back to the bus. "Hey," he said, "Where'd you eat lunch, Mr. L?"

"I have a friend who works here. We ate in the cafeteria," said David, gesturing with his coffee as if to an invisible cafeteria. Only half of that was true, though."What did you think of the presentation? Think you'd ever work here?"

"Oh, man, that'd be cool. I could be one of those tower workers—" he mimed climbing the ladder, as the woman had done in the demonstration, his doughy fists fearlessly grasping hand-over-hand—"except that I'm kind of scared of heights."

"Yeah, me too! Did your palms get sweaty when they showed the video of the guy replacing the transmitter, and he kept clipping himself in and out of the harness?"

Brett gestured so wildly that he almost dropped his drink. "Same! My palms are wet right now, just thinking about it!"

"Yeah! Same!" said David. This was not true. When he'd watched the video, safely having loaded some very heavily regulated cellular networking technology into the pole vault holder in the back of the bus, he sighed almost audibly to himself out of nostalgia. In hindsight, one was inclined only to remember the good parts of past exploits and block out the unpleasant. He had once jumped off a radio tower outside of Shanghai after installing some "firmware updates." Of course, he was wearing a parachute, but what made David nervous at the time was not knowing where he would land, much less how he would lose the Shanghai police force once he did. Climbing the tower had been, well, fun, and the view up where the air was clear had been fantastic. Seeing the first three PRC army trucks park at the base of the tower—yes, that was a feeling better forgotten.

He followed Brett into the bus. He wanted to go to the back and check on his merchandise—the true reason for the InterCell trip—but that wouldn't do. Instead, he moved a seat in and greeted Carl the Bus Driver with a smile. Kids were rolling the windows down and sharing stories about what they'd seen that day, especially the cornucopia of soda flavors that had been available in the InterCell cafeteria. This led to an animated discussion about the number of side dishes and provided desserts each had ordered in the cafeteria.

When David had meekly asked if the students should bring a bag lunch, Dhip, as David knew he would, dismissed the idea with a wave of his hand. "They can eat in the cafeteria. I'll let our lunch staff know." Carl, for one, could scarcely believe his luck for being invited in to eat, forgoing his wife's two peanut butter sandwiches.

Dhip didn't add that the student-dazzling feast would amount to a tiny rounding error for the multibillion-dollar contract company, and Dhip would be able to use the money to prove the company's Long-Term Investment in the Community. Everyone wins, and no one questions that the self-sacrificing teacher setting up the field trip is returning to the school with a long plastic tube of semi-legal communications equipment, with plans to use it in a very illegal way.

"You still think you can get this track stuff outta my bus?" asked Carl.

"Oh, no problem," said David, settling into his seat.

"Hey, thanks for that. And thanks for thinking of your bus driver at lunchtime."

"For you, Carl," said David, leaning back in the seat and closing his eyes for a moment, "anything."

15 - Saturday Visit

Seventeen hours later, the late fall weather was still warm, though around sunrise, it was beginning to show signs of that wintry bite. David's motorcycle was put away today, and as he arrived at the Elm Ridge parking lot on this Saturday morning, he wore the hybrid khaki pants and orange safety vest of a junior project manager since he had learned in his time here that no one in a school seemed to ever question a construction worker around the building. Parents were directed to the main office; kids with long black coats and permanent scowls who spouted angry self-talk were directed gently to the counselors' area. But you could have a duffel bag full of C4 and a forehead tattoo that read "We Don't Need No Education," and if you were carrying a ladder and wearing a hard hat, everyone greeted you with a smile—if they noticed you at all.

Not that there were many people there on a Saturday, which was handy, because he didn't have keys for a few of the rooms he needed to access.

First stop: the data closet. Any large building or school with an established wifi network operating through a fiber optic trunk needed at least three data closets to house the routers and switches, so naturally, a public high school had only one: a shared cramped space with an old metal shelf filled with hardened art supplies. David had his set of rakes to open any keyed door—but again, this was a public school with public school facilities, so he simply slipped the edge of his school ID between the door jamb and the door and pulled it open.

The first thing David noticed was that the room was about one hundred degrees. All data closets should have adequate ventilation, but of course, this was an old art storage closet that no one wanted to clean out, so some new tech who left for a higher-paying job after three weeks had set up shop here. If David didn't do some upkeep now, there would be no wifi traffic to intercept here because there'd be no wireless network at all.

"Well," he said aloud, "you're wearing this costume—might as well do some actual construction upkeep." His buoyant mood persisted as he easily let an hour or two slip by while he cleaned up the spaghetti twist of Ethernet cables, vacuumed off the router and switches, and brought yesteryear's art materials to the dumpster. He even found, bolted to the back wall, two unused switches, with twenty-four ports each—simply sitting there, like soldiers buried with the pharaoh. He stacked unused and cut-up Ethernet and power cables on the mummified switches just behind the main shelf.

Meanwhile, his portable speaker softly whispered Farsi phrases of intermediate difficulty at him, which he dutifully whispered back.

After cleaning up the closet, he stepped back into the hallway to admire his handiwork and let out an involuntary gasp. The hallway was still about forty degrees cooler than the closet—he'd been so bound up in his closet reorganization that he'd forgotten it wasn't July. But now he realized he needed to reroute some HVAC into this closet, or his job would get a whole lot harder very quickly.

"Again," he reminded himself out loud, "the construction truck is a great cover this morning because you're actually going to use it."

He trudged back out to the van and grabbed some six-inch ductwork, some snips, and a few hangers, and made his way back into the building.

And it was perhaps this "trudging" that explained why David Legnagyszerübb, who had survived no fewer than four spy campaigns that involved breaking into heavily armed, overseas financial institutions, was nearly murdered in an empty public high school on a Saturday in November.

He dumped his HVAC materials and tools in front of the data closet door, sighed, stretched his back, and sighed again. He turned the handle to enter the data closet—and, in a split second, remembered that he had gained access to the room with a credit card swiped through the big, dumb gap between the jamb and the door, which meant that he did not unlock the handle. Only the real key could do that.

His instincts did the work for him. He did not panic and try to slam the door quickly. Rather, while his mind determined that someone was now in the data closet, his hand continued to open the door as normal to make the occupier believe he had no clue that anything was amiss. If the assailant wanted to shoot or stab him, the attacker would let David take the milliseconds he needed because the closet's occupant believed he had the drop on him.

While his hand continued to open the door, he pivoted instantly to the other side of the metal door. No one inside could possibly see him now, and he had the safety of the door/shield, which he needed because the knife thrust at him nearly hit his forehead.

This quick head thrust was followed by an equally quick midsection stab and then a pause as the attacker tried to figure out where David was. At that moment, David knew the final attempt to kill him would be almost imperceptibly perfunctory, as it wouldn't immediately be clear where he, the intended target, was. That hesitation was all he needed.

David quickly locked the arm that now protruded past the data closet entryway under his elbow while retaining his body position on the other side of the door. From here, he had a lock on his attacker, and again he predicted what came next: two foot strikes. The first caught his midsection, but again the door prevented the full impact, and when the second came, he pulled the ankle up and towards his head, smashing it against the door's edge. There was no grunt of pain from inside the closet, despite nearly having shattered the attacker's shin on the door. At this point, he thought he knew who his Saturday school visitor might be.

The hand holding the knife jerked forward to free itself, but he torqued the wrist until the knife dropped to the ground. They were now completely locked together, wrist to hand.

David decided to gamble that the person he thought was trying to kill him was indeed the person he'd known. He lowered his weight, stepped out in front of the door, and threw the body over his shoulder, where it collided loudly with some loose ductwork on the floor. There was a flash of metal mixed with a dark splash of ponytail. He did not want blood everywhere, so he must get his assailant back in the data closet.

She was already standing up and shooting for his midsection with another knife. He pivoted, lifting her up by the karate belt he knew she wore to work assignments, and threw them both, judo-style, into the closet.

In close quarters her speed now gave her an advantage as she struck him in the throat with the back of her hand. He made the first noise of the fight—a sputter combined with the classic downward-chin, oh-my-windpipe face—but he had her original knife now, and she had stepped into the only real space on the floor of the closet: into several coils of yellow Ethernet cable.

He threw his weight into her, pressing her against the wall and the two old switches and router. He cut the excess cable on the floor and pulled, lassoing her ankles, and immediately started plugging cables into the old switches. One cable plug would obviously not hold her, but he snapped ten or twelve in as she struck at his head, and soon she stopped struggling. Nearly instantly, she controlled her breath, and in the dimness of the closet, he saw her eyes close.

Yes, he had guessed correctly, but he'd only been lucky that she'd stepped into the turns of the Ethernet cable. Otherwise, he'd be bleeding out in the closet right now, and if he knew her at all, she'd be forcing him into a heavy-duty garbage bag while he was still alive. She was several shades more deadly in combat, and the longer he held her here, the more likely she'd escape the makeshift restraints and finish the job.

He plugged in almost all of the ports in the old switch, wondering how tightly it was bolted to the wall. She was slight, but that certainly wouldn't stop her from using leverage to break out. And, as sure as a magician had half-dollars hidden in every available fold of clothing, she had several more knives of varying ferocity hidden on her person, so he used her own belt to secure her hands.

She did not struggle or curse, or spout clever jabs, or hint at some long-smoldering love affair between the two—as former co-workers, they'd be more likely to inquire if the other ever finished that mystery novel they used to read during the weeks spent out in the wilderness. Her eyes remained closed and her breathing calm.

"Neve," he asked, "do you think I'm going to torture you?"

"David," she responded, eyes still closed. Her sweat had stopped glinting on her temples; she had controlled her physical traits as quickly as if she'd transported herself to some beach. "I guess I'd be shocked if you didn't."

David frowned. This was an involuntary frown, to be sure, but it seemed to have some effect on students, so he tried it anyway. "Neve, that doesn't fit with my current gig."

"What—IT repair man?"

"No, I'm teaching here at the high school."

Neve almost laughed—it was more like a shallow exhale. "Teaching? Sure, sure, David—you just gave up the life and decided to teach high school English. What, for its edifying qualities? To write a bestseller about it? *Dangerous Minds 2*, starring Coolio and David Legnagyszerübb as Himself?"

David did not answer, but she knew she'd crossed a line, so she said nothing for a few moments in penance—ironic, considering that she came to kill him and would have done just that if his agent's intuition weren't always so high.

"Sorry," she said more quietly. Again, he could almost feel her will to control her breathing, her sweat, her heart rate. He noted the sweat drying under her black hair near the dark, fibrous curve on her forehead. The scar that circled her left temple was not a movie-star glamor mark. It had been cut there by a Liberian human trafficker while they were working in Algiers. She had pretended to faint when the middle-management trafficker cut her, and an hour later, she was receiving stitches, and the trafficker was at the bottom of the Mediterranean.

"Why the termination?" he asked, not expecting an answer, though he received one nonetheless.

"David, Cuconotti is dead, and my bosses were fairly sure you eliminated him. Since they had no idea why, the simple solution was to eliminate you." Her eyes were still closed, and her breathing was now normal.

He froze.

"What do you mean he's dead?"

Her eyes opened. "Stabbed to death. It was either torture or amateur hour."

Her face was implacable, even though she and David had worked with Ray Cuconotti for over a decade. "By high school students, David. In the street, by a whole group of teenagers. I talked with the agents who cleaned it up. So what—you gave it out as a homework assignment under the guise of your new… job?"

Moment-to-moment decisions were always clear and, more importantly, instinctual for David Legnagyszerübb. It was why he was still alive. But big-picture ideas took a lot longer for him to piece together, and that wasn't good because Neve was about to slip out of her restraints, end his life and disappear quietly into the suburban afternoon. He and his maintenance van would disappear off the face of the Earth.

"What was Ray Cuconotti doing around here?"

She exhale-laughed again. The scar did not crease when she did it. It moved up and down as a unit.

He wondered if she was somehow forcing him to look at the scar to distract him.

"Seriously."

"David. You had a reason to eliminate Cuconotti, a.k.a. Larry Yearson. I have my own background for him, but there's clearly something I missed. When you ask what that tubby old spook was doing around here, David—that was my glove-compartment question for you."

Even for a hardened operative like David, nostalgia could seep in through the cracks of the levee where he blocked off whole years of his life. The "glove-compartment question" was a reference to an instructor they'd both had in training in Kamchatka. When you're trying to sink a car to the bottom of a lake, the lesson went, don't start pulling things out of the glove box. When you're trying to murder someone on the job, don't solicit or even allow an exchange of information, as you might end up knowing something you shouldn't. Let the glove box items stay as such, securely locked away at the bottom of the lake.

"Glove-compartment question." He smiled. She shifted almost imperceptibly. It was like watching a hungry tiger bat at the door handle of its enclosure. "Does that mean I will survive the day? Now that you've asked me that question?"

She paused and bit her lip.

"There's part of me," she began, licking blood from her lip, "that wants to just extract the information from you, and then let you fall victim to whatever it is that's going on around here. One more teacher-spy, duly eliminated by his students in the most bloody, inefficient way possible."

He didn't get a chance to answer before the Ethernet cable's thin wires plunged into his neck. He heard himself screaming—fifteen amps was not bad as a shock, but the current traveling through the thin wire created heat that felt—and smelled—as if it were cauterizing his skin and melting into him. Instantly, the cords were now around his neck. There were three loops made by two quick, lithe hands, and then the loops tightened. She flung off the cords and sprinted past him as he fell to his knees.

He managed to get the Ethernet noose off and the makeshift electrical knife out of his neck, rolling over onto his side and gasping for breath. A shadow darkened his face.

"Like you, he was trying to establish some kind of cover in a high school. 'Mr. Yearson' actually worked his way up to a head volleyball coach." She paused. "I'm actually not sure if you knew that or not. Either way—"

She almost told him that it was good to see him, but she didn't. After five quick footfalls, she was gone.

David Legnagyszerübb lay there for a moment. So—another "teacher" was dead, and she thought he had done it or made it happen. He thought briefly of Cuconotti, imagining him as that archetypal, demanding "throwback" high school coach and teacher. Not too far of a stretch from his work as an agent, it turned out. David knew how to deal with the deaths of people he knew well and to accept that he might not know what became of those individuals. He had psychological tools and training to box it up and put it away, though the box tended to jostle and make noise in the closet of his psyche if it was someone he cared about.

In this case, it wasn't. Cuconotti was not likable in any way, and in his several months' experience as a high school teacher (slightly different than the six years listed on his incredibly false resume), David could see him being a pain to work with. The mourning box of his time with Cuconotti was easy to place on the closet shelf.

David picked up the HVAC ducting, which was only slightly bent, grabbed a ladder and started to do the necessary work for the closet. As he worked, he processed the "big picture" while his hands measured, snipped, screwed and taped.

Rather than worry about the dead man's legacy, it was more constructive to think about the implications of Cuconotti's presence at the other high school and his fate. Who would be working to thwart agents operating in the area? Who would choose to have them cut apart by amateurs? Or was the old man just unlucky, cut up by some group of psychotics he'd pissed off at a watering hole? Or at a junior varsity volleyball game?

He opened the damper in the new ductwork. Air could now circulate throughout the closet, meaning that the data equipment might actually work for most of the school year. He cleaned up the mess from the scuffle—he'd almost been eliminated by a former co-worker; *that* was worth putting away in a box—and installed his own Ethernet transmitters in a few key ports.

"That's why I'm here," he said, addressing the hardware in the closet.

Next point of data gathering to install: the cell signal hijacker.

He walked down to the athletic closet where he had been kind enough to "put away" the "pole vault equipment." The black market transmitters and antennae came out and were soon under his arm as he trudged back upstairs to the roof of the school, thanks to his contacts at InterCell.

Perhaps he could enjoy the warm, pleasant November weather as he worked to install the signal hijacker on the roof, with the view of the surrounding suburban maples in their late-fall burgundies and reds. Perhaps no one would try and murder him for the rest of the afternoon.

16 – Happy Hour, Part 1

Teachers' Happy Hour—that joyous pressure-valve release that made a Friday in December feel like the beer-soaked last day before Spring Break—was different at Maple Valley High School. Instead of being perched atop a bar stool, new teacher Dave Legnagyszerübb found himself lying prone on a gymnastics mat.

And as he lay on the mat where he'd landed, Dave looked past the open doors of the gym, through the glass exterior panels on the west entrance of the school, and saw the sun slip under the horizon just past the evergreen trees that framed the teacher's parking lot. The red of the sun made the wet snow on the tree boughs glow purple—a few weeks before Winter Break, it was still warm enough on some afternoons to melt the snow.

He wondered if the hit he'd just taken was a result of a mistake he'd made, and if so, which one it could be: murdering a colleague? That one, strangely, had seemingly few repercussions around here. Letting students steal his keys? That had come with some consequences, as the group of students who had accessed weaponry had gone on a short melee before being rounded up by a group of custodians—custodians with serious skills in jiu-jitsu as well as faucet repair.

Once again, the question arose in Dave's head, "What am I doing here?"

These topics clanged around in Dave's head like a bell clapper as his hands, seemingly of their own volition, slid underneath his own chest to lift himself back up, though his eyes still seemed transfixed on that winter evening tableau that was so perfectly framed, albeit sideways, through the school's rear entry doors.

He blinked hard. There were no noises in the gym right now, which he had learned over the last several happy hours meant that everyone else was in some sort of ready stance while he was peeling himself off the floor. Sure enough, his co-workers stood in two lines facing a partner, some stealing sideways glances at him—and like the rest, his partner, Nassir, stood with his bare feet slightly spread and his fists slightly apart in front of his belt. Which, like many of the belts in the Maple Valley auxiliary gym right now, was black with gold-embossed symbols on it.

Dave did not own a belt or a uniform. He had tried to use this as an excuse to duck the first happy hour he'd been invited to when Derrick, the new phy ed teacher who looked like one of those men who pick up trucks in streets during cable television contests, had held out a set of reclaimed sweats from the locker room's Lost and Found. Luckily, they fit, but less luckily, they smelled like—well, a student.

"Wear these, brah," he'd said. "And don't worry—I know you're new to the Mammoth happy hour traditions. I was, too, until last month." His grin moved the lower half of his face like a spare tire being dropped out of a trunk.

"Look," responded Dave. He found himself starting many exchanges with that imperative lately—even though he often had nothing to follow up with. It just seemed important to raise some type of protest when a co-worker casually mentioned a student munitions test happening out on the practice soccer field or that the group of kids who regularly cheated on Spanish tests was using a cipher to communicate test answers via text message.

But Derrick had simply held up his giant paw to stifle any further debate. "Don't worry—I'm actually new to martial arts, too. We'll go together, 3:15 in the wrestling room. I think you're gonna like it, and I think you need it. You look a little tense lately." Two hours later, Dave had ended the week with an ice pack and seven ibuprofen pills. Derrick, for his part, had left with an eye that looked like a bleeding prune—but he'd had a smile on his face, too. There was some platitude about learning styles here, though Dave had been in no state to discern it. Yet he kept coming, week after week.

The master of ceremonies at Happy Hour was, of course, Principal-cum-Sensei Don Carter. He wore a purple gi and a black belt that appeared to have accolades, certificates and God knows what other esoteric awesomeness stitched into it with golden thread. Dave once got a good look at it when Carter was demonstrating a hold on a fellow teacher. The belt had writing on it in what appeared to be Japanese, Russian and Hebrew, as well as what looked like an image of the North Korean flag.

During last week's happy hour, Derrick partnered with Nassir. At one point, Carter was teaching some basic kicks to the class, and although Dave had felt like a dandelion among roses, he'd noticed that Derrick struggled to lift his knee high enough for the "basic" kick.

And several minutes later, during a sparring session, Dave saw the lithe Nassir dance in front of Derrick, dodging his kicks with what looked like disingenuous effort. After a particularly lumbering round kick, Nassir struck Derrick in the side with two kicks whose quick successions reminded Dave of a whip being cracked. Derrick did not fall—could people that size fall at all?—but collapsed, clutching his side like a building whose supports had buckled. Nassir let him get up, bouncing lightly on his toes. After a beat, Derrick stood up slowly, took a deep breath and gave Nassir a conciliatory grimace.

Nassir had responded with an instantaneous turn on one foot, and suddenly his roundhouse connected with Derrick's shoulder, which was about at Nassir's head level. Derrick's bulk shuddered, and Dave thought he might go down again.

Nassir's face remained blank, betraying nothing.

When the stony-faced Nassir turned on his heel to deliver another surgical strike, Derrick charged him. For a moment, he was leaning forward, and the next, he was flying through the air horizontally. Even after being struck three times, the giant gym teacher was quick and agile, but those qualities expressed by someone with that frame made it seem unreal.

Derrick's shoulder hit Nassir on his left side before the kick flew, and he drove the slender man into the mat like a delivery truck T-boning a cheap sedan. Nassir, of course, twisted himself in the air using some combination of judo and magic, but the end result was unavoidable: he suffered the crushing piston action of Derrick's enormous body.

Dave's first reaction upon seeing this was simple—he was glad it wasn't him. His second reaction was that he would pay money to see Derrick do that to some student who was instigating a fight—though he derived no pleasure from seeing the soft-spoken Nassir get pile-driven into the ground. Perhaps a wrist injury would prevent the young man from writing so many comments on kids' chemistry tests, which was the only negative thing Dave had thought about Nassir, especially since he was the only first-year teacher Dave knew who'd escaped government custody during a morning new-teacher meeting.

Dave was able to see the whole Derrick-as-ICBM incident because he was being held up in the air by his wrist. Julia—who Dave had once thought might also have been clueless as to the school's true purpose but now seemed to be just another lethal assassin-cum-teacher—was showing him a defense for a wrist grab.

"And you're just going to have to try it yourself, you know, and once you have it, it just requires the teensiest bit of pressure, David." He let out an involuntary gasp and got on his toes. "And you can really do anything, David, as long as you grip the, you know, heel of the hand with your—"

Dave, of course, was far beyond the emasculation of being called by his incorrect name or of being physically dominated by someone he had assumed to be a chatty bit of a know-it-all housemarm teacher. He just kept nodding, and that's when he saw Derrick slam into the cat-like Nassir.

"Oh, man, I am *sorry*," Derrick said, leaping off Nassir with his hands.

Luckily, the lithe science teacher lifted his head up off the mat and puffed out a "Not a problem," though Dave could easily imagine the man having a collapsed lung. However, Nassir was inscrutable. And was he surprised at all that Derrick was built like a rhino but moved like a viper?

Don Carter was suddenly standing over both men. He did not offer either his hand or ask if Nassir had broken a rib. Rather, he simply waited, cinching his who's-who-of-murderous-combat-degrees belt as the two men stood up—Derrick as if he'd been fired out of a hole, Nassir quite a bit more slowly.

"Happy hour goers," said Carter, not looking at the two men but not looking at any single person in particular, "if this were a traditional martial arts *dojo*, we would offer some platitude here about the rock and the river or the crocodile and the hippo." Many people chuckled. Dave assumed they'd heard such a pithy quote given out in sweaty, concrete training gyms in… who knew where? Tel Aviv? Buenos Aires?

"But remember that we have a job to do. Sometimes we have to look at all the rules that govern us—that try and help us, yet in some cases, end up preventing us—from teaching students the hard skills that they need to know."

There were small nods of assent throughout the gym. Dave found himself nodding, too, barely aware that Julia had released him from a grip that, given a few more minutes, might have inspired him to try out his health insurance.

Carter called them back into lines, and Dave stole a look at the clock. There were forty minutes or so left in happy hour—time for some weapon disarmament training. Julia was suddenly holding a plastic knife, and the learning continued.

Two partner switches later, Dave felt as if he might, given a slow and possibly stoned high school attacker, be able to disarm an assailant. The parts of the moves were disjointed—not fluidly strung together as Julia had demonstrated or as Zen-like in their efficiency as when Carter had led them—but they came one after the other without a ton of thinking.

But if there was a lesson here about the brutality of learning, the test—the part when the student realizes he clearly doesn't "get it"—came after another partner shift when Sarah greeted him with a smile. That smile had quickened Dave's pulse until he realized that it was less of a girl-is-interested-in-boy greeting and more of a grizzly-is-interested-in-salmon greeting.

And that's how he'd ended up where he was now, with his head on the floor, asking himself—again—what he was doing here.

They were doing more disarmament exercises, and although the music teacher might elevate his heartbeat at school when he saw her, Dave was fairly focused on learning the tasks at hand because his life might depend on it, literally. He had been holding the weapon, completely focused on learning from her hands and feet as she took the weapon from him and stepped back, took it and stepped back, over and over. He was grateful and upset at the same time at how little physical contact there was in this particular mini-lesson.

Then he lost his focus for a moment and approached too low. The "weapon" (just a long piece of PVC) swung at her thigh, just below where her black belt (with white, not gold) embossed Chinese characters hung. Instantly, rather than pulling the staff from him, she struck it against the ground, and then suddenly her foot was on his chest, and he was on the mat, taking in those oranges and yellows on the fir trees in the parking lot.

Unlike a "meet-cute" scene in a movie, she did not fawn over him or kneel down and apologize. Sarah, she of the oboe and the wave in the gym and the yellow skirts, now stood in the ready position, not acknowledging Dave in the least, which was surely part of some martial arts master training or something. Or, possibly, Sarah Lehner was so accustomed to crushing her opponents that it did not occur to her to acknowledge them any more than it might occur to a flyswatter to acknowledge a lump of fly guts.

His colleagues stood in straight-facing lines as he managed to place his feet underneath his torso, like an android downloading a new standing algorithm. He lost sight of the view outside, and a pang of sadness that he couldn't explain made his chest tighten. If he'd been asked to explain it, Dave would have probably said that the colors—the burnt reds on the pine tree snow, the purples in the evening sky, the various crystalline whites on the lawns—were something that he could no longer enjoy. Either that, or it was his nervous system warning him that another blow could lead to a long-term coma.

Yet he took his spot across from Sarah on the gym floor, setting his limbs in position for another trouncing. Carter said a Korean phrase to the class, which they repeated, and they bowed to their opponent—Sarah seemed to look right through him—and switched partners again.

Now he was across from Nassir, who seemed to show no ill effects from having been rugby-tackled by a seven-foot-tall man-boulder earlier. They bowed, repeated another Korean phrase and Carter led them through some close-quarter grappling moves.

Several minutes later, Nassir was holding Dave over his right hip, pulling his midsection up off the ground while at the same time yanking him down by the head. Like everything else they were doing, it made Dave feel helpless. Carter repeated the cue, and Nassir made Dave weightless again, blood filling his head. Their faces were next to each other when Nassir whispered, "Keep fighting through this whole-group stuff." He pulled down on Dave's head again.

"What?" Dave managed to whisper.

"These 'happy hour' exercises—they're just hand-to-hand combat refreshers for most of the group, so we don't lose our training while we're stationed here at the high school." He flung Dave halfway over his shoulder, and Dave grunted involuntarily. Nassir continued. "This isn't a basic class, but you need a few basic things to get started."

Was this a trap? Carter and Young had told him, in no uncertain terms, that he was not to let any of the other staff know that he'd been hired despite knowing nothing about espionage, the military, or any of that kind of thing. Yet he supposed he couldn't hide it for very long here at "happy hour."

They switched sides. He was now at Nassir's left hip, and they continued talking when the throws drill put Dave's red and sweaty face near Nassir's carefully combed black hair.

"How am I supposed to 'get started'? What can I do?" he asked into Nassir's neck.

"I'll train you." Nassir repositioned him briefly. "If you need it," he added, throwing Dave onto his back with a *whomp* that didn't knock the wind out of him so much as vaporize any functioning cells located in his torso. As the gym swirling around Dave regained its color, Nassir reached down and helped him up—the first time this had happened in a Maple Valley happy hour.

"Meet me Monday at seven in the weight room," Nassir said, pulling him to his feet.

Before Dave could thank Nassir for the invite—and for treating him like a person rather than just a punching dummy—they switched partners again.

17 - Happy Hour, Part 2

Two and a half weeks later, the two men walked into Erik's brewery, knocking the snow off their boots as they made their way to the bar. Indoor string lights were strewn in that half-chaotic, half-trying-to-be-chaotic brewery decor, and flashing outdoor lights twinkled in through the windows. The familiar huge ceiling fans now pushed around heated December air, and the square wooden tables' polished tops reflected the holiday lights.

Dave and Nassir stopped to check out the holiday brews list: a set of five imperial stouts that became progressively darker and more alcoholic, starting with the oatmeal Monday Before Break and ending with the barrel-aged Friday Before Break, which could only be purchased in five-ounce quantities.

"So your friend owns this place?" asked Nassir as they scanned the selection.

"Yeah—a former teacher, in case you couldn't tell by the beer names," said Dave, absentmindedly rubbing his fist. "So, what can I get for you?"

Nassir just smiled. "You know, I don't mind giving you the extra training. I know it's tough to buy anything on a new teacher's salary, much less an extra beer for a coworker."

"You might be literally saving my life," said Dave. He quickly moved on. "I'm having a Tuesday to start with—"

"And don't think you're going to pay for those drinks here, either," said Erik, who had materialized next to the bar and was already clapping his shoulder.

They exchanged how-ya-doins, and Dave introduced Nassir as a chemistry teacher—not as the man who was giving him semi-clandestine hand-to-hand combat lessons—to Erik.

"Geez," said Erik, pouring several taps at once for other thirsty teachers farther down the bar, "one minute, I'm thinking that you'll be my prodigal son who needs a barback job because no one wants him to teach, and the next minute you're rolling into Winter Break and bringing more Maple Valley staff into my brewery! It's a Christmas miracle!"

Dave smiled and looked a bit sheepishly at Nassir. Erik gave them their beers and promised to return. Dave quaffed his and felt the black stout warm his stomach. He'd probably have heartburn later, but he didn't care.

"Seems like a nice guy," said Nassir. He took a sip, eyebrows raised in anticipation, and then Dave saw his nostrils flare in the enjoyment of the beer's multisensory attack—well, less of an attack than a coordinated ballet of earthy, grainy scents and tastes all along the mouth and down the throat. Nassir gave the thousand-yard stare of beer consideration seen in microbreweries around the country over the past decade. He nodded, the holiday lights accenting his midnight shade of hair. "It's good, dark beer. Not too overpowering, so it's not too weird to drink after a workout of sorts. Perfect for this time of year. For a Tuesday Ale on a Thursday." He laughed.

When the familiar question surfaced in his head—"What am I doing here?"—several answers actually presented themselves.

First, he realized this chat with Nassir Sahil was the only small talk he'd been able to make in his short time at Maple Valley. Dave Legnagyszerübb had realized early on, as most smart and socially awkward people do, that he would never be able to get by on charisma and that he'd have to work hard to form interpersonal bonds, which was tough enough in a line of work that depended on bonding with other humans. But students in class were a captive audience—the JBs and Ninas and Golfs almost *had* to chit-chat with Dave, their teacher. Adults, however, were never required to speak to him, and he was just realizing that during his time as a Mammoth, they generally chose not to.

But this led to intersecting realization number two. Nassir was all of these things he was not, and yet he'd reached out, shown him some survival skills—Dave had even controlled his wrist for a moment during their "sparring," which he figured that Nassir did at a quarter speed—and agreed to have a beer with him.

The final intersecting realization was this: it was great to have a beer and talk to the young, impossible-to-arrest science teacher because Nassir was not Sarah Lehner. Sarah had not given him the time of day since their chat in the gym a few months ago, and he guessed it was entirely due to the fact that he'd had his faculty keys snatched that same day. He was infatuated with her, which was both horrible and undeniable, and it got worse every time she a) saved his sorry butt in the bathroom during Unstructured Time and b) kicked his sorry butt during happy hour. So—

"Thank you, Nassir," he said, breaking the cardinal rule that dudes/men never said each others' first names unless they were about to mock one another. "Thanks for the instruction. And the beer. You know, when we sat in that new-teacher meeting earlier—when you got arrested, or whatever—"

Nassir didn't stop him but just took another sip of the Tuesday Stout.

"—I noticed all that feedback you wrote on kids' tests, and I thought, 'Here's a guy who, like me, has no idea what he's doing.'"

Dave, so desperate for regular-teacher small talk, realized as it came out of his mouth that he'd just criticized another teacher's work, which was all-time *verboten*. For one horrible beat, the ambient brewery noise filled the space, and the holiday lights twinkled in a shifting rhythm that seemed to amplify the perceived slight. But then Nassir guffawed right into his beer.

"I know, right? I feel like when a kid says something dumb on a biology test, I have to justify taking points away. So I write this small essay on each kid's short-answer—"

"In light green pen."

"—Yes! I'm burning through green pen!" Nassir was now animated in a way Dave hadn't seen. His fingers waved perpendicularly to his face as he spoke, and he seemed to be talking down at his beer now, which he'd set on the knotty-pine counter. "I'm writing *War and Peace* on Golf's half-baked answers—"

"Ah, Tipuan. His whole everything is half-baked."

"—Yes, yes, you know! And I'm sitting in PLC meetings with people who are just writing the score on the test in red pen, and I'm shocked and disappointed by my Mammoth colleagues, especially my mentor teacher, who's supposed to be showing me *how* to grade. She looks like she only spent an hour and a half grading, unlike foolish me, who spent the whole weekend. Don't they *care* enough about these kids to let them know how to get better—to become better scientists?"

He took a gulp of his beer. Whether the alcohol had quickly injected itself into Nassir's forebrain, or maybe another teacher had been waiting for a chance to make real happy-hour small talk, too, Dave was flummoxed at how a man who had effortlessly parried and survived attacks by a bear masquerading as a man only weeks before would be so stymied by something like student feedback.

"Aaaaaand then I hand the tests back, and I see that my mentor's kids have all recycled their tests, rather than look over any feedback, and then I watch *my* kids—" he gulped his Tuesday Ale with relish now, and almost finished it, "throw my handwritten, personalized essays of feedback right on top of the other classes'. In the recycle bin. Genius." As so often during a good happy hour, the end of the story coincided with the end of the beer. Nassir shook his head to make it final.

"So, you've stopped giving so much feedback? Writing a shorter novel on each test? Spending days instead of weeks on each?" Dave was gulping his now, trying to keep up with Nassir, heartburn be damned.

"Of course not," smiled the new science teacher. "Can't stop writing paragraphs of test-taking strategies and helpful short-answer feedback on each stupid one."

They laughed. Dave broached the subject before he even knew he was doing it. "Don't kick yourself," he said. "All that feedback is really helping my self-defense."

Nassir's smile blanched almost imperceptibly. "You'll want to call it 'hand-to-hand combat.'"

"Oh, yeah, yeah," said Dave quickly, burying his mouth in his beer. He was pushing it, he knew, but he couldn't go on pretending that they were just two random new teachers at a random school, where no one possessed anything other than run-of-the-mill skills or talents. "But I do need the help."

"Yeah, you do. Even if everyone else is convinced, you're still just in deep cover." He paused, looking briefly over Dave's shoulder, and with the slightest neck tilt, over his own. "They're convinced that your woe-is-me-ya-hired-the-wrong-guy story was a smokescreen and a fairly unsophisticated one at that." His voice lowered a level. "But I know."

"How?" Dave asked before he could stop himself.

"We're in the business of seeing past the act, right? To detecting the microexpressions that might expose someone's true feelings?" Nassir had, suddenly, another full stout in his hand, and he took a careful sip. Dave supposed that professional spies were full of these types of entertaining party tricks—and that Erik wouldn't let a glass go empty near Dave.

"Well, I completed that 'escape' exercise during the meeting closer to the beginning of the school year, and when I slipped back in, I saw the look on your face, and if there were ever a more genuine show of shock on a man's face, I haven't seen it."

Unbidden, the question popped into Dave's mind, "What am I doing here?" He shoved it away, pushing his mental palm against the contents of the stuff-sack of memory. His head just nodded.

Nassir moved the beer up to his mouth and then paused, his eyes flicking side-to-side, his hands and the beer moving to obscure his mouth from any would-be listeners or watchers.

"The other teachers are convinced, mostly due to Carter and Young's work, that you are pretending to be the confused new guy who's not aware he's teaching at a prep school for government agents. They were, for a while, genuinely confused at the... let's call it *strange* nature of your backstory—that you, a guy with a fourteen-letter, nearly-mathematically-unique last name, were mistakenly hired here due to a case of mistaken identity, and that you're wading haplessly through the year like some kind of Monty Python character. No one was quite sure what you were trying to do with that cover. It's so stupid." Rather than looking away after this statement, Nassir only lifted his head at Dave and met his gaze steadily.

Dave clenched his fist around his beer, and his nostrils flared. He was actually making conversation with a colleague who seemed willing to talk to him. There was no reason to get testy. He exhaled and, in his mind, kept his hand firmly on the stuff-sack of memory.

"Nassir, it's my life, and it's true, even though it's cosmically stupid. And now I'm not only worried about the first-year teacher stuff but about not getting murdered here on the job as some kind of authentic learning forensics lab example."

Nassir raised his eyebrows. "That's a good point. I'm surprised the science class doesn't do more real-time work with data collection in the field."

"You mean, you're surprised the crime scene investigation teacher doesn't just murder someone for a lab experiment."

Nassir looked at him blankly. "Well, yes."

"Okay," said Dave, with his eyes closed. "This leads me to my next question. Do they really think I ordered the murder of the tubby volleyball coach?"

"Oh, yes, they do," he answered immediately. "That's why they're convinced you're undercover. They just haven't sussed out who you're working for, or why, or anything." He took a long draught and added, suppressing a hiccup, "Before he was a volleyball coach, Larry Yearson went by several other identities, but most of us in the intelligence community think he was a man named Cuconotti."

Dave took a shallow breath. He had hoped for a while that if he proved able to engage any of his coworkers in real conversation, they'd let on that there was some trap door, some "out," to this existence. "Oh, you're not a *real* spy? Clap twelve times in the mailroom, and you'll be whisked away to Witness Protection and live the rest of your life as an overqualified mail carrier. Sorry for the mistake." But that wasn't going to happen, and now that he finally realized it, his good options seemed to vaporize into the brewery's chilly, humid air.

"But—you believe me. That I'm actually an underemployed, long-term substitute teacher that may have been hired because, according to our principal, there were multiple Mr. Legnagyszerübbs who applied for the job."

He was not thinking about drinking his beer now, nor was he basking in the pleasant collegial glow of a post-workout happy hour. It was about keeping that question—"What am I doing here?"—at bay. It was keeping his hand on the stuff-sack and figuring out Maple Valley High School. And how he would survive it without ending up like Rotundo. Or Larry Yearson. Or Calzone, or whatever his real name was, when he'd been rubbed off by a miscommunication between a fledgling English teacher and his tenth graders.

"Yes," said Nassir. He was drinking enough for the both of them now, big gulps that left frothy evidence on his rather delicate upper lip. "And a few of the rest of us do—Julia, for one. But Carter and Young are convinced that it would be a great student project to determine why you ordered Cuconotti killed."

"And then, my guess is, I would disappear. Fall down my elevator shaft at home, or the like."

Nassir raised his eyebrows as if to question the naïveté of Dave's comment. But after a moment, he nodded, followed by a sip of beer. A slender young science teacher had slowly turned into a great martial arts mentor, only to develop into an almost heartless John le Carré character, all in the course of an evening.

Dave tapped the bottom of his beer glass on the wooden table, and the two-person silence of a two-person happy hour suddenly blanketed the glasses, the square pine table, the stools. It wasn't an awkward silence, but it wasn't far away. Nassir, Dave realized, had been excited just to share the frustrations and idiosyncrasies of teaching without worrying about espionage for an evening, but Dave wanted to pounce on the chance to find out more about how to survive accidentally being hired at a school where kids learned how to steal, spy and kill. They both eyed their glasses, which reflected the tinsel-esque colors of the flashing LED lights.

Dave conjectured further, as he tapped his glass and Nassir swayed slightly atop his stool, that their reasons for the after-school martial arts sessions were also complementary. Nassir welcomed a chance to teach a willing student in any capacity, and Dave was trying to prevent being physically dominated by students during, say, more unstructured time, or pickup basketball while subbing in gym class.

"Here they are," Erik said, looking back down past a group of people.

A young woman was looking down demurely as she slid past the cluster of tall workmen just past Dave's shoulder. When she passed, Erik held out a beer to her—much lighter than the heavy fuel Nassir and Dave had been enjoying. Then Erik addressed the woman, Nassir and Dave all at the same time.

"Dave and—sorry didn't catch your name, man."

"It's Nassir." Suddenly, no more swaying on the stool from Nassir.

"Dave and Nasser, this is Melody."

"Melanie, actually," she said, extending her hand. She had a black leather jacket and jet-black hair in a long bob. She shook both their hands with a firm grip.

"Melanie was just telling me that she's been subbing long-term over at Oak Creek Middle School, and so far, she hadn't been able to find a full-time gig. I told her that my former student teacher used to hang out here, talking about the same problems, and now he's got himself a full-time teaching English over at…" He trailed off, clearly impressed with his own networking in the way that men of a certain age were.

"Maple Valley High," said Dave. Nassir was scooting his stool over closer, and he was shaking that slight-but-firm hand as well. Dave straightened up a bit.

"Oh, congratulations!" she said. "And what do you two teach?"

Dave looked over at Nassir and almost fell off his stool. The starting-to-slur, chatty bio teacher had been replaced by a relaxed, pleasant professional who leaned forward, Dave thought, as if he smelled something. His eyes were clear and direct.

"I teach English," Dave said.

"I teach high school science," said Nassir with a smile. With some men his own age, Dave would have seen a pose struck, a pithy remark thrown out, a leading question dropped, all to gauge Melanie's interest. And some pairs of guys would turn it into a contest: who makes her laugh more? Who does she address when she talks? But with Nassir, there was none of that—just that sudden alertness and that look that he sensed something on the wind. His thin frame was like a Leaning Tower of Pisa on the stool, and even his faded yet chic gray sweatshirt seemed to "lean in" to Melanie a bit.

Erik, satisfied with his introductions, nodded and disappeared past the clump of people down the bar.

"How do you like Oak Creek Middle?" asked Nassir.

"You know, I'm glad to get some good experience under my belt, but honestly—middle school is not the grade level I really want to be doing. High school is what I'm hoping for." She nodded as if to reaffirm herself, as she took a drink of her pilsner. "Though I'd take anything at this point." She brushed her dark hair behind her ear and turned her head almost reflexively. Dave noticed a purple, circular scar on her temple.

"Maple Valley might have an opening at the semester," chimed Nassir, leaning even farther forward. "In fact, let me get you the number for—" He pulled out his phone and scrolled through his lists. "—for the HR department. A number where the guy who schedules the interviews for the district might actually pick up and get you in an interview. Because once you get in the office for an interview—" Dave thought he saw Nassir smile at him, almost imperceptibly, "you've got some kind of chance, right?"

"Oh, that would be great!" Melanie's eyebrows arched in gratitude, though the scar didn't move with the rest of her forehead. Her phone was now in her hand. "I'll send you a text, and you can... What's your number?"

Nassir spelled out the numbers, and they both looked at their phones, trying to add a contact. Nassir held up his phone, looking at the bars. He sighed. "Might have to step outside to get this in my phone."

Melanie did not look up from her device but stood up and said, "And I have to visit the ladies' room. I do want to talk to you both, though, about working at that school, so don't ditch me." Both of their faces, tilted toward the exit, were tinted in electric blue by the phones, as well as an assorted shift of colors from the holiday lights.

Dave sat, suddenly in the limbo of bar solitude. But it wasn't unpleasant, now that a bit of awkwardness between him and his—friend? Coworker?—had been interrupted. And he was still enjoying the Wednesday, or maybe this one was the Thursday, stout. Either way, it was stronger than when he started out earlier, and pretty soon, he'd have to stop, but for now, there was the pleasant buzz of—

His phone. He pulled it out and saw a message from an unlisted number: *Leave now, through the southeastern exit.*

He froze. As if recognizing his hesitation, the phone buzzed again with a follow-up: *Now.*

He stood up, and it sounded as if the background noise of the bar was suddenly amplified. Individual conversations around him seemed indistinct, and the whole place felt colder. He moved as if in slow motion as he put on his coat and left a twenty on the pine bar, right where it would absorb a ring of condensation.

He looked around. The only familiar face was Erik's, and he was filling glasses. Was the text a joke? Maybe before working at Maple Valley, he would have believed that. Now, though, he started walking toward the main exit. He placed his hand on the glass door when a sound, audible through the din, made him stop.

He heard a motorcycle outside, probably to his right. The two heavy ales he'd had made him say out loud, "Who drives a bike in December?"

The sound got louder, and a single headlight illuminated the side street in front of the brewery. It was the type of area where breweries were prone to spring up: industrial zones with not much traffic and not much of anything else except maybe loading docks, concrete with exposed rebar and steel roofs. Yet since it was dark, most of these details were indistinct, and Dave still sat with his fingertips on the glass pane as the motorcycle passed under the only streetlight in front of the building.

Her black leather jacket shone under the vapor bulb, and even from here, Dave could see the arc of the scar on her forehead, its protruding curve casting a sliver of a shadow across her face. In the flash he saw that all of "Melanie's" networking joviality had been peeled off her face—now she looked more like a tigress that had picked up a scent. Behind her was a figure wrapped in a giant black coat, its face obscured by a helmet dropped over a hood. The hood kept the figure in darkness for anyone not looking too closely, and it kept the figure anonymous for anyone who did. Dave realized that the passenger was probably bound under that coat, but at the moment, he could see a set of slim brown fingers that protruded from underneath the furry hem, gripping the side bar.

The text had warned him to leave through the... which exit was he at? He distinctly remembered looking back at Nassir on their way in hours earlier and seeing the last hint of purple and orange light on the horizon through this main entrance.

"So this is the west exit, and I was supposed to go through the southeastern exit, and now I know why," he said aloud. No one was near the door to hear him.

Several months ago, had Dave seen the scene he witnessed now, with an assassin holding a bound, captive colleague on a motorcycle in the velvety December night, he would have frozen here in the doorway. She would have seen him, and by the time his feet got around to listening to his brain screaming at him to run, she'd have a syringe plunged into his neck, and she'd be holding him up while any brewery patron inside who happened to look might think they were seeing an amorous, maybe alcohol-fueled holiday encounter out front. And then he'd be dead. Or worse. But, like a good comedian or a cage fighter, Dave had developed split-second instincts—as well as the fearlessness to accompany them—by working in front of hostile crowds.

So instead of freezing in panic, Dave Legnagyszerübb pivoted smoothly at the doorway and strode back into the brewery, pulling his hood up on his winter jacket as he did.

Out of decorum, Pre-Mammoth Dave would probably never have worn his hood up indoors. And Pre-Mammoth Dave would never, ever have done what Dave Legnagyszerübb did right now, which was to sidle by a cluster of thirtysomethings into an open door that led into the glass brewery area marked "Employees Only" where overhead bulbs lit up the gleaming metal mash tuns, and the rubber floor's water splashed Dave's cross trainers.

No one yelled at him for trespassing. He saw a few guys carrying five-gallon buckets in an open space across the way from the tuns, but none looked over at him. He saw an Emergency Exit sign in a darker corner of the brewery and had a flashback to the poorly lit corner of the Maple Valley gym—though he kept his hand firmly on the stuff-sack in his brain.

The hesitation spurred by that memory may have saved him. Another worker with requisite flannel and mustache opened the exit door, presumably to throw out whatever was in the bucket. Dave threw himself behind a long horizontal tank, and as soon as the brewer opened the door, the unmistakable sound of a carbureted engine filled the room, and the bright halogen headlight of the bike poured in. The motorcycle must have been six inches past the door sweep—waiting for someone.

The flannelled employee threw his free hand in front of his face. He yelled something out past the southeast exit, but from where he was hiding and with the idling motorcycle engine, Dave couldn't hear it. A woman's voice, indistinct but clearly flirtily apologetic, answered, and a tire squeal cut through the air as the engine roared away.

The brewer said a few confused and profane words about motorcycles and winter, tossed the bucket contents into the night, and walked back towards the lighted area, greeting his co-workers with some kind of "getta load of this" address.

What was going to happen to Nassir? It didn't feel as if he'd blithely slide through a lower-level window again and return to school during a staff meeting on Monday. But before worrying about Nassir, he needed to think about his own escape.

Dave stuck his head over the horizontal tank once, twice, and then on the third time, scoped around. No one was on this side of the brewery. But they would be back to look if the guy's story warranted a check.

He stayed low and tried not to slosh his feet in the water or squeak on the rubber floor. He leaned into the door opener as gently as possible, looked to make sure no one waited for him behind the building, and then stepped out into the night.

"What am I doing here?" he whispered aloud. Eyes scanning the parking lot, he took off toward his car.

18 – The Guitar Player

"Man," said Jayson.

The small group of students in the circle laughed in agreement, but Jayson was the only one allowed to verbalize, per high school social rules. He fingered the silver-and-black ball necklace hanging over his chest, pulling the purple translucent guitar pick back and forth across the small gleaming spheres. It was loud in the Elm Ridge High School hallway among the gray locker banks during C and D lunch—otherwise, any of Jayson's friends would be able to identify that distinctive purr from the quieter classroom setting.

Jayson smiled wider. His even white teeth shone through in that teenage rarity: the genuine smile of enjoyment. The teeth were a shade whiter than the lettering on his Billie Eilish T-shirt, just as the gauges in his ear were a shade blacker than the black background of Eilish perched moodily upon her bed. He pulled the pick more frantically and repeated the sentiment.

"*Man!*" The other teens who'd been monitoring Jayson's response were then allowed to let out their own declarations of amazement:

"Dude!" a girl with long pink-and-green hair and an anime shirt grunted.

"Bro, why you gotta flex on us so hard?" asked a kid with frosted tips and an oversized Nike sweatshirt.

"Mr. L, tell me you are *not good at anything!*" admonished a burly sophomore who, as the owner of several weight room records and a nearly-unspoken desire to be a ballad-playing, eyes-closed guitarist with

133

a rose between his teeth, carried the second-highest amount of clout in the circle, and, along with Jayson, the status to be somewhat genuine in his emotions.

David Legnagyszerübb was not scheduled for hallway duty that late-winter morning, but he had "accidentally" met Jayson in the hallway and now played a slightly bluesy run to get back to the root note of the little four-chord ditty he just improvised, to the astonishment of the students around him. It was February, and he'd just arrived at school, walking over the stained maroon carpet in the main hallway through the one semi-open area where kids could congregate between the rows of dull gray lockers that stood like stone-age computer servers on the periphery of the passageway. The main office was on one end of the "court," and a few science classrooms were on the other end. It was where David had orchestrated the events of the morning, starting with this little one-man jam. It kept him out conversing with this group of kids for a few minutes, which, as a harried new teacher this year, he shouldn't have any reason to do in the middle of the hallway. And his guitar playing, conducted by the slightly numb fingers of a February morning, wasn't stellar by any means. But kids were a largely untalented, unsophisticated lot, and as the saying went, it didn't take much.

"Man," said Jayson again. The smile was winsome and attracted Jayson much attention from the young women of Elm Creek High School. The image of the songsmith certainly didn't hurt either, an image that wouldn't be buoyed by seeing his English teacher play his guitar in ways that seemed almost adulterous to a high schooler like Jayson, who looked the part—but hadn't mastered barre chords yet.

David took the guitar strap expertly off his shoulder, not too nonchalantly, but also to give the impression that he did, in fact, easily throw out blues riffs when it suited him. He followed it with a little shrug and a smile—the humble teacher, just lucky to shine a bit of light in some kids' morning with a few tasty licks—as he handed it back to Jayson.

Jayson looked at his guitar as if it had betrayed him—which it had, in a way. But he beamed the smile around gamely, laughed, and vowed to take up a new instrument.

The beam of sunlight that shone through the front entrance struck the muscular sophomore straight in the chest, making him look like a superhero's understudy. It was a good late-winter bit of sun for students and a teacher who hadn't seen such a thing in several months. Suddenly, everything in the "court" area seemed to loosen a bit, and everyone relaxed and talked a tone louder.

David smiled, too, ostensibly in reaction to Jayson but also in the way that the weather was going to contribute to this morning's choreographed events. Some younger agents at the CSS might claim that David was just incredibly lucky in these types of things. Others would argue the other side of the spectrum: that what appeared to be serendipity—a beam of light that obscured the activities of the front end of the school, for example— was just a result of the type of fastidious planning that started to happen in your second decade of this type of work. David knew the truth: it lay squarely in the middle. When planning the destabilization of a country's currency or the poisoning of a religious figure, careful preparation took care of the effects of Murphy's Law and other bad fortune. Then the universe filled the gaps with the circumstance you needed at the right time—hence this sunlight.

The muscular sophomore, a bit less scared now that people knew the extent of his passion for song, pressed David to go beyond a little "aw-shucks" shrug. "So, like, how'd you learn to play like that, Mr..." He knew David's name, but the charade almost always took top priority. In high school, caring enough to know a stranger's name was like getting thrown into the contest of popularity judo.

"I'm Mr. Legnagyszerübb," he said, shaking the sophomore's hand. He needed to keep this group of kids around him until the time was right. It would help with the overall effect of the situation's final outcome, or at least his role in it.

"I'm Angel," responded the sophomore, shifting his weight from one foot to the other.

"There was this time after college," began David, "when I was living in Philadelphia and working in a bar. I used to clean the place after musicians would play, and I'd give them, you know, a free soda—"

The kids laughed. It fell under a specific high school humor category: Let's pretend the adult has never drank and you pretend you don't know what alcohol is.

"—if they showed me some chord progressions or how to play a certain lick. I learned a little something from each act, and now I can put it all together into something coherent. At the time, you couldn't just sit down with a YouTube video and learn a song."

Jayson pulled the pick on his necklace and laughed. That was probably how he spent many an evening, ducking girls' texts and trying to play the intro to "What's My Age Again?" at one-quarter speed.

The only problem was that this folksy story, with its inclusion of late nights and alcohol for the kids' benefit, was completely untrue. David Legnagyszerübb had learned to play guitar as part of his work as a CSS agent, of course.

19 - El Guitarrista

Twelve years ago, on a dusty highway in the southern Durango state, hidden in plain view by being the same dirt-streaked beige as the entire surrounding area, was a warehouse used by a midsized narcotics cartel. The small community around the warehouse had no school, and so David Legnagyszerübb had gone down in a pickup loaded with old books and a guitar as a Peace Corps member, looking to set up some literacy programs.

Across the street from the warehouse were some ancient picnic tables that stood out in the hot sun like fossils. Soon, the *gabacho*, who barely spoke any Spanish, and certainly no local Tepehuán, was teaching kids to read, and when he'd spoon out *arroz y frijoles* during the lunch break, the kids would talk about how nice he was. After the afternoon lessons, the kids would sit around the skeletal picnic tables, and he would play songs—he was a bit proud of "La Playa," his version of "Boardwalk," because he had only just learned guitar for this particular mission— sometimes in bastardized Spanish just to prove how little he knew of the language. He avoided being kidnapped for long enough—partially by his ability to perfectly understand all the Spanish and enough of the local Tepehuan to know what was going on all the time—to be a fixture in the villages. David—"Paul" to the folks here in the village—was just a *norteño* interloper who sweat profusely in the desert sun, trying to get kids to read by bribing them with lunch every day and then singing.

One day after lunch, the young Peace Corps member was cleaning up the paper plates when he heard someone clear their throat behind him. He turned to see a man in full denim, one cowboy boot up on a picnic table, holding a guitar and looking off into the desert. David resisted the urge to grin, tied off the garbage bag and hoisted his own guitar as well. And without looking at each other, the two launched into David's version of "La Playa."

That's how David met Vincente Calderon. Vincente showed up twice again to jam and then, in halting English, invited David to visit him at his job, where he had plenty of downtime to play music regularly at an old warehouse out in the desert. He could even give him a ride out—it would be fun, promised Vincente.

And it was. Every night, they'd start with "La Playa" and then launch into minor-key ballads and major-key jams. Along the way, David learned about Mexican pop and rock music. Out in the cooling desert evening, the men played, smiling at one another at each guitar run or improvised harmony. But not too much could be said without someone striking up a phrase or melody line reminiscent of El Tri or Cafe Tacuba, and the music would fill the dry air again.

It was a regular gig—if David declined a ride from Vincente to the jam session more than once a week, Vincente would get a little surly. After all, Vincente's one job task was to stand in the dark heat and stop anyone who tried to get into the warehouse, which was precisely no one, so his and David's sessions were all he had to look forward to.

A frown from the driver's seat of the pickup regarding any of David's absences, however, was about as tough as Vincente got. As far as David could tell, Vincente had earned the cartel's trust by sheer availability. Everyone in the surrounding area knew him to be by far the laziest of the Ortuño brothers, unable to get a serious girlfriend or a factory job, and therefore available at night to stand guard. Though after he pulled an old office chair out of the warehouse, he preferred to sit guard. Every country, it turns out, has dudes who have no gumption for anything but six strings. Had Vincente been born in L.A. in 1976, things might have been different, but in south Durango, he was a lookout and an easily manipulated one at that.

David had stopped by early one evening to *tomar la guitarra,* and had seen several sets of eyes in the dark behind the beige metal door to the beige metal warehouse. One set materialized into a large man with sunglasses, a tan and the sleeves cut off his flannel shirt. Up until now, Vincente was the only person "Paul" ever saw out here.

After some awkward initial conversation—David was still pretending to have very limited Spanish—David was able to mention his work with the books and the kids to show the heavy in the flannel shirt that he was no threat to anyone.

"*Por eso, que estoy aquí,*" he said, even though it wasn't true, but it did fit with the James Taylor chord structure he was currently playing. Then David mentioned the version of "La Playa" he and Vincente had been working on.

At that point, Vincente had nearly stood up from the office chair but instead had leaned forward, his dusty brown belt loops straining in straight lines against the Euclidean geometry of his black jeans' waistband and the white-brown of his side rolls. In the dark, his eyes twinkled, and he began in an untrained yet pleasant voice, "*Caminando por el paseo...*"

The man in the flannel shirt didn't smile. But he moved his index finger in a circle parallel to the ground, in the universal imperative to "go on."

David's fingers grabbed the chords by habit, and they began to play together. At that moment, David had found something of a transcendence. He didn't forget that he was on the job, but it didn't detract from the way Vincente's imperfect voice intertwined with the warmth of his nylon strings in the cooling Durango night. After all, he'd never played guitar before this, and before the "Peace Corps" gig began, he'd never performed music with anyone. Vincente's boot tapped a soft backbeat in the dust—though it quickly went away, as even for *las baladas,* too much work was too much—and they branched out to other songs.

He showed up again the next night with a few beers to share. Several guys in the warehouse came out to listen to Vincente and his *norteño* friend jam.

And the night after that, only one set of eyes looked out from the doorway. Everyone else sat out in the darkness to sing with Vincente, "Paul," and the other musicians.

And the night after that, three men came out right away, their smiles evident in the dark even under their thick mustaches. The next night they had beer too, and after a few *cervezas*, Sleeveless Flannel sang in a lovely falsetto as if to cool the night off with an icy alto tone. The "band" even kept jamming as "Paul" walked into the warehouse without being stopped, ostensibly to look for some cups in one of the warehouse's old steel filing cabinets.

Night after night, it became easier for David to pick up the chords to the folk songs and the pop standards. But each night, as he steadied his hands on the dash and kept up the slurry conversation with Vincente in the pitch dark, he lamented that he'd have to get up and teach in about five hours. However, he couldn't lapse into unconsciousness on those truck rides home. One, he had to keep Vincente awake and semi-focused. Two, he clutched his guitar to make sure it didn't get broken on the bumpy roads.

And three—no matter how bleary and drunk he got, he had to make sure that the extra car battery Vincente kept on the floor stayed there and didn't tip over, spill or get thrown out into the desert night through the hole in the floorboard. Each night when Vincente dropped him off, he wouldn't see the reassuring pat that David gave that battery before leaving it and stumbling off to bed.

And then waking to teach reading only a few hours later. Luckily, his exhausted morning demeanor offered no loss of faith among those *arroz*-scarfing, *libro*-reading kids. Occasionally he'd think about some of his fellow agents, wearing dark blue suits as they stepped into the office at 5:30 a.m., being searched until 5:40, and then trudging up to their offices, hoping to be seen arriving early to fill out paperwork dealing with the latest rounds of faceless, uncatchable identity thieves. At night he shuddered thinking of his colleagues as he drank another warm Tecate and stumbled through something that sounded vaguely of "Hey Joe" with the late-night security-cum-singing crew.

But what he remembered the most about those days was the guitar study. There was no paperwork here—nothing to busy his hands or his mind—nor would there be until he returned. It was liberating for a day or two, but in this dry, barren scrubland, he couldn't risk keeping his shooting skills up with some target practice on Tecate cans or find a spry sixteen-year-old with whom to practice hand-to-hand. No, this was the land and the time signature of Vincente & Co.—wake, work for the cartel or a cartel-owned business in town, lunch, nap out of the scorching sun, back to work, several beers after work, fall asleep with mouth open, repeat.

But David Legnagyszerübb was not an idle-hands kind of guy. So he'd practice, occasionally singing along with himself but mostly working on the technical skill of playing his fingerstyle well enough to do Durango justice. No subterfuge, no murder. Just the simple act of practicing a discrete skill every single day and making it better.

Eventually, as his hands found the music, he could take recommendations from the boys over at the warehouse, and they could sing along with him, too. Soon he slipped a bit more into the bar-piano-playing role, as the "security team" would stumble in and out of the door, talk loosely around him about the warehouse's daily action (again, *no hable Ingles,* so it was all good), all while he'd ride a modified twelve-bar blues into a steady stream of background music.

The initial compliments paid to him by the group of warehouse guys started to fade as he became part of the background noise for them. Headlights flooded the entrance to the warehouse each night as he sat on the back of Vincente's pickup, watching the sparse insects reveal themselves like sleet in the night air as he riffed on "Oye Como Va," playing a bit louder when the men would join in. But even Vincente had started to forget that he was there, forgot that he brought most of the *cervezas* and, on this particular tonight, the rum, too. An hour in, there was still light in the sky as the men passed out, slumped in chairs or, in the case of the Flannel Falsetto Singer, directly in the dust.

He would look back on those moments fondly when he had rejoined the ranks of the agents with their morning coffees and gleaming desks with quartz clocks upon them and sterile, always-emptied wastebaskets. As he pressed his pen neatly into the fibers of the paper under the soft fluorescent lights, his tie crisply lighting up his white shirt with a splash of verdant green, he'd think about being unwashed, bug-bitten and ignored in a warehouse at dusk in Mexico, and he would remember stopping himself before he got off the truck.

Now, as he sat among the warehouse men, he stopped playing guitar for a moment and thought he'd heard one of the men stir—or at least that's the excuse he gave himself—so he immediately gave an open A chord a thumb-brush. All was quiet again—but the guitar could not stop. So he played the chords and melody for "Auld Lang Syne," singing slightly flat but in flawless Spanish with only a hint of an Anglo accent. The nylon and the calluses on his fingers, and even the beat-up truck he perched on, seemed to come together, and for the first time in his guitar education, rather than generate ideas to play with David Legnagyszerübb, listened to the snores of the men sprawled around him, to the sound of the wind in the scrub brush, to the sand that hit the bumper of the truck as the wind sprayed it through the open warehouse door.

He finished on a barre A up the neck, and it was perfect, so he had to smile. He was still smiling as he made his way lightly across the open cement floor of the warehouse, unconsciously wedging his toes into the ground so as not to make the loud crunching sounds that the guys made with their boots. He stopped at the old filing cabinet and listened for a sound, either within or without, and heard nothing but the men's snores. In the bottom drawer was the cartel's big Glock pistol, which they had long since forgotten about, but David had seen last week when "looking around for some cups."

He regarded the gun, which he had loaded two mornings ago, in the filthy yellow light coming through a hole between the crumbling concrete and the broken glass block. The edges of his sleeve prevented his fingers from making any direct contact with the metal, and he held it low enough on his stomach so that anyone who saw his silhouette would not see the weapon.

He made his way, slowly and patiently, thinking about those two beautiful A chords, back to the circle of men. Vincente was the hardest sleeper, drunk or not, and David stooped in the darkness, caressed his wrist and held it. David put the gun firmly in Vincente's hand, pushed the muzzle into the base of his neck where it met his skull and fired.

The report echoed impossibly through the warehouse and out into the night. David's mind, previously perturbed by the natural beauty of his own steel-string creation, flattened itself into that blank bed of sand necessary for these kinds of tasks. Vincente's hand went slack, but David held it firmly in his own, even as the back of the corpse's hand slid against his palm, and the pad of his trigger finger struggled to find purchase against the dead man's fingernail.

His mind did not race. He didn't frantically point the gun around or put a few rounds into the air. Some of the men roused, and even a few opened their eyes long enough to offer one last look of disbelief. He used Vincente's hand and shot them all, and the last retort bounced around the rusty metal interior walls of the warehouse like a cymbal.

He set down Vincente's hand and hopped into the back of the truck, where he lay for about four minutes, per the protocol he'd learned when he tested for his termination license all those years ago. He scanned the warehouse with a mirror, as protocol dictated. He looked for anyone who heard the shots—but no one would be out here in the Durango emptiness. Instead, he mentally reviewed the information he'd learned and tried to consider if there was anything he needed to take from the warehouse. After the four minutes, he didn't hear any approaching vehicles or see any confused passerby stopping in to see what the noise was.

He took out an extra car battery from the back of the pickup and set it next to a translucent plastic container. The next moment he was unwinding his guitar strings, stopping once every few moments to make sure no one was approaching the warehouse. He produced a roll of electrical tape and fixed a few of the thickest guitar strings to the posts of the battery. The wound strings, acting as resistors, would keep the bomb from pulling all the amperage it needed for at least three minutes. As he touched the strings, he realized he'd remember the hot desert afternoons spent spooning rice, the evenings spent playing real music, and the mornings trying to wake up before sunrise—in fact, he'd remember them all fondly.

By the time the warehouse blew, he was twelve miles out of town, headed to a cove south of Navolato on the ocean where a boat would be waiting for him—about a three-hour drive. He'd left all the rice and dried beans he had outside for the kids and their mothers to find the next day. The truck would be found by a wrecking company whose cousin had very loose contacts in American security, and the stringless guitar would be wrapped in Peace Corps long sleeves and thrown into the ocean. The warehouse would burn to the ground. The cartel's investigation would reveal that Vincente Amarillo, known as *Pies Pesados* among the cartel's brethren, killed his compatriots after a night of hard drinking and then turned the gun on himself. No one had seen it coming from *Pesados*, yet you could never tell, could you? The local school also received a letter saying their Peace Corps literacy worker had been withdrawn due to cartel violence and safety concerns for the children.

And yes, there'd been a lot of paperwork to file when he returned home.

20 - The Fight

The square of morning sun hitting Angel's chest, compounded with the feel of playing guitar for a small circle of onlookers, reminded him so poignantly of that time in Mexico's Durango state that his throat clamped shut. As a man who had to keep his marksman's certifications up for the Bureau and then later for a few other clandestine organizations, he spent lots of time putting bullets into pieces of cardstock, which was beautiful by way of precision engineering but would never make you look at the world in a different way—not the way the right note on a guitar, bent to the major third at just the right time, held there like a rare insect, and then shaken lovingly with vibrato could change the very taste of the air around your head. With this reverie in mind, he played a little dancing lick that descended and then climbed back up before you could notice and shook the last note like he was coaxing honey out of it. It was something he'd always play at the end of "La Playa," and it always made Vincente, his unfortunate friend, smile.

"Yeeeeaasss," said Jayson, hand frozen on the pick around his neck. His eyes shone with a gray intensity that, like a winning lottery ticket, most girls wanted but couldn't handle.

At last, David saw the school resource officer, Graig LaMonde, stride past on his way to the front office. His jaw was set, and his stubble seemed to point out from his face as if it, too, had been put on high alert. Students could instantly tell that something was up as they looked away from their phones and conversations to watch Officer LaMonde stride through the commons.

Even better: one of the assistant principals, Mr. Craisel, strode out of the main office and joined Officer LaMonde on his march. Craisel was short and combed his thinning hair over and wore suits whose blue palettes never quite matched his pasty skin. Craisel instantly addressed LaMonde and started asking questions, his face turned ninety degrees toward LaMonde's stubble. It was clear from how LaMonde kept his cops' face forward and did not turn his head toward Craisel—nor did he slow his walk—that this was a one-sided conversation between someone who got excited about the possibility of some real threat and adventure and someone else who had to take these "exciting" moments seriously, lest people lose their lives.

Even better still: as they approached the front door, Carlson, the lead principal, joined them at the front entrance. Carlson never wore a suit—only worn but clean dress shirts that varied predictably throughout the week and strained at his large belly. He said little and smiled even less, and for that, most of the teachers that David had met here at Elm Creek were grateful for him, even if he visibly couldn't stand his own second-in-command, Craisel.

These three men were far from being in David's earshot, but when Carlson addressed LaMonde, they paused their march, sending Craisel, whose head still bent obsequiously towards the officer's face, into a metal part of the doorframe. It was great, and David wished more people would have been around to see it, though the two Hispanic girls sitting on the one bench at the entrance of the school, who covered their mouths politely and laughed mostly with their eyes at Craisel's slapstick, had their mornings made.

An officer whom David did not recognize—and neither did the kids, from the way they stopped and suddenly stared at the silhouette, replete with taser, baton, gun and even beard outline—stepped in through the main entrance from the parking lot. Again, David could hear nothing, but he saw the officer explain to Principal Carlson why he'd been requested at Elm Creek High this morning.

The four outlines stood in the February morning sun. Carlson spoke and gestured with his hands, the outline of a folder in one and a walkie-talkie in the other. LaMonde stood stock straight with his hands on his hips, having been clearly updated several times on what was occurring this morning and quite familiar with the situation. The new street officer (name: Carlos Harris) stood directly across from Carlson, nodding his head with his arms folded in thought as he listened. And, last and least, Craisel leaned in so far that it seemed he might topple over and, judging by his hand gestures, attempted to chime in several times with more commentary than Carlson was offering. Each time the inane assistant principal offered something—again, David couldn't make out the words but could guess at their stupidity—Officer Harris turned towards him. Carlson and LaMonde ignored him, and neither looked his way. Carlson invariably continued the explanation as if he hadn't been interrupted.

David could see that the new officer held what looked like a phone in his hand and was showing it to Carlson. Carlson pulled out his own phone and held it up in kind. It was kind of like watching indigenous tribe members communicate, except that David alone knew what the officer and the principal were talking about.

Craisel, leaning almost impossibly forward now, received a "Don't Talk Right Now" hand from Carlson. Administrators like Craisel were always looking to make it seem as if they knew more than they did while always trying to slyly figure out an answer to the question of the day at Elm Creek: What in the world was going on?

The answer was that there was about to be a drug search of the student parking lot. Usually, drug searches were performed with all the surprise of a fake punt in football, with someone noticing that the quarterback, not the kicker, was standing back to catch the long snap or that the kicker was still warming up on the sidelines as the players got into position at the line of scrimmage. In the case of searches of the students' cars, there would usually be a K-9 squad car parked in front of the school about fifty minutes before 1st hour started, which may have well been a sign saying, "If you're high, trying to get high, or making money off of getting people high, please call in sick today, or at least be cognizant enough of your surroundings to skip."

Today, however, there was no such squad car.

The K-9 unit was here for a demonstration, not a search—at least according to Officer Carlos Harris, who had arrived in the K-9 squad car this morning with his partner, Laser. Officer Harris's face rarely betrayed emotion of any kind, but today showed a hint of an excited smile behind his beard. Talking to students about Laser and the training and experiences the two of them had together—it was guaranteed to get at least a couple of kids roped in. And sanctioned teenage excitement was not something that Harris and Laser got to see very often on the drug task force.

Harris was now showing Principal Carlson a text message he'd received from him, proposing this morning's visit. The only problem was that Carlson had not sent the message. David had spoofed his phone, using the cell tower components he had installed in the building after the InterCell field trip, as well as a cloned SIM card obtained from the foolish customer service agent over at Principal Carlson's network provider. This allowed him to send the fake text, and then when the service provider uploaded a copy of the sent text to Carlson's phone, delete it from that device. No harm, no foul.

But Carlson was not holding up his own phone right now. Rather, he was showing Harris a phone that had been brought to his office this morning by a student who used the bathroom each morning at 6:30. And though "serendipity" was not a word ever used by any of the men standing at the entrance to Elm Ridge High School, at this moment it was the essence of their conversation. The phone was unlocked, and when Carlson thumbed the screen, it displayed several text conversations about the sale of Adderall, Vicodin and marijuana at Elm Ridge today.

The phone belonged to one Nelson Delamont, a "B" Honor Roll Student and known drug dealer at Elm Ridge. David had stolen the phone from the boys' locker room during gym class, as Nelson left his phone in the locker each day so that Leeia Mitchum would share an earbud with him during their in-class aerobic walks. He learned this by intercepting a series of Instagram messages between Nelson and a friend, describing the "game" he was "dropping" on Leeia. It was clear that Nelson actually cared for Leeia by the way that he referenced her in the direct messages; David had even let out an "Aw" during his extended reading of these communiqués.

However, Nelson had served no fewer than eleven days of OSS last spring for having a Ziplock bag full of one-hitters that was also full of cash. Officer LaMonde had not needed to cut open a seat cushion in Nelson's Geo Prism to find the goodie bag, nor had he been forced to decode some sort of tag on a bathroom wall indicating that the bag was buried in a planter in front of the school under some neatly repotted geraniums. Rather, Nelson had run back for his Algebra II textbook and left a full quarter of the bag sticking out of his locker, cutting several of the one-hitters in half and exposing several corners of the drug money bills. It wasn't quite the *Scarface* level of moving weight; when LaMonde had completed a proper search of the bag—which was quite easy when it turned out that not only had Nelson left a chunk of the bag hanging out of his locker, but he had also forgotten to latch the lock properly—it had revealed a total of $16, which made many of the authority figures in the building realize that although Nelson Delamont was selling drugs in this building, he was doing it quite poorly (from a financial standpoint) despite his B Honor Roll status.

A touchscreen field pressure recorder and a gyroscope reader had been installed on Nelson's phone by a friendly network administrator on the Elm Ridge public Wi-Fi that the students all used and signed into it each day, allowing their devices to remember to allow it unfettered access to their devices' data, as agreed to in the never-before-read EULA. The touchscreen and gyroscope information were brilliant little pieces of data that, when relayed to any government agency's deep learning algorithms running perpetually, could determine a six-digit passcode typed into a smartphone screen—even one with randomly rotating number fields. Nelson's phone had begun relaying this data on the first day that David started to watch Nelson, but when David had seen Nelson type in a 1111 passcode while holding his phone up to take a picture of the clock, any other information to access the phone of Nelson Delamont, B Honor Roll Student and Two-Digit Drug Kingpin, became superfluous.

During Nelson's phy ed walks with Leeia, David had set up a series of equally underwhelming and poorly articulated drug deals around the school via spoofed text. Then it was simply a matter of leaving the "unlocked" phone, along with a few hundred dollars worth of cash, in the bathroom for someone to find.

Officer Harris kept his poker face as he read the phone that Carlson had given him, but even at this distance, David could see a smirk on his face as he addressed LaMonde. He even thought he noticed an "All right, let's do this" play out on the K-9 officer's lips.

And so now, on a sleepy February morning, as the newly powerful sun broke over the cars in the Elm Ridge student parking lot and cast arrows of silver light back into the high school entrance, the main administrative weight of the high school—Principal Carlson and Officer LaMonde, as well as the sycophant Craisel and the interloper Officer Harris—exited the building at the same time.

But for every Assistant Principal Craisel who goes outside to get in on the action, there must be another administrator who stays behind to unceremoniously do all the work. Craisel's yang was named Daphne Moua, and David Legnagyszerübb knew that in the parking lot DEA raid he'd set up Assistant Principal Moua would be the one to assess the situation as a whole, notice the administrative boys in their fire truck, and realize that someone needed to stay in the building. At six foot with bold highlights in her long black hair, APs like Moua needed only to stand in the center of the commons area with her arms folded to maintain order. And for David, today, that wouldn't do.

So he'd easily fabricated an email from HR pointing out that Moua had accumulated vacation days which would be lost at the end of the year if she did not use them.

Moua, of course, considered the email briefly, but then also considered what the imbecile Craisel might do in her absence, like accidentally share the unpublished spreadsheet about staffing decisions with the whole district. Or neglect a call on his walkie-talkie because he was on the phone with his brother about some sports bets he'd made. Or look through signposts of Principal Carlson's life on social media in order to get some clues as to how to suck up to the boss.

But then, inexplicably, Daphne Moua had also received an invitation to the early spring plant sale at the university's horticulture building. The date was February 20. The plant sale was real, for the record—David just had to send the email Moua's way. And the last chance to take a personal day was February 20. David interspersed the two emails a few times, trying not to press too hard, but then he finally got the alert on his phone: she'd taken the 20th off, her second personal day in her nine years in the district. So, the only person with enough sense to realize that every zookeeper should not go into the same tiger exhibit at the same time was out of the building.

Later, Dr. Moua would feel hugely guilty about it once the phone videos were circulated on the evening news. And she shouldn't have felt guilty about it. Craisel had blown through his entire stock of personal, sick and emergency days when he'd won a cruise through a mail-order contest, and Carlson had done similarly after his divorce tore a year of his principalship apart. But then again, of course, both men would later drop the "It's not her fault, but Daphne wasn't here that day" in interviews with the superintendent.

So there was no tall, sensible administrative presence in the main commons. And all the less sensible administrative presence had left with the police through the exit to the parking lot to find some drugs. And David Legnagyszerübb, surrounded by admiring students who were still discussing his guitar abilities, was the lone adult in the morning sea of near-adults. He smiled as he got the same feeling he had outside the warehouse in Durango state in Mexico when he launched into the version of "La Playa" to begin the process of finishing the job.

On the west side of the commons area, Kadar Rodriquez opened his locker with one hand while smoothing the thighs of his jet-black jeans with his other. The silver pattern of fleur-de-lis on the back pocket of these pants matched the one on his equally jet-black backpack, and it paired well with the various tiger and rose imagery on his none-more-black jacket with white sleeve cuffs. He reached over the locker bank to exchange finger handshakes with Garret Myka, who leaned against his own locker, his arm protectively (or possessively) around his girlfriend's neck.

Kadar did this, not because he was friends with Garret or because the two shared an affinity for expensive-looking jackets with vaguely Asian imagery on them. He did it so that no one would see the knife he now pulled out of his backpack, as anyone, save a trained professional like David, would look at the intertwining handshake above the lockers, not the weapons surreptitiously pulled into coat sleeves below.

Kadar kept glancing at Jayson, who was still trying to keep the guitar-centered conversation going, pulling at the guitar pick around his neck, making the *thc-thc-thc-thc* sound as he raked it over the beads. Jayson, facing David Legnagyszerübb, never looked behind him to see Kadar since he was completely engrossed in a conversation with a musician that, up until four minutes ago, he didn't know that he wanted to be. After all, who wants to be an English teacher at a faceless suburban high school? But normal people forget how fast the young can become infatuated—with a girl, with a game, with a shoe—and so any adult who ever uses the term "callous youth" should see Jayson Whittier as he frantically asks questions of someone who just played an intoxicating guitar melody for him and his acquaintances.

This is why Jayson did not see Kadar looking at him. The two boys had a smattering of shared classes (Algebra II, Health) and even a handful of shared presentation assignments ("Remembering the Holocaust" in US History, "The Holocaust Today" in World History), but no real friendship—hence Kadar's consternation when Jayson began attacking Kadar's sister on Instagram.

Kadar had hopped in, even offering deferential outs for Jayson to walk back his comments. Jayson, his account taken over using the school's newly compromised cellular and Wi-Fi networks, stated in no uncertain terms that he would be happy to leave Kadar's sister alone, but he would be administering a beating to Kadar himself that would put him in the hospital. The hospital mention was enough for the aggrieved black-jacket fanatic to bring the knife to school.

Kadar would not preemptively attack Jayson this morning, but he would focus all his attention on the young guitar disciple, and Jayson, having no idea the part that his fabricated online persona was playing in all this, would not turn around to check out a sometimes acquaintance staring at him. And so the final pieces came into play in the largely unsupervised morning commons area: the Yangs.

One of the Yangs was in ninth grade, and the second was in eleventh, though it was impossible for most students and staff to tell them apart. A Yang sister was in eighth grade and looked, sadly enough, like the boys, though, unlike her brothers, she was a decent academic and one of the captains of Elm Ridge Jr's Knowledge Bowl team. There was almost no chance either Yang boy could spell "knowledge" and only a slightly better chance that they might be able to pull off "bowl." Cherie Yang hated her brothers, and she hated them even more every time someone mistook her for one of them.

Now, the two Yang boys approached Kadar: the taller ninth grader in front, the older and more muscular eleventh grader behind him.

The Yangs gamed hard on the school's network and were known to be available to game before, after and mostly during the school day. One brother was visible as "xyangx" and the other as "yang2014" at almost any time since the handheld consoles were used in every class, and the Yang's father (name: Yang), who attended parent-teacher conferences, learned four times a year from as many as eighteen different teachers that the gaming systems the old man thought had been thrown away had, in fact, been brought to school to distract from the annoying practices and procedures of learning.

And it was these consoles that enabled David Legnagyszerübb to, as the kids and online-savvy adults called it, "troll" the Yangs so easily.

It involved absolutely no packet-sniffing or phone-tower tomfoolery. All David did here was set up a fake gaming account (kandarrod69) on the PlayStation website, play online with the Yangs for a few days, purport to become upset over some experienced slight in a late-night *Bullets and Honor* game, and then start trading some serious insults. Baiting the Yang boys was easier than convincing an angry dog to bark.

And now, the Yangs IRL power-strutted down the corridor in between the two locker banks as only young males can, in fully puffy vests, with the elder's hair slicked back and the younger sporting a tenth-grade mustache over his sneering ninth-grade lip. Kadar still leaned lightly against the locker with laser eyes on Jayson. And with no Dr. Moua to keep watch over the hallway, the place was free of supervision, all administrators being in the parking lot for a K-9 drug bust.

David Legnagyszerübb's chess board was set up. All he had to do was play.

David grudgingly agreed to play Jayson's guitar one more time before first hour. As he put the strap over his head, he waited half a beat—and

Angel took out his phone to record the teacher-cum-guitar impresario. The rest of the teens smiled and followed suit. Seven tiny red eyes faced David Legnagyszerübb as he launched into John Mayer's "Neon," and as he finished the sixth bar of the intro, the older Yang hit Kadar Rodriquez's upper back with a hammer fist, and the two spilled into the common area.

David did not look as the younger Yang sprung on the other half of Kadar's scrawny back and began raining punches down on the back of his head. David continued playing until the crowd of students became quiet for half a beat: the de facto opening bell for any good school fight.

A girl yelled, and phones came out of jackets in concentric waves. The pitch of the crowd changed as girls covered their mouths and boys hit each other on the shoulder in anticipation and excitement.

Kadar was trying to stand up, but the two Yangs were, at the moment, too much. One punch hit the back of his head, and it rebounded; the crowd let out a gasp. The older Yang was trying to extricate himself in order to really fight, but all he'd manage to do was insult Kadar's mother a few times. His brother was inadvertently cinching his head against a tiger on the back of Kadar's jacket, making a fight sandwich sandwiching the three of them together.

David set the guitar gently against a locker. There was no use holding it out for Jayson to take, as a fight always had and will always supersede any other event in a school, a law as immutable as any of Newton's revelations. He stretched his arms behind his head for a moment, and no one noticed. For a few minutes, he'd considered performing the denouement in this play with the guitar in his hand but realized that it would look a little flamenco-Mexican-folk-hero ridiculous, and even though these were idiot high school students and not the professionals he'd spent his whole life training with and combating in close quarters, one might land a wayward punch that would slip his guard if he didn't have all four limbs available.

He edged past the throng of onlookers and heard one or two "Aw, it's Mr. L!" as he made his way into the melee, but none of them sounded disappointed at the change from fight to fight breakup. Good.

The older Yang let out a curse word as he finally squeezed to his feet. His brother had stopped throwing his fists wildly around and seemed intent on actually finding the back of Kadar's head to smash. This was dangerous for the prone Kadar, for at this point in the fight, there were no administrators or police to save him. Good.

David did not throw himself in like a rugby player to break it up the way a normal teacher might. Rather, he planted his right foot behind Yang's bent right leg and inserted his forearm in the space behind the now-outstretched fist of the Yang, who was about to get his revenge on a student who barely knew him. As he'd done a million times in the gym, David pulled his body down and threw the elder Yang over his hip.

There was that beautiful moment when his victim's weight just seemed to disappear, as if the earth had forgotten about gravity for a moment and then remembered just as fast. David heard the stunned Yang lose all his breath at once as his face and chest smashed into the carpet.

Wordless cries of shock rose up from the crowd, and later phone videos would show the telltale shake of an unplanned, excited reaction. David, however, simply let go of his hold on the older Yang and turned quickly to face the other two combatants.

The younger Yang was frozen mid-punch as he realized what had happened to his brother, but before he had a chance to do anything, it was Kadar's turn to pounce. A right hook from the kid who had just been jumped elicited another round of cheers and yells from the crowd, even though the flailing, blind-white anger of the punch knocked the hard part of Freshman Yang's skull, damaging Kadar's hand more than Yang's head.

According to eyewitness statements, at that point Mr. Legnagyszerübb simply appeared between the two students, and as Kadar and Yang flailed, David gained control of Kadar's right hand, pinning it against the locker by leveraging his wrist. The most important move came in the form of another judo throw against the small Yang. David meant to put his knee behind Yang's and place his shin on the opposite side of Yang's opposite leg in order to throw him to the ground against his brother. But the older Yang was on his feet a bit faster than David had guessed, and any conscious thought about how this was supposed to occur suddenly slipped to the side.

Grasping at the air, the younger Yang was pivoted and thrown—not as high as his brother, but with enough obvious force that the crowd gave an even louder cheer. And he completely missed his brother in the fall, who was already up and going at Kadar.

David moved towards the older Yang, striking him with a straight punch that broke his jaw. He then gave Kadar a side kick to the ribs that sent the victim sprawling against the lockers. And when David Legnagyszerübb, high school English teacher and the newest, coolest, most popular staff member of Elm Creek High School, reeled in his natural instincts, he spun around to see three students lying on the floor in various states of injury, a crowd of students cheering as he spun around—and then, he heard gasps.

"Oh my God, they stabbed him! They stabbed him!" screamed one girl, and students began running. This, thought David, would get the administrators to leave their failed drug bust in the parking lot and come back into school.

It was Jayson, unintentional almost-Franz-Ferdinand of this battle royale, who first moved toward poor Mr. Legnagzsrübb. His cheap teacher dress shirt, right from where Kadar's knife—though in reviewing multiple videos provided by the single working school camera, the police would not see exactly where the stabbing occurred, though there had been opportunity—stuck out on the left side of his abdomen, right above the belt line.

"Jayson," he said, and pretended to lose consciousness.

21 – Study Hall Duty

Study hall had seemed to be the ideal place for Dave to recruit students to help him find Nassir Salhi, his fellow young teacher who'd been abducted under his nose while drinking beers at a brewery. But the problem was that there wasn't a single brain cell in the whole commons area where 5th period study hall was held.

He looked around at the brutalist-style metal table from which every study hall supervisor in America was required to take attendance. Fluorescent bulbs seemed unable to fill the common area, often used for lunch and smelling the part, with any kind of steady, usable light. The custodians kept the place clean, but no detergent could fill the craters in the gray linoleum floor that years of moving lunch tables, and desks like the one he sat in now, had created.

But hope springs eternal in the mind of the young teacher, even in the dead zone of study hall. A young figure approached in a hoodie, and Dave Legnagyszerübb would both help this Palpatine-esque figure with homework and determine whether or not he could help Dave find Nassir.

He was not quite certain how to identify the students who were—what was Carter's phrase again?—on the "operative" career path. There were a few kids surely on that list, but they'd done things like steal his staff keys and almost blow up the school, or assault him in the bathroom. Dave had to try to find more students like this. He was sure they would be at least a smidgen smarter than the "regular" kids at Maple Valley High School and, therefore, easier to pick out if he just continued to do the caring-teacher thing and helped every kid in Study Hall with some kind of schoolwork.

"Hey!" said Dave, leaning forward on the metal table and smiling. "What can I help you with?" He pushed his gradebook to the side to further indicate his desire to help.

The young man across from him said nothing as he sat down and made no eye contact. His black backpack looked depressed as if it had once held stacks of High Potential reading novels and now contained empty chip bags and dead batteries from calculators. The kid pulled his hood over his face until only his eyes and nose were showing and then pulled a notebook out with a crumpled purple cover. Out of the notebook swung two different folded pieces of paper—in Dave's brief glance, one appeared to be a mole conversion worksheet for Chemistry, the other, a syllabus for Basic Pastry Baking.

Dave picked up the one near him and held it out to the boy. The young scholar reared his head back—with his hoodie obscuring most of his face, it was the only way to accurately see anything below the horizontal. It made him look a bit like a Muppet. He somehow saw the Baking syllabus and put it in his backpack. David sat still as his new-teacher patience continued to wither. Watching this Muppet was like watching a dog paw at a ball that it could quite easily pick up with its mouth. But it was study hall, so apparently, no one was going anywhere in the immediate future, both figuratively and literally.

"Looks like we're working on some chemistry?" Dave offered. Since the boy moved so slowly, he wondered if he heard Dave speaking in double time. Under his hoodie, could he hear Dave at all?

The boy fished in the backpack for what felt like a half an hour and pulled a dull pencil out of the very bottom, probably next to a few fossilized Jolly Ranchers and some lint. He then proceeded to set it on the purple college-ruled notebook as if making some kind of statement about his postsecondary readiness.

A few months ago, Dave would have seen the hoodie and the whole three-ring backpack circus as a cry for help—a student so uncomfortable and traumatized by the myriad injustices of life who sought to shield himself from the school by pulling his comfort hoodie over his face, as far as it would go. The poor soul needed reassurance from Mr. Legnagyszerübb that everything was going to be okay.

But now? In early March (which, impossibly like February and April, was the cruelest month), Dave saw something different—another kid whose weaknesses had been indulged too many times in his educational history. Hide in your sweatshirt, provide materials, however feebly, and an adult will help you. Then, when you still do nothing, the adult will do it for you. Learn nothing, pass the class and move on. Or fail the class, learn nothing and still take the next course in sequence. It didn't seem to matter.

But Dave's heart, like the weather outside, might have been thawing a bit lately, bits of caring-for-young-people dripping off the icicles in the sun, the days getting longer, allowing more radiating warmth to penetrate the frozen stone his heart had become through nearly seven months of full-time public-school teaching. So, he leaned his head down and peered through the hole in the hoodie. Dave could see a set of eyes and nose and thick black glasses frames. The hood leaned back again, reminding Dave once more of a puppet tilted backward comically by an unseen hand. In his imagination, Dave posed his question to the puppet under the hood: "What am I doing here?"

Instead, Dave Legnagyszerübb asked, "How are you today?" His welcoming smile was waning quickly.

Dave could not immediately understand the muffled words that emerged from the hoodie, but he guessed it was "I'm Gucci." Which made no sense, syntactically or metaphorically or historically or fiscally, but it was what kids said to indicate positivity.

"Great. Need any help with this worksheet? Or with anything?"

"Wha?"

"Is there *an-y-thing* I can help you with?"

"Yeah." A pasty hand emerged from the hoodie's muff and pushed the chemistry sheet across the table to Dave, then returned to the safety and comfort of the hoodie.

Dave leaned away from the worksheet. Again, five months ago, he would have eagerly snatched it up and begun parsing it out, learning the atomic weights of the relevant elements in order to write the conversions, so the student could copy them down, thereby learning the material with his help, and then, gloriously, applying the learning to new, unfamiliar chemistry problems! Kilograms to pounds, cubic centimeters to liters—nothing would stop the young mind from converting units. And someday, as the student clutched his Nobel Prize, he would remember the soul who shepherded him through study hall all those years ago in a suburb of—

No. None of that was true.

Dave wondered idly in the silence: at one point, had this boy backed his feces-caked bottom into his mother's face expectantly, saying nothing until prompted except a "Yeah" in response to "Do you need me to wipe you before we go take your driver's test?"

Dave would not play the game, which is why he set the sheet down and said in a helpful tone, "What part of it don't you understand?"

"Nuh." All that this human could manage, it seemed, was a single syllable that began with "n."

"I'm sorry, what?"

"I don't get any of it."

"Do you have any notes?"

"Wha?"

At this point, Dave realized that under the hoodie was a pair of earbuds. He mimed the universal teaching sign for "take your goddamned earbuds out, you infant." The two eyes squeezed into the hoodie-hole rolled, but his pasty hands did, indeed, weasel their way into the hood to grudgingly remove the earbuds.

Dave repeated his question about the notes and, this time, received a nearly human response, "Yeah, I think so." Back to the deflated backpack, the young man, the vessel which held the future of America, pawed through his backpack, where half-folded sheets of notebook paper intermingled with multicolored worksheets, as well as crumbs of all sorts and the cracked plastic shells of mechanical pencils.

While the young man searched, Dave scanned the dim recesses of the study hall, though the term "study" was used very loosely. He seemed to have lost a sheep or two, though as he regarded the arrangement of seats and tables in the commons area, he could not pinpoint one specific soul as missing.

One girl scanned her phone while a movie played on the laptop in front of her; Dave couldn't tell which device her headphones were plugged into. Another young lady held a phone in one hand and a sweet sticky bun, still halfway in the wrapper, in the other hand. Occasionally, she gingerly set the bun down so that the packaging kept it separate from the table—and then proceeded to type, transferring the maximum amount of frosting to the keys of her laptop with the single non-phone-holding hand.

In this morning's staff meeting, Assistant Principal Cathy Young showed a short video in which a scrolling Star-Wars-esque diatribe about the callous youth of today ("It will be evident that... My generation is lost and lethargic... It is foolish to presume that... There is hope") displayed a different message when played in reverse ("There is hope... It is foolish to presume that... My generation is lost and lethargic..."). At one time, videos like this may have inspired the young Daves of the world about the power of teaching, but all he could think about, while Young shook her bracelets at the staff and implored that they reverse their thinking about kids, was that the video truly illustrated the dangers of definite articles such as "which."

He thought about the video as he watched the young lady smear sugar across the spacebar on the computer. She laughed at whatever video she was watching, and bits of sticky bun cascaded onto her computer.

Hoodie Boy finally procured a yellow sheet from his backpack. It was, miraculously, a printout guide to mole conversions. He looked at the first problem, which asked how many moles of helium were present in 3.01×10^{24} atoms of helium, and showed the steps to get to the answer, which was four moles.

"Okay," he said to the hoodie. "What part don't you understand?"

The hoodie produced a finger, which pointed at the worksheet's first question: How many atoms of helium were in four moles of helium?

Dave took a deep breath. "Have you looked at any of these examples?"

Hoodie gave his quickest reply yet, "I don't like chemistry."

"Can you look at the example, though?"

Hoodie pursed his lips—at least, the bit of his face that Dave could see seemed to do this—and regarded the example, again with the Muppet-esque look down his nose. He looked back at Dave expectantly.

"So?"

Hoodie shrugged. It was the biggest physical movement Dave had seen from him in terms of caloric expense.

"Now, look at the first problem on the sheet."

Hoodie looked at the problem, which was identical to the example. Dave thought that someone who had never spoken a word of English could solve the chemistry problem cleanly and accurately, and after completing the problem, they would say through a translator, "Is that it? I just figured out which number was missing. I don't even know what 'chemistry' is." The student would then be granted a high school diploma and an embarrassing anecdote about the state of the US educational system.

"I told you, I hate chemistry," said the Muppet.

"Let me write out what it looks like," said Dave. He grabbed an attendance sheet and started to write "4 moles He" on the back.

And that was the sign the young woman who'd been crouched a few feet away from Muppet and Dave's table had been waiting for. He had noticed her bright yellow fingernails wrapped discreetly around the bathroom pass and a request to use the restroom that was quiet enough not to pull Dave's head up from the Muppet's chem problem. She then dropped the pass on the ground, an innocuous moment that happens twenty times a second at high schools across the United States.

All in a moment, Dave's ankle was pulled away from his foot at a strange angle—and then the force simply disappeared, and his foot was sticking out from under the table, hanging in midair. He looked under the table.

Nina dos Santos Pandlay's hand held his keys strangely, with each of his four keys (classroom, front door, loading dock, upstairs East Wing doors) sticking out from its own spot between her fingers, like some kind of bioengineered killer reptile claw. He realized when he saw it that it was a technique to prevent the keys from making any noise. Her limbs were spread out in order to let her crawl almost silently on the floor, under the table. The look on her round, cherubic face didn't plead for him to say or do anything. She just regarded him with surprise.

Dave stuck his hand through the loop of the fishing line around his ankle and slipped it off his foot. Nina let go of the keys—but it was too late, as her wrist was still stuck in his lanyard. With the fishing line now wrapped around his wrist, the line tied to the lanyard, and the lanyard tight around Nina's wrist, they were bound together at the forearm, and she was still under the table. He looked up from this surreal scene to see the Muppet still staring off into the distance through the hole in his stupid sweatshirt.

Dave was now physically restraining with one hand a student he needed to talk to and with the other continuing to tutor a student as disengaged as a loose U-Haul trailer careening down the hallway.

"Do you have a calculator? That's probably the easiest way to get the answer," said Dave in a perfectly normal tone. The Muppet, tempted by the prospect of yet another small computer doing any and all thinking for him, went for the non-educational emptiness of his backpack.

Immediately, Dave ducked his head under the table to address Nina, who was trying to twist her whole body around her wrist to extricate herself.

"Nina!" he whispered hoarsely and pulled her above the table, careful not to hit her head. At one point in history, the entire study hall would have noticed this move, and ripples of disbelief would have bounced around the group of students. No one looked up from their sticky screens or even stickier keyboards, and the Muppet had barely gotten the zipper going on his backpack.

He needed to get Nina out of the study hall, but he couldn't let her disentangle her arm from his lanyard/fishing line combination. This was tricky. With a male student, a male teacher could always do the pat-on-the-shoulder/caring-father-figure walk; in fact, many male students needed that. Everyone knew—well, anyone with designs to work in a school for more than a few hours—without ever being explicitly told that you did not walk close to a female student and you did not engage in any contact beyond the high-five.

So how would he walk her out of here, basically chained to her forearm? Suddenly the answer revealed itself.

He put his hand on her back and said, "Let's get you to the nurse, kiddo," loud enough to cut through the study hall, and then whispered, "Pretend to get sick." He walked her three steps before she dove for the nearest garbage can with Dave right alongside her. He held the can under her face, and she played it well, sticking her head far enough in it to obscure the visual implied by her loud retching.

She stood up and wiped her mouth—she was quite good, especially while being tied to Dave's limb. At a normal school, Nina dos Santos Pandlay would have been the lead in both the fall musical and the spring play. Here she was a "pre-operative," as the phrase went. She leaned on his forearm, and they walked out of study hall with only a few loud whispers ("That girl just yakked in the garbage! Ungh!") following them out.

He led her to the end of the south hallway. Here they weren't out of view of anyone but too far away from any eavesdroppers who might glean that this was different from the usual "let's talk about when the paper was *actually* due" conversation.

They sat on one of the long wooden tables in the wing area, and he produced a pair of scissors, cutting the fishing line and pulling his keys and lanyard back into his possession.

"Mr. L," she began, rubbing her hands. Her eyebrows were arched in a convincing plea for innocence, her large brown eyes swimming. The fishing line hadn't cut her skin, but it must have hurt quite a bit. "I saw you drop your keys, and then my hand was all wrapped in up in that… that stuff, and then—"

Dave held up his hands halfway between the "stop talking" gesture and the "spare me" gesture. "Nina, you just appeared out of nowhere, trying to grab my keys—that's happened this year to me already."

She leveled her gaze past Dave, and he got the distinct sense she was making a decision about what to tell him. Instead, she tried one more parry. "Mr. L, we know each other. Do I seem like a key thief to you?" Her bright, perfectly even yellow fingernails brushed some dark curls out of her cherubic face, and her wet eyes widened even further in shock and amazement.

A few months ago, Dave would have walked this back in full deference to the students' thoughts and, more importantly, feelings. Now, he just let his face sink stonily into a stare of his own and said nothing.

"So, Mr. L, I was trying to just grab your keys for you, but if it was actually the wrong thing to do, I—I'm so sorry. Can I go back to class now?"

"Nina, I need your help. And we need to be honest with each other." He didn't change his face. Like Nina, he had been forced to decide how to proceed.

"Mr. L, I can—"

"Nina." He stopped. "I'm asking you to drop the charade. Please." He took a deep breath. "I know that you're what the other staff around here call 'pre-op.' I used my keys as bait because I need a student who's capable of tracking down a—" He paused. "A colleague and a friend. I saw someone—an agent, I think—take him from outside a brewery, and I have no idea where he is."

"Mr. Salhi," she said. "The sub said he's got the flu."

"But you know better," he said, keeping his gaze level. "Nassir Salhi does not have the flu."

"Well, yeah," she said. "But it's not that weird to have our teachers at this school be gone for different... jobs," she said, looking down and letting her curls obscure her eyes. "If you really don't know where he is, how am I supposed to help find someone like Mr. Salhi? I haven't even taken Asset and Location II yet. I got a B- in A&L I last semester. You're a *teacher*." A less-likable kid than Nina would have added, "Find him yourself."

"Nina," he said, drawing a deep breath.

He pushed the memory stuff-sack down in his mind, and the question came back up, "What am I doing here?"

Perhaps an answer was starting to reveal itself.

He took a deep breath. "I'm not a Jason-Bourne-type spy-agent-assassin, Nina. I'm a normal—some would even sub-par—English teacher who got hired here by some kind of accident."

Nina's mask seemed to slip off in indignation. "But Mr. L," she whispered harshly, "you killed Mr. Y! You ordered your students to terminate him, and they did!" Then, predictably, her face turned to horror before he could interrupt. "Are you going to kill me, too? Here at school?"

Dave pulled his cheeks down with his fingers in exasperation. "Nina, you have to understand." He stopped as a student rounded the corner, checking her pouty lips in her cell phone. It gave Nina just enough time to drop her face into the garbage can nearest the bathroom and continue retching; Lip Girl must be in their study hall. Man, thought Dave. This girl doesn't miss much. No wonder she's pre-operative.

Lip Girl walked by and only raised her eyebrows at the poor girl barfing into the garbage can. She looked back with that same look of sympathy mixed with a haughtiness that she clearly used for students of lower castes and, by proxy, teachers.

Dave responded with an open-palmed "What can you do?" gesture, and Lip Girl shoved her phone in her back pocket, straining the bleached denim on her mom jeans. She raised her hand high enough to push the bathroom door open while simultaneously lifting her sweater, which appeared as if it had been cut off accidentally at the ribcage. Dave mused for a moment that a high school was the perfect playground to train operatives: on the balance, the population was only interested in themselves. You could get away with anything around here.

Nina peeked one eye above the rim of the garbage can. Was this the result of educating these kids in such an espionage-saturated environment? Did they just develop these instincts? Maybe they'd end up being terrible spies, in the same way they were terrible future engineers, or nurses, or writers, but maybe the education system was doing them *some* favors. After all, messy or not, Larry Yearson was dead.

"Nina, I'm not going to hurt you. I swear I was hired here by accident, and now my friend Nassir—Mr. Salhi—is missing. And I need someone who can help me find him. So I left my keys out and twisted some fishing line around my leg, and I—I caught you." Yes, that seemed silly, especially as an English teacher trained to see every metaphor. "Again, I'm not some agent who can hunt people down. Mr. Salhi and I were at a brewery—"

"A what?" She'd finally removed her whole head from the garbage can.

"A bar, and this woman was talking to us, and she rode off with him on a motorcycle."

Nina held her chin in her hands, her bright yellow fingernails again sticking out like sun rays bouncing off ocean rocks. "You know, Elm Creek High School has a few motorcycles in their, like, gas engines class? Do you think—"

"Good! I can go over there and look."

Nina's eyes widened. "No, Mr. L! You can't just, like, go over there! That place is dangerous!"

She threw her head back into the garbage can. A moment later, the bathroom door flew open again for Lip Girl. She kept her hand up in the air, this time after pushing the door wide open, and paused at the sight of Nina, still retching.

"Is she, like..." Lip Girl raised her comically sculpted eyebrows.

"No, she's going to be okay. I just have to get her to the nurse's office," replied Dave with a frown.

Lip Girl shrugged. She wasn't offering to help, and Dave would have bet that she'd been about to snap a picture of the girl as fodder for some "hilarious" caption. She sauntered away.

Nina didn't miss a beat, popping her head back out. "They are trying to murder teachers over there, Mr. L! They stabbed this dude yesterday! In a fight in the morning, right in the damn—sorry—cafeteria!"

Dave furrowed his eyebrows. "What? Stabbed? Is he—"

"No," said Nina, shaking her head. "I think he's, like, okay or whatever."

Dave Legnagyszerübb thought if only that poor bastard had been a teacher at this school, he might have had a chance.

22 – The Other Performance Review

"Five steak tacos, *al pastor*," said the young cook/server, as the steam from the meat waved its fingers over the bed of cilantro, onions and *salsa rojo*. Cooper Baird looked up at the young man's jet-black goatee and combed-back hair under his White Sox hat.

Baird, David Legnagyszerübb, and the restaurateur had to squint in the sun as deft hands slid paper plates of incomparable food onto the bench tops. The sun seemed to revel in the outdoor seating. Though it was early April and almost 60 degrees, a recent snowstorm had left piles of wet cotton around the metal benches, as if reminding people that though they could eat outside, they risked being blanketed by sloppy, heavy snow.

"Thank you," said Baird. David knew the young agent hadn't eaten in almost forty hours but showed no interest in the food, even though the scent of chile and lime must have been shooting through his nose right now, too.

"And three more steak tacos… and four *papadillas*." Then, as if by magic, he produced two lime Jarritos bottles from behind his back. "Figured you guys could probably use something to drink out here in the hot sun."

It was a joke—sort of. The radiation did make one want to shed layers, despite the surrounding snow piles. Moreover, he was a Mexican man serving authentic (read: spicy) food to a couple of *Norteños,* hundreds or thousands of miles away from any kind of desert that would promote the unquenchable thirst that Jarritos soda slaked so well.

"Appreciate it, sir," said Baird. The young operative wore a blue flannel shirt and a backwards Nashville Predators hat. Anyone in the Taco Listo diner who looked quite closely at Cooper Baird would think that the shirt and the mesh hat were too new—a disguise that didn't quite "fit in." But Baird also knew how to carry a low profile, in many senses of the word—rounding his shoulders without overtly slouching, looking down at the stubs of his fingers, etc.—and so he seemed to almost disappear into the outdoor bench, becoming one more nondescript customer. Cooper Baird was an up-and-comer, and the CSS, according to rumor, had been a bit too cocky with the bosses, but his skills were still impressive.

On the other hand, David Legnagyszerübb, who wore what looked like ratty old workout sweats and a really old Old Navy sweatshirt, had a harder time keeping a low profile lately. He regarded his tacos and papadillas with the same kind of restraint that Baird did.

Once the young cook/waiter/host had walked away, Baird looked at David Legnagyszerübb with what could have been an icy stare. Or an expectant gaze. Or an inscrutable half-smile. Whatever it was, it came from practice, and it had built up to an impassability that would be the envy of any poker player. David himself, who divined others' intentions as easily as most people spotted a sales pitch, had no clue what the young agent was thinking. So he volleyed first as they sat over their steaming plates of perfect Mexican food.

"Perfectly leavened, easy-to-assemble *sopapillas* enter local eateries today, son. Every avenue traveled nearly overturns waste." One of the first birds of spring whistled as if in agreement, but the steam rose off the untouched food for another moment.

Was that a hint of a smile on the agent's face?

Baird reached for the tacos; David did immediately as well. Baird closed his eyes as the steak and cilantro overwhelmed his senses. So much for the poker face. Still chewing the taco—he held the rest in a mass in front of his face, the vapor off the steak dancing in the spring air like a genie—he reached for the Jarritos and, in one swift movement, popped the bottle top off the electric lime drink. He had brought it to his lips before he froze.

He leveled that same inscrutable gaze at David, setting the soda bottle down without moving his eyes. The contents of the bottle sloshed, and David caught a whiff of its delicious fake fruitiness, even through the spring smell of mud fed by melting snow. His taco was still an inch or two in front of his mouth.

"Wow, Legnagyszerübb," said Baird, readjusting his Predators hat. "I'm glad you're sticking to procedure. I *get* it. But we've known each other for a while now. Did you really think I'd have our food poisoned? What would be the point in that?"

David said nothing—he just sat in the April sun, holding the taco.

A flicker of expression, invisible to all but the most highly trained interrogators and observers in the business, rippled over Baird's face.

"*Did* you poison this? If so, I need to eat more poison. It's incredible."

"You think I'm poisoning my co-worker right now? If I did, I certainly wouldn't despoil a delicious Taco Listo with some rotten-tasting poison." It was well-known in the trade that the tasteless poison was largely a myth. Poison was terrible. It tasted like poison.

"So quit playing spy games. Eat your damn food." Apparently, Baird had decided the poison threat was paranoia as he polished off the first taco and slugged the Jarritos, leaving bits of cilantro and onion around the neck.

"It's been an… off-putting few months, Baird," said Dave, who still hadn't taken a bite of his taco. "I would say that my work at the school is going as well as it possibly could. I've got hearts and minds. I'm knee-deep—socially, academically, politically, even charismatically." He finally tore into his taco, feeling the steam on his cheek, and the rest of the known universe took a backseat for a moment.

"So," managed Baird, cheeks full of the second taco. "What's the problem?"

"These kids!" he said. He nearly raised his voice but restrained himself. "They're so deep in the cover of the school that they won't betray anything. I got myself stabbed, Baird."

"You stabbed yourself. I saw the video online, David."

"Po-tay-to, po-tah-to. Anyway, I went the extra mile, and it all worked. The principal owes me because he was out of the building finding non-existent drugs when I was so violently attacked."

"The drug bust was a nice touch, by the way."

"Thanks." They both cashed another taco and drained their Jarritos.

"But," began David, mouth still full, "what… what did it get me? I have the undying adoration of the whole school population. I did a stint in the hospital and got cards from over 80 percent of the student body. But I'm no closer to being 'in' with whatever student group is training operatives. Orchestrating the inter-student combat, gathering intel via telecom—"

"And excellent work in both those regards," interjected Baird. Then he adjusted his Predators hat and seemed to grasp for a more fitting register of speech. "I mean, killer work on the fight and spot-on Wi-Fi and cell snooping." Baird examined a *papadilla*. "Speaking of excellent work, I hope this place makes these—" he caught himself again "—these beauties as well as they make the tacos."

"They're good too, but for some reason, the cilantro in the green sauce skews the taste a bit." He grabbed one of his own and dipped it in the red sauce.

Baird bit into the *papadilla* and closed his eyes briefly. Chewing, he shut his eyes again for a few seconds. David savored the burn of the *rojo*, wishing he had another Jarritos or three to wash it down.

"Sorry," managed Baird, wiping his chin, "please continue."

David held up an index finger; his other digits grasped the papadilla. The coals in his mouth were relentless and caused him to tap his leg in a quick staccato while the edge of his sweatpants touched the muddy area under the picnic table with every hot foot tap. But underneath the table, his right hand tapped a steady rhythm against his knee, the digit bouncing with the kind of rebound a better-than-average drummer could muster. With each tap, he counted a beat in his head—1, 2, 3, 4, and so on. Meanwhile, he ate the tacos *y papadillas* with great pleasure, but he was able to keep counting regardless of the distraction. He swallowed.

"For all my work at this school, I am not even remotely close to determining where these operative students are. So I'm doing my work—and it's a, well, fertile ground for our, ah, craft—but these kids are deep. Clandestine." He kept count with his finger: 46, 47, 48…

Baird nodded. He paused for a moment. "Maybe you should try to go to bat."

David knew that Baird was about to give him a contact name, probably using their established first-letter "cipher."

"Clearly, all rendezvous telegrams exist remotely." Baird raised his eyebrows.

David continued with the tapping, now approaching seventy. Suddenly Baird was slumping down in his chair, and David was smoothly moving to jam his fist under Baird's armpit to keep him from falling over. Bits of papadilla were falling out of his mouth, though David's other hand now held up his face, so it wasn't quite as *Weekend at Bernie's* as it might have been.

David pulled the man forward to rest on his own arms and pulled the Predators hat around to cover his forehead. It was, all in all, not a very astute disguise. Baird looked like a guy who wore tailored suits and expensive shoes who realized that he should "dress down" to ride, say, the bus. The hat's brim was bent in a subtle arc, but the blues were too bright, and the whites gleamed with no tan swaths from sweat.

As he adjusted the man's elbows for a more natural-looking "afternoon nap" look, he heard the two Jarritos bottles being picked up. He looked up to see the White Sox hat and then to the *taqueria's* co-owner underneath it, adding "busboy" to his small-business resumé of doing every job at once.

"How's everything tasting?" he asked, smoothly slipping the scraped-clean plates beneath his deft fingers.

"Oh, it was delicious," said David, without making eye contact. "I'm not as impressed, however, in this stooge's getup. It was his hat that gave him away, by the way. Next time, send someone who can wear the clothes you're stuffing them into."

"Was it that obvious?" asked the man with the goatee. His White Sox hat just seemed to fit him better than his proxy's Predators hat, which had rolled off the table and into the mud. And his right hand, which deftly held all the plates and Jarritos bottles, had a slender rectangular watch perched just inside the sleeve of his black shirt. If David knew his technology, he'd bet it was a universal remote car starter with multiple satellite communication and GPS capabilities that only looked like Target's highest-end, lower-middle-class social-climber watch.

"You've walked over here twice with food, and it's in the 50s in April. Your footwear should be making a racket in the mud like something at a suction-cup-test facility, but yet I haven't heard any footsteps."

The man's cool dark eyes regarded him for a moment. Whatever reason David might give for seeing through his boss's ruse, the eyes would have eventually given it away. Clearly, this busboy/cook/server was David's boss, who probably reported to Clefthorne herself at CSS. Eyes like those—never squinting, never wide open—didn't miss much. David knew he would not learn this man's name (though it surely wasn't "Baird") or his exact position, but he was no cubicle paper-pusher. Years of fieldwork had turned him into some kind of nearly omniscient human sensor.

"Mr. Legnagyszerübb, will you give me a hand with our sleepy friend?" The two men picked up the man formerly in a Predators hat, using a hug-lift familiar to anyone who's ever walked a drunk friend down the street.

Through the mud, they walk-dragged the man into Taco Listo's side doors, depositing Cooper Baird in a chair just inside the kitchen door, next to the dishwasher. David noticed that there was, indeed, another employee here, who raised his eyebrows at the man in the White Sox hat.

David's boss shouted, in Spanish, over the dish sprayer that although he enjoyed foot traffic from the nearby bar, it wasn't worth it to have to babysit drunks who just vomited up the food later. The man laughed and replied that it was his food to do what he wanted with after he purchased it, and who didn't like having a buddy in the dishroom?

David's boss laughed, and David just smiled—a force of habit from a time when it was beneficial to pretend one's knowledge of Spanish was limited. For a moment, he thought about Durango and his time there, playing guitar and preparing to murder, serving a bit of food to kids under the sun's unyielding sear that was so different than this timid April warmth.

The boss set the plates down in front of the dishwasher and walked out the back door as David followed. They sat on another metal bench that was on the parking lot asphalt. A warm-ish breeze sent the puddles in the cracked surface to ripple.

"You know, when you were in Durango, Mr. Legnagyszerübb, I stopped in to see your work." Those eyes again were scanning David's eyes, forehead, neck—not frantically, but methodically. This mentalism-type work always seemed to David to be some kind of pseudo-magic trick: reading, if not the exact details of your mind's eye, at least the main chunks of ideas that floated at the forefront, apparently written all over your face.

"And?" asked David without hesitating. "How did I do?"

Those dark brown eyes stopped back on David's eyes. Every word was a threat, a code, a veiled request. "Very competent. You handled the interpersonal nuance of that job with extraordinary—" Again, he didn't seem to be searching for the right word; rather, he seemed to be pulling in gigabytes of data through every pore, directly into his brain. "—aplomb." He then produced a Jarritos bottle from—from somewhere. The magic-trick effect was strong here. He popped the cap off on the edge of the metal bench and handed it to David.

"Thanks. For the drink, and the compliment, and the tacos. And not being mad that I knocked out your puppet-slash-proxy guy." When he got impatient—which wasn't often—he'd slip back into the language he used growing up before he'd changed himself into an agent of limitless poise with the flexibility of an eel. Cryptic bosses tended to make him impatient.

"Who says I'm *not* upset, Agent Legnagyszerübb? But Director Clefthorne was unequivocally unhappy with everything ex-Agent Baird here had told her. Anyway, back in the day, I took notes and reported to my superiors about your work down in Durango." His eyes scanned the parking lot again as if his superiors were hiding in the backseat of a Corolla, looking at the two of them through binoculars and taking fervent notes into their recorders. Just a bunch of spooks watching their fellow spooks. David hated that because it was probably true: enemy spies often seemed far less bent on destroying you and your career than your co-workers.

And again, there was that sense that his brain was being picked apart. Clefthorne's proxy continued: "What I didn't mention in my reports, but what I admired about you was your sense of earnestness. I didn't get the impression that you were helping out Mexican kids only out of cover or singing *canciones del amor* only because the assignment required it. You seemed to be truly—" he scanned the parking lot again and then came back to David, "experiencing your cover in a way that most of our operatives do not."

"Okay," David replied evenly. "That's why I'm here." Was this a fault that his boss was pointing out?

"In certain situations, it can play as a weakness, Mr. Legnagyszerübb, this… *zest* for the cover that serves to hide our real work. As much as we *try* to pretend to be heartless automatons, we are not, nor will we ever be. And though usually a healthy dispassionate streak is called for, we also need people with a bit of heart. In a profession that serves the ruthless and the psychopathic quite well, that extra facet of humanity can be both rare and valuable."

Ah, thought David, a job pitch. He took a slower swig of Jarritos and tried a quick parry before his boss laid an offer he couldn't refuse at his feet.

"But I'm not Mother Theresa. In my report, did you see the students I used in the process of winning over Elm Ridge High School?"

"That is precisely it, David. I'm not pitching you a job but rather explaining the assignment you have right now."

David took a moment and tried to mask his face from being read, even though it was futile. "I am primarily a telecommunications operative. I assumed that was the reason for the assignment. It was relatively easy for me to control the school since every person in it is entirely dependent on their poorly secured wireless and cellular networks for communication." That was not a deflection. David would wager that he was one of the top communication infiltration techs at the agency.

His boss narrowed his eyes at him almost imperceptibly. It was almost as if he'd committed to fully and transparently reading David's mind now. He lowered his voice, too, saying, "Your old colleague says that she got to see you working your tech magic in real time, and that you're still as sharp as ever."

Now, it was David's turn to narrow his eyes. "Neve?" he asked. "When did *you*—"

"About the time my own bosses needed to know why Ray Cuconotti was murdered." He returned to scanning the parking lot, flicking his eyes up above their heads to make sure no one was on the roof of the *taqueria*. David said nothing, and though his face betrayed little, his immediate, difficult-to-restrain impulse was to sit and let his jaw hang open. Ray Cuconotti, a.k.a Larry Yearson? Again? Apparently, a great number of people were convinced that David had terminated the old man.

David took a long, slow final sip from his Jarritos, draining it while he thought frantically. Here he was, trying to do a job and doing it well, yet failing, and all anyone ever accosted him about was this Cuconotti issue.

He almost began with a "Sir," but didn't think it would land in the right place. If earnestness was what he was being praised for, then—so be it. "I do not understand why people think I murdered this agent. I didn't come to Elm Ridge to—"

"What?" shot out of the man's mouth, cutting David's blunt rhetoric off. "Did you say Elm Ridge?"

"Yes," said David, restraining his voice.

"You have been at Elm Ridge High School during this mission? *Not* Maple Valley High School?"

David met his gaze. This time, his boss did not stop to scan the parking lot.

"Yes," said David.

"The school you've been working on for the better part of the year is *Elm Ridge* High School? Where you were stabbed? Where you installed a mountain of surveillance equipment? *Elm Ridge* High School?"

"Yes," said David. There was no more Jarritos to drink.

Again, it was extraordinarily disquieting how this man, wearing a White Sox hat and smelling of ground corn, had stopped looking through the parking lot, stopped glancing at the rooftop behind his head, stopped scanning the corners of the brick building.

"Agent Legnagyszerübb, the difficulty you have experienced in uncovering and taking over the pre-op program at your high school is due entirely to the fact that there is no pre-op program at your high school. There is no secret subset of students who practice our professional work." His eyes seemed to bore into David's. "Does your school offer unstructured time when the student body is ostensibly working on independent projects in, say, the arts or tech ed?"

He could have said, "I'm confused," but this man could read it all over his face like a tattoo. "No."

"Maple Valley High School, located just across town from Elm Ridge, offers this 'open time.' It gives the pre-operative students an opportunity to field-test their skills in recon, codebreaking—even extraordinary rendition. In fact, especially gifted students can earn rankings by obtaining pieces of teacher property."

"There's nothing like that at Elm Ridge," said David.

"This year, several students have earned high marks—and even started a bit of a ruckus—by taking a teacher's keys and breaking into a secure vault. Hence the name: M-VAULT. I thought that, perhaps, you had snared some of these students by allowing them to take your keys. But it seems that conjecture was incorrect."

Several minutes ago, he was wolfing down delicious, authentic tacos and sedating his lunch partner almost as a lark, ready to enumerate his successes at Elm Ridge and receive some guidance on how to proceed. The warmth of spring had seemed ready to break through, if only at their table in the gravel outside of Taco Listo. Now, sitting at the back of the same restaurant, it seemed the steel-gray clouds of March had returned, and the wind had picked up.

He thought he knew why he was here.

Like a series of fast-forwarded videos, David's mind seemed to make sense only in fractional clips. Everything else was a whirr of all the interactions he'd had with students and staff over the last seven months—yet before he even had to ask the question, he'd answered it himself.

Because they're teenagers, he said clearly in his head, ordering the 32x speed video to a halt. *All the circumspect stories, all the nonsensical explanations, all the irrational and inexplicable behavior—they're high schoolers, not masters of deception. Unless it's self-deception.*

"So," began David. His boss's eyes had never left his own. "If I am here—then who is operating at Maple Valley High School?"

14 – The Hunt

Dave took out the small, knobby key and unlocked the seat of the motorcycle, swinging it open as rainwater spilled over the leather and splashed down on his foot. He paused for only a moment and wiped the bottom of his foot on his dark khakis so that it wouldn't slip off the shifter once he was on the bike. Several months ago, the fastidious young teacher would have done nothing of the sort, including both dirtying his new-teacher khakis and taking a motorcycle to and from school. Now his only concern was to get the motorcycle ready to go so that when his passenger came out of the building, the two could drive out of the parking lot at as low of a profile as two people can leave a high school on a motorcycle on a gray, post-rain April afternoon.

He pulled the rag out of the space next to the battery under the seat and tilted the metal frame of the seat back, wiping as he went. As he dried off the tachometer and the handlebars, he caught a glimpse of himself in the left-hand mirror. It was as if time had folded in on itself, making a closed loop between the Maple Valley parking lot nine months ago and today. He could still see himself in the mirror of his Hyundai, shoving memories down in the stuff-sack while asking himself, "What am I doing here?"

Like any good teacher, Dave Legnagyszerübb knew that some questions shouldn't be answered right at the beginning of class. They carried the class forward, pushing it towards a destination like a motorcycle engine.

But as he stared into his own face, he knew he was almost ready to answer the question and just about ready to pull everything out from that cramped stuff-sack.

But first, he had to finish wiping down the bike he'd borrowed from Erik. And, for the time being, keep his hand firmly pressed on the pile at the bottom of the sack.

Now, with the bike dry, he sat with his helmet on and checked his phone: there were four minutes before school was out. Nina was supposed to ask to go to the counselor with ten minutes left and then meet him outside. If someone had stopped her, he had faith, given the skills she'd demonstrated already, that she would be able to get out of it.

But as he balanced on the bike and listened to the gas slosh in the brown-and-maroon metal tank, he felt like he'd made a stupid gamble. In his normal teacher mind, it was all about whether or not Nina would get caught skipping a few minutes of seventh hour. But she was a teenager training to be an agent: a congenital liar, a born sneak. Would she simply flip on him, turning him into Carter for a few credits and a good letter of recommendation? With his helmet on, was he unable to hear Young, whose bracelets and bangles kept time with her heels clicking on the asphalt as she came up behind him? "Nassir quit months ago," she might say, and then clench her fists and don that strained smile, "but it was a great opportunity for us to catch you and fire you for doing something so patently counterintuitive to student—" Her hands would shake in harmless fists at this moment, trying to find the right word, since "learning" was not the right word, since it excluded kids who refused to learn, nor was "life" correct, even though it was what she meant. "—*development*," she would say, and then murder him on the spot with a silenced gun. Or worse, fire him. He'd never even get to explain that he was going to try and find Mr. Salhi before he met the same fate as Mr. Yearson.

But his fears proved unfounded when, in the reflection of his helmet visor, he saw a hand—with bright yellow fingernail polish.

He nodded, and he felt her weight lower the back of the bike, and the realization hit: he was getting on a motorcycle with an underage female student after convincing her to skip part of class. He looked around to see if any police or school monitors were around, but the only things populating the parking lot were the fat drops of rain that dripped off chrome, forming April puddles that reflected themselves in damp gray on the underside bevels of the car bumpers.

He hit the ignition, and the 750cc engine fired as if to remind Dave that it was bigger than it looked from the side. Taking a deep breath, he adjusted the rearview mirror—and saw Nina looking at her phone behind him. She wasn't even trying to hide it, holding it directly out in front of her.

Talking through helmets over a roaring motorcycle engine was always fraught, requiring one to be loud, direct and simple enough to get the point across. "Nina! You need to put your phone away!" He reached over his right shoulder and tapped the phone with two fingers, a classic teacher move.

Instead, she leaned in, and again Dave's danger-alert system fired, warning him that a female student was leaning in too close. But he could tell she was shouting, "Just trust me and drive!" He shook his helmeted head, put the bike in gear and turned the throttle. The four-cylinder engine hardly noticed there was another person back there as he swooped out of the parking lot.

He parked on a residential street two blocks away, gently maneuvering around the puddles in the asphalt's cracks as he did so. He turned around to see Nina, who looked up from her phone. He had to take his helmet off and address her directly, turning around as far as he kinesiologically could.

"Nina," he began, almost finishing with, "You can't have your phone out while we're on the motorcycle!" Instead, the slightly wiser high school teacher chose, "Nina—why do you have your phone out?"

She pulled her helmet off with a painful one-handed effort, but the helmet snagged her nose. After forcing more of the helmet off, more hair was stuck in her hoop earrings and plastered to her forehead, and her sweat had made her mascara run. It was not how one expected the next great American spy to remove safety equipment.

As Dave sat parked next to a curb, she took a moment to re-focus on her phone screen. Nina then looked up at the teacher who caught her in a study hall using a fishing line and had now quasi-abducted her outside the high school; then, she looked back at her phone without a word.

"Nina, what are you doing?"

"What?" She pulled a tracer of black hair off her forehead using the nail of a finger. Her usually endearing round face was suddenly maddening.

"What are you *doing?*"

"I'm trying to do an Instagram match to figure out which way Mr. Salhi was taken," she said, arching her eyebrows and holding her palms toward the sky in the universal teenage sign for exasperation at the short-sightedness of the old.

He somehow managed to turn his body even more on the bike. "What?"

"I'm thinking that Mr. Salhi always seemed cool, you know?"

He felt like simply driving her back to the high school, dropping her back off, and ordering her not to tell anyone about this. Ever.

Instead, he closed his eyes, took a deep breath, and opened them again. "Okay. So?"

"Like, he always wrote lots of stuff on my biology tests."

Dave said nothing.

"So, I'm thinking, what if when he got abducted or whatever, he might not have been able to get his arms out if he was tied up and tied to the bike, but what if he got his phone out and took a video and put it on social media? Like, an attempt to let people know where he was?"

The teacher's shield of instantly believing that every student's idea was inherently foolish crumpled a bit. This seemed unlikely, but at least she wasn't just on the back of the motorcycle Snapchatting. "Do you think a secret agent teacher instructing kids on the arts of espionage would post things on social media?"

Nina smiled. "I thought that, too. But I remembered from Digital Information, or whatever that class was called, that people using multiple identities might have, like, fake profiles set up, so they can observe other people..." She snapped her fingers, looking for the right word.

"Anonymously?"

"Yes!" She pointed at him in acknowledgment, smiling with her whole face. "So I have an app that will try and match, like, the surroundings in a video I'm taking to a video on social media. If he was on a bike, and I'm on a bike, that should help the app match up—that's why I suggested for you to bring a, um, motorcycle."

Dave felt reaffirmed. He had brought the right student. "So if it matches the geographical features with random social media videos—"

"Well, not random ones, Mr. Legnagyszerübb. It narrows it down to, like, the surrounding areas. It can't search the whole internet, so it uses our location to help filter out motorcycle videos from China or whatever."

Of all the poor young souls trudging through school systems in America that fit them as poorly as an older sister's hand-me-downs, at least Nina dos Santos Pandlay had found a school that fit her skills.

"Oh, okay. Either way, we should start recording at the brewery, right? Make a video while we drive, and see if it matches?"

"Yeah, Mr. Legnagyszerübb." She was now reaching for her helmet. "And if I can get a match right away, I can pull up the video Mr. Salhi made, if he made one, and run it ahead of where we are so we can use it to, like, navigate."

"Nina," he shouted over his shoulder as he started the motorcycle, "brilliant. Let's do it."

Within a few minutes, he was over by the brewery. Both of their pant cuffs were muddy from the April roads, but it was warm out (especially inside the bulky helmets) for this particular sub-season of spring. Had it really been that long, when holiday lights were strewn with the intent to look haphazard since he and Nassir came here for a drink? What kind of ridiculous school was this, where a teacher could be missing for so long, and yet there was no type of search party out and about trying to find them? He felt as if Nassir was more important than that. Were kids at this school used to teachers being mysteriously "let go" so often that it wasn't worth even a bit of lunchtime conversation?

Nina tapped him on the shoulder, nodded and pointed at her phone. She'd had a hit on an account for the video—and to answer his question before he asked it, yes, he should turn right.

He leaned into the turn, leaving a large enough radius to account for the wet ground and the weight of two people on the back of the large bike. Accelerating after a turn—pulling on the throttle and feeling the engine try to respond for a moment, trying to drag two people and a tank full of gas and a heavy metal engine in a straight line over the blacktop—that felt good.

After a few lefts and several splashes through a few wet intersections, they developed a system: She would tap his left or right shoulder a block before the required turn, but otherwise, he would keep going straight.

They turned onto a side street. Dave saw older houses with sprawling, unkempt trees lining the boulevard. The road was cracked, and of course, the puddles in the asphalt were significant enough for him to slow his bike down. Nina pulled hard on his jacket, and he leaned back. She shouted for him to pull over, which he did, behind an old SUV that looked as if it hadn't moved in years. He cut the engine, coasted to a stop and removed his helmet.

Nina did the same, and he put the kickstand down and turned around to tell her to get off—but she was already doing the light-footed leap straight up off of both foot pegs, which was the only way to dismount a bike that heavy without tipping its center of gravity, heavy gas tank and all, over to the side.

He opened his mouth to ask her where she'd learn how to do—and her bright yellow fingernail stood insistently against her lips. She was crouched, hidden behind the rusty, giant SUV, gesturing to him to follow her. He set his helmet on the seat of the bike and crouch-walked around the motorcycle, following her lead.

She held up the cell phone and scrubbed the video left with her thumb, and instantly the old SUV came into view, recognizable even under the bright halogen street lamps of a winter's night in Nassir's video. The edges of the SUV's roof were covered in snow and ice, but this was it for sure. The right flank of the woman who took Nassir obscured about half of the frame, but it was clear that he'd been holding his phone with his fingertips, despite his restraints. The video showed them slowing a few houses after passing the SUV. As soon as it went to turn into the driveway, the video cut out. Dave nodded, stooped low and began to creep out.

Nina grabbed the collar of his shirt. He turned around, wide-eyed. Sure, they were away from school, on a "mission" that was beyond the bounds of educational instruction—but he definitely had a gut reaction to being grabbed by a kid.

"Sorry, Mr. L," she said in a low voice—not a whisper, but with enough deference to make him feel bad. He had brought her because, well, she was the expert, right?

"No," he said, frowning at himself and shaking his head. "I'm sorry. What should we do?"

"You can't just go, like, creeping through the bushes for half a block. I learned that in C. Move, day 2."

"'C. Move?'"

"Candlestein Movement."

"You mean *clandestine* movement."

"Oh. Yeah. Whatever—the idea is that nobody's probably going to notice you if you just walk normal, but everyone's going to notice if a grown person starts hiding behind bushes."

"That's a good point. So do we just walk normally down the block and then approach the house?" He thought he could see the house from the video: brick with white and red trim.

"Yes," she said and stood up normally to walk.

It was true—he did feel a lot less like a felon just walking normally. But as the house grew larger, he wondered: had Nassir, the escape expert from earlier this year, really been unable to leave this very normal-looking house? If he had, or hadn't, then what had he been doing this whole time?

Nina had her hands in her hoodie pockets, her face obscured by the hood. She looked up and over at him. "Put your hood up, Mr. L, so they can't see you."

He raised his hands in a what-can-you-do face. "No hood, Nina."

"Okay, I guess, like, either way, walk down the street here to the house where Mr. Salhi is. But what are we gonna do when we get there?"

Dave Legnagyszerübb stopped.

"You mean," he asked, "what am I doing here?"

She wrinkled her nose and squinted at him, but he wasn't looking at her. He was looking at a tree on the boulevard.

It was covered in April buds as if ready to grow hands to push the icy waters of late spring away. Everything about it seemed to herald the change of the seasons.

But then the sun pushed a hazy eye through the April drizzle and fog, casting a purple and orange shadow on the lawn of the house they were going to. The shadow of the tree seemed so different than the real-life model—yet, they were the same being. Dave froze.

"What am I doing here, Nina?"

They were standing on the street in a nondescript suburban neighborhood, but he was thinking about a young man staring back at him in a rearview mirror before a job interview. A young man who kept the truth about what he was indeed doing there stuffed away in a memory sack. But now, standing next to Maple Valley's greatest student, only moments before a rescue operation, it was time to pull everything out of that sack and stop pretending he was that young man.

He closed his eyes.

"I'm certainly not here to teach."

Part III

24 – The Mentor

"Mr. L?" Nina dos Santos Pandlay asked. She was trying to keep a blank expression on her face, but her slightly wrinkled brow betrayed her.

He could not answer her right now but could see the house: a white one-story with red trim around the doors and windows, rounded shrubs in front, a chimney, a red garage door that was open to reveal—yes, a motorcycle, framed against the bare concrete floor and flat white wall of the garage. He held up his hand to Nina in a just-a-minute gesture.

He thought one more time about that naïve young man looking at himself in the mirror before the interview, asking the question. He thought about a rattlesnake, its new skin making first contact with the dirt as it leaves its sloughed, dead outer layer behind.

He thought about his protegé—the type of student to try to fly under the radar, the type to underplay her own ability, the one that the CSS agents should have sought and HRB operatives should have been more protective of—standing in front of him, pointing at the house.

It wasn't time to tell her just yet. Shedding skin was not an instantaneous process.

"Nina," he said. His voice felt lower than before, though he wasn't sure if she could tell. "You've been chosen for this real-time operative test. Mr. Carter, Ms. Young—everyone has agreed that you're ready for this assessment. We're going to do some authentic learning here."

Nina's face still showed some skepticism. Again, in everything, she was proving herself to be the ideal Maple Valley pre-operative student:

creative, cunning and more than a little untrusting. "Is Mr. Salhi really in danger, Mr. L? Or is, like, this part of the test?"

"No, it's not part of the test, but yes, Mr. Salhi's in great danger." It felt liberating to tell the truth. "That's what makes this a real-life learning experience."

She opened her mouth to protest, but Dave cut her off. "We wouldn't have picked you, Nina, if you weren't ready. Do your best because lives are always depending on how well we do our jobs." He knew she picked up on the deliberate "we" here.

In his brief foray into education, Dave had learned that, although each student fought unique battles, common problems emerged with high school students: wealthy privilege. Technology use. Sports obsession. And one of the most common and most crippling, difficulties: female self-esteem.

When challenged with a dangerous task that could ostensibly be done by someone else, the pragmatic high school female with low self-esteem tended to shrink within herself rather than accept the challenge. She would blush, frown and examine her shoes before listing reasons that she could not accept the task—when she'd been only gauging her own self-confidence, determining it to be too low when push came to shove, and ultimately, deeming herself unworthy of the task. It was true that some students, male and female, avoided difficult tasks because they were difficult, but most brands of high-school females simply did not have the self-confidence to do them.

Nina, however, straightened her spine, looked directly at Dave, and took a quick, deep breath between her lips. Past shortcomings were behind her. This was her chance.

"I can do this, Mr. L."

A hundred sci-fi/fantasy novels sung in chorus: "She is The One!"

He gave her the sign to go up to the house and crouched behind the old van to wait.

He could hear the front door open, and a woman's voice—not unfriendly, yet not warm—addressed Nina. He heard Nina's voice pitch up an octave as she pleaded whatever story she'd made up.

There was no hesitation from the resident. Nina was able to walk straight into the house.

Dave pulled his head back from observing his student's trespass and considered the van he'd planted here yesterday—the same one he now crouched behind.

Grabbing the metal pulls of the door, he threw them open and vaulted himself into the back of the van, which was like a small, tidy Ace-Hardware-and-Radio-Shack. Plastic trays lined the walls, loops of cable and wire hung from the ceiling, and building materials covered the floor in neat piles. He grabbed six 2Xs, including a pair that were screwed together with a notch cut in them, a pouch full of hardware, a powder-actuated fastener, and a tool belt.

There was also a gray hard plastic case fitted with a strap that he knew so very well. He slung it over his shoulder and tightened it to his body. Somewhere in the back of his mind, he considered that a horse might feel the same way when a rider she knew well hopped in the saddle.

He paused and regarded the metal container near the driver's seat. It looked like a giant coffee thermos with wires running down the side and a few analog readouts on the bottom. In the movies, these wires would be exposed so that some intrepid young agent could cut them after a sweaty conversation over a walkie-talkie with an older, maybe alcoholic, definitely troubled mentor. Not so here. These wires were encased in hard clear epoxy, with several ports for diode inserts. He wanted to tell someone, somewhere, at some time, that he had won it at a basketball game. He laughed out loud, which was something he would have never done on the job before his teaching gig.

Still crouching, he hopped out of the van, deftly holding the 2Xs at floor height and then pulling them quickly but carefully towards his chest. He then made his way toward the house, holding the 2Xs at their fulcrum point, standing straight up like any better-than-novice homeowner starting a spring project on an ambitious April evening.

In the driveway of the house that Nina was infiltrating, he broke into a jog, tossing a few of the studs onto the wet lawn. With three quick steps, he was on the stoop, holding the stud against the door with his knee. Using only his right hand, he loaded the charge and the nail into the fastener; with his left, he pulled a large cylinder from his toolbelt that looked a bit like a two-liter plastic bottle, cut up and stuffed with tape and foam insulation. He held the makeshift silencer against the 2X, pressed the barrel of the fastener against the wood, pulled the trigger, and felt the violent recoil as the nail was driven into the concrete foundation wall. Pulling a driver out of his toolbelt's loop, he affixed the wood to the door. He switched hands and repeated on the other side.

They might have noticed the noise and the vibrations on the inside of the house, but they would be so busy trying to figure out why Nina was there that no one would be poking their heads outside anytime in the next few seconds. And that's all he would need.

He sprinted around to the back door and bolted the door closed with six more fasteners, repeating the process for the two windows. Because he'd still heard no scrambling-at-the-noises-outside, Dave pulled the garage door down, jumping up with both feet so as to make it move quickly since the sound of a garage door alerted most homeowners, even the plainly ignorant ones, that someone was outside. He slid the screwed and notched 2Xs over the riveted opening handle to the garage door and bolted them to the threshold of the garage floor with two more shots from the powder-actuated fastener.

Who would come out of the house first, and how? He had a plan for each contingency, but each started with him getting on the roof. He jumped up and grabbed a gutter bracket with one hand; hanging in the air, he placed his feet firmly on the garage door. Dave bounced off the door once, and the bracket held. He bounced again, pushing off with his feet and pulling up with his hand, squinting for a moment in the setting sun's light. Good—he would make that element of the surroundings work for him. Again, it was as if he was renewed and reborn. His skills were rested and, therefore, fresh but novel and exciting, like they were years ago.

Dave could almost look behind him and see the shed skin. He could definitely take his hand off all the dirty, compressed contents of the stuff-sack.

His shoulder hit the roof, and he bit into it by turning down and rolling onto his back. A grin spread across his face.

He rolled again, this time across the roof so that he wouldn't be visible from the window directly behind him now. If the agents inside the house went quiet, he'd get in through that window.

His hands and fingers did all the work while the conscious part of his brain focused on holding himself right on the pitched roof. The gray case flew open, and the rifle and tripod came out almost of their own accord. Within seconds, the entire apparatus was set up.

Underneath his feet, he felt the asphalt shingles vibrating. That was what he'd predicted she would do: cut the garage door tracks off their struts. He heard a pause and imagined her walking the bike back far away enough so that the door wouldn't fall on her. There was a crash, and a second later, the motorcycle shot out of the garage.

It was all he needed. One shot took out her back wheel, and the motorcycle that had once taken off from a brewery with Nassir restrained to the backseat suddenly slid on its flat pancake of rubber and threw Neve into the grass. No neighbors were out to witness this because the NSA's Central Security Service owned all the houses on the street. There were no neighbors.

Before the bike had hit the ground, Dave had rolled off the side of the roof and, steadying himself with the same hand-on-the-gutter-bracket trick, made his way silently to the ground. The sun was setting, which meant he only had a few minutes to get the old van and its cargo on their way. First, there was the problem of Neve.

She had held Nassir all the way out here for the last few months, and it had made everything else work. Now, he had a plan for her.

He heard the window open on the roof above him, and Neve immediately looked up from the ground.

"Do not come out here," she said in a clear voice. It was impossible to tell whether she had been seriously hurt or not, as her voice did not reveal any pain or injury but rather issued clear directives to Nina and Nassir, who would be looking down at her, trying desperately to determine what had just happened.

"If you come out here, he will shoot you. Go inside and stay away from any windows or doors."

She got gingerly on her injured foot first, but again, there was no way of telling how badly hurt she was—if at all.

It was quiet enough that he heard his work friend and his protegé—neither of whom truly knew who he was—relocating inside the house, far from any openings to the outside. Good. Now, it was time to talk to Neve.

He tapped the edge of the garage with a knuckle. Instantly, she pulled a 9mm from her boot and aimed it at his head, though he was already behind a recycling bin on the side of the garage. He held one hand up above the bin and one hand to the side, beckoning her to come over.

She made her way off the grass and towards the old blue bins, which contrasted sharply with the still-gleaming, shiny, jet-black helmet now under her arm. Her limp as she walked over was real.

"Hi, Neve."

"What are you—oh, no," she began, as the math started to whirl inside her mind.

"Yeah, it's me," he said evenly.

"You brought Nassir to the brew hall. So that means…"

"You took him off my hands while I could get the last of my work done at Maple Valley. And there was a lot of work to do. So, thank you."

"You know," she began, still leveling the barrel perfectly at Dave, "I should have guessed you were behind all this."

He almost sneered—but teachers never sneered, so he offered a smile. Neve's tense muscles fell almost imperceptibly, and his first instinct was to disarm her of her weapon, which he could have done. But he didn't. It wouldn't do any good, and he needed Neve to be receptive to what he was going to say.

She instantly caught herself and pointed the gun directly between his temples. But when she opened her mouth to say something, nothing came out.

He smiled again. He'd never smiled before on a job. Was this particular assignment making him sharper or looser? Maybe both?

"Neve, I liked that you never tried to… pad anyone with fluffy words or filler. You know that I have all sorts of contingency plans in place in the event that I am terminated or forced to swallow the pill." He was tempted to switch his squatting position, but he found that it was good to get back into the ascetic self-control of his old life, so he held it. "And once I took out Cuocotti and managed to get away with it—even though I ordered the termination to a bunch of kids—I knew I'd gained control. Of everything."

Now it was her turn to repress a sneer. "It *was* you."

"Neve, I appreciate it that you didn't add 'I suspected all along' or anything like that. I played a fairly deep cover, even convincing myself I was a lab victim during my job interview. That sure felt like authenticity."

Neve clenched her teeth and re-leveled the weapon.

"I'd never worked with Carter or Young, so I was free to slip under the radar. Eliminating 'Yearson' gave the distraction and destabilization that I needed to move forward. It was a hornet's nest after that one."

Neve was unable to suppress an eye roll. Fair, thought Dave. He waited.

"So, what after that? Why did you need Salhi out of the way?"

"I needed space—no other close colleagues—to get at the weapon."

He saw the confusion displayed right in her eyebrow. "The student project from a few years back. The one that brought me out here to slip into that CSS agent's teaching job."

"What student project?"

"A very portable, very functional small-scale nuclear weapon." His face betrayed nothing about the lie.

She lowered her weapon all the way. Bird calls reverberated in the warm April air.

"Where? Where is it?"

"In the school. In the M-VAULT. Some students got it for me." He smiled again.

"I don't know what you're talking about," she said. She was telling the truth.

"Well, that's the idea, isn't it?"

He stood up quickly—too quickly, for she leaped back one step. Again, reading her face, he could see her frustration at not being completely in control here. He held up his palms in a gesture of "Hey, it's fine." He could see the question behind her eyes. And she must have thought she was about to be killed because she just went ahead and asked it.

"Why didn't you just shoot me off the bike?" She raised the gun at him. "Why not just—"

He looked over to his left, into the garage, and interrupted her. "Nina?" he asked.

That was it. Neve looked where he was looking. By the time she realized Nina was not, in fact, standing there, he had already hit the back of her wrist with the stick he had slid up his sleeve from the ground. It hit her bone, and she dropped the gun, which he covered with his foot. When she went to kick his leg, he rotated backward, caught her heel with the top of his foot, and continued her leg's momentum, pulling her up in the air and then landing her on her back. She looked up at him in shock and—

Again, her face made it easy for him. He rolled to the side just as Nassir tried a quick ax kick in the air, which would have knocked him out cold. He'd gotten out the window and jumped off the roof. Nice.

"Nassir?" Dave asked. "You're okay?"

Neve started to say something from his right, but Nassir spoke first. "You know I'm okay," he said, his voice low. "You set me up at that brewery so that she could take me away, Da—" He stopped himself. "What is your real name, anyway?"

He let another smile leak out. "It's best if you just remember me as Dave Legnagyszerübb, the rookie teacher."

"Who turned out not to be a rookie?"

"Yes. Sure," nodded Dave. "But teaching-wise—definitely a rookie."

Nassir smirked. Dave realized he had missed Nassir over the last few weeks.

"You're probably not someone who needs a basic self-defense course every day after school—but you have me convinced," said Nassir. Then, the science teacher let it out: "Your name's probably not Dave at all. Who are you? Who do you work for?"

"It's easier if you just think of me as the Dave Legnagyszerübb you work with."

Dave followed it up with a shrug, and Neve let loose a roundhouse kick to his side. He leaned away, but just as quickly, Nassir swung what looked to be a galvanized steel pipe at his head.

There was no laxity, feigned or otherwise, in this Dave. Not now, not ever—even if during his time as a new high school teacher, he had forced himself to ignore threatening details about his environment, about his students, about his colleagues. Now he was himself again.

As Nassir swung the pipe, he pulled back so as not to leave an opening, but that made it simple to avoid both the pipe and Neve's kick. He let a straight sidekick bury the pipe back in Nassir's stomach, and the young biology teacher's usually expressionless face belied the pain of that force. At the same time, Neve went to throw a straight punch, a combination she should have known better than to use on an agent who'd seen it countless times himself. Instantly, he pivoted, and Neve was between Dave and the stifled Nassir. A high kick to her chin buried Neve into Nassir.

"Dave" pivoted again, using his left hand to shove the two onto the ground, a messy mass of limbs. He wanted to use them to accomplish the mission, but it might not be necessary. He glanced back up on the roof, calculating whether it would be faster to hop back up there to his rifle or relieve Neve of hers and finish the job that way.

Nassir—the man who had allowed himself to be arrested by a team of agents at a morning staff meeting and managed to free himself within the hour—lasted almost a full second against the agent who had called himself Dave Legnagyszerübb.

"Mr. L."

Nina was standing in the garage, a look of confusion on her face.

"He's not Mr. L, Nina," grunted Nassir, trying to untangle himself from Neve, who was bleeding from her mouth.

"What do you mean? I know him, Mr. Salhi." Her perfect round cheeks hardened in indignation.

"He's not on our side, Nina," said Dave. "See? He faked the whole 'abduction' thing. We've got to take that vehicle over there and get back to the high school. We'll leave the motorcycle here. But there's a really dangerous weapon that we need to get out of their hands, and I need you to help me do it."

Nina blanched, but it was clear, even at that moment, that she had a handle on it in a way that you couldn't train a person to do. That kind of self-control would make Nina great someday. Maybe even right now.

Without a word, the teenager looped a finger through an extension cord hanging in the garage and flung it, underhanded, to the man she still thought was Mr. Legnagyszerübb, who snagged the cord from its arc.

Neve moved when she should have waited, and suddenly one of her hands was stuck inside the loop of the coiled extension cord. She moved again, and it tightened like a snare. He whirled around her so quickly and tightly that she had no time to strike him. Nassir then stood up at the wrong time—though suddenly every counterpunch was thrown at the wrong time, the angle of every elbow strike was at the wrong angle, and every kick seemed just as effective as throwing yourself on the ground. The agent pulled the orange noose taut around Neve's hands and Nassir's neck in a double snare.

His lessons with Nassir and the rest of the Maple Valley staff had sharpened his skills. During those afternoons in the gym and the evenings with Nassir, freed of the thought requirements of expert combat, he had noticed all sorts of shortcomings—even some laziness—in the combat techniques of his fellow teachers.

The kidnapper and the science teacher were now tethered together in the grass in front of the house where he had come back into his full self. Neve was beaten but not foolish. She tried to hold her "handcuffs" over her shoulders as far as she could, so Nassir would not be strangled to death. Yet the science teacher was beginning to look ashen. No matter. He turned towards the garage to look for Nina.

The garage was empty. The sun had set; the pale orange and purple sand mix of the spring evening reflected off the two windows of the garage, but there were no shadows inside or out.

Dave didn't know quite what to make of this, so for efficiency's sake, he started to grab his equipment. He once again vaulted with one hand onto the roof with a somersault, and within seconds his rifle was packed up. Next, he hopped off the roof, shouldered up the motorcycle Neve had tried to escape with and rolled it back into the garage. In between the floppy sounds of the flat rear wheel, he heard a foot scrape against concrete. Setting the stand down, he pulled the collapsed door against the frame of the garage. Not that many prying eyes ever drove by here, but if they did, they might not notice anything except one-and-a-half dead agents on the front lawn.

He looked over at his restrained enemies, knowing what he'd see.

"Nina, please don't free them. You have to trust me."

She had a pair of tin snips from the garage and had already managed to hack through the loop that was around Nassir's neck. The gasp from the young science teacher cut through the evening. She looked up at Dave, unapologetic. Nassir's gasps were more spread out as he calmed himself, but he and Neve were still intertwined, even if he could now breathe. Would she cut her biology teacher free?

"Nina, this is part of the business."

She didn't respond but moved quickly over the driveway and tossed the snips in through the giant gap between the broken door and the frame.

"I'm not going to be responsible for anyone's death, Mr. L," she said. Had she been less mature, less ready, she might have said it with her arms crossed, her hips jutting to one side, her eyes squinting. Instead, she stood straight up, looking him in the eye.

He tried not to smile.

Instead, he returned her gaze, thinking of all the ways they would get her to kill in her first few months at the training facility in Libya or the one in Myanmar. And one day, she would forget how it felt to object to the forfeiture of life as surely as she'd forget her given name.

He'd had a given name, too—though maybe that had fallen out of the stuff-sack of his memory during the various shoves and unpackings. He had been a real person with a real name long before there had been Dave, the new teacher, or Lawrence, the rookie footballer, or Shakir, the fresh software architect. He even remembered his big ideas about morality and what quasi-government agencies could do to make the world a better place. And he had held on to those ideals as long as he could until they were subsumed by promotions and intrigue and assignment after assignment. Nina would be placed in a box and held wherever Marguerite or Dominica or Christine had room for her.

Was this job making him nostalgic? Wistful? Yet one more effect of teaching: a connection to youth. Not the youth that goes in and out with each fad ("What are the kids saying these days?"), but the primordial youth that has always and will always think the same, even when it's on scattered agricultural outposts, or in an isolated tribe in the Amazon, or in an international school. Young, burning, distracted, infatuated youth.

And a small part of him—that kid with the lost name who was good at everything and foolishly believed he would use that particular talent to make the world better at everything—wanted to shield Nina from this loss. So he said, "Enjoy your freedom to make that decision now—either way, we've got to get you and this van back to school. You drive. I'll be in the back working out a plan to avoid accidentally irradiating every single person in the greater metropolitan area."

She made a puzzled face. "Mr. L, " she said, "I am not able to drive. I don't have a permit. Or nothing."

"Nina," he said, "I wouldn't be here if you had 'nothing.'"

25 – The Chase

"Wait, what?"

David Legnagyszerübb did not take his eyes off the road but arched his back and mashed the pedal into the floor. This brought the white truck's speed from 50 to 52 miles per hour in just over four seconds. So he had plenty of time to look comically over at Neve and regard her with shock.

"Yes. he stole your CSS assignment. He then ordered students to kill Larry Yearson, which was Cuocotti's alias—and they did."

"Wait." It seemed to be all he could say. "Wait. He *did* kill Cuocotti? How?"

"He convinced students to do it. For a school assignment."

David imagined his own students attempting such a thing: they might hold a victim down and club his foot until he cried. Or hold his arms underwater until he got cold. But there was a real, practicing operative training facility for youth masquerading as a school in this district—and he wasn't at it. He'd been leading field trips and breaking up fights at Elm Creek High School, a facility that had nothing to do with any national security apparatus.

"Wait—" He knew he'd been outplayed, but it wasn't just ego fueling his incredulity.

"Who did he work for? Who does he work for? The SVR? Mossad?"

Nassir and Neve both gave small grunts. Neve had a look on her face as if she'd heard something offensive but couldn't stop smiling.

"What?"

"When people discussed this—people who should know more than the rest of us, like Don Carter or Courtney Young—the joke is that he works for Lakota County Independent School District 517. Because beyond that, Dave Legnagyszerübb does not exist."

"Wait—wait?" His toes mashed the accelerator into the floor. Neve looked out the rear window to see the old Ford Transit belch out a small rain cloud of carbon monoxide.

"Doesn't exist? Even if he were that good—especially if he were that good—the NSA'd at least have him in the system somewhere. It's the freaking NSA. There could not be a pet goldfish in the United States that they didn't have in their database of databases. There is absolutely no way we don't know who this person actually is unless he's an extra-extraterrestrial."

David's incredulity was met with silence.

"Goes by Dave?"

"Yeah. Insists on it."

"Well, then, call me David."

"I already do."

He saw Nassir smile in the rearview mirror. What was with these grinning idiots? Maybe it was a lack of oxygen—even in the dim light of the Ford Transit, the bruises from the extension cord were visible along Nassir's neck.

Again, he held the van's pedal to the floor, and again the van waited several seconds to respond. He couldn't even go fast enough to get around the Hyundai in front of him.

When he'd sprinted out of Elm Ridge High School this afternoon, none of the vehicles he tried to jump would start—except this one. This white van accelerated as if someone had put retardant in the fuel tank. Someone who knew that David Legnagyszerübb would need to be slowed, but not stopped, today.

"Wait," he said, for what felt like the hundredth time. It was just so strange not being in control. His mind was churning questions out faster than his mouth could articulate them. And all this was happening faster than this God-forsaken van could drive. "Okay, so he's—"

A pause hung in the air above the whinnying transmission of the strained van. "Not 'he.' It's 'they,' David. He's got the girl with him." David caught it. "Wait—who?" Whoever she was, she was significant; he could see it on their faces in the rearview mirror. His foot was still on the floor, and he still saw faster cars approaching through the rear windows. He'd be better off hijacking a car. But—what was Neve not telling him?

"*Who?*" he repeated. He couldn't look back as he was finally about to overtake a Hyundai.

"The girl's a problem," said Neve. David caught her glance at Nassir. "How so?"

"We've had the feeling at Maple Valley for some time," said Nassir, obviously hesitant to share the information, "that Nina dos Santos Pandlay was falsifying her school records."

"Don't kids do that all the time at your spy school?"

Nassir nodded with a grimace. "Oh, all the time. We even have a sandbox grade server to lure kids into attacking, even though it contains no live grading and transcript information. And it's hard to fault a kid who has the capability to get into our main architecture, secure routers and servers, especially when obtaining information is a major component for any of the main assignments at Maple Valley."

"So," began David. He felt like he was standing on the pedal. The van continued on, unhurriedly. "She's got digital exploitation skills, right? If she got into her grades, that means she's good. Probably earned that B."

Nassir rubbed his cheek where the bruise was spreading. "Except," he said, just loudly enough to be heard over the strains of the engine, "she was actually going in and *lowering* her grades."

The van crept up from 54 to 55 miles per hour. David did something he hadn't done in years, which was to reach for the shifter on his right as if he were still driving a high-performance vehicle as he'd done, Bond style, while working in Tunisia about ten years ago. After Durango. About the time when he'd felt as an agent—not in a proud way, but just as a matter of course—that he could walk into any situation, anywhere in the world, and take control in a few days or weeks. Everyone was seeing the chess game about six moves too late, and he had the rook and the queen in a fork, his opponent's king pinned behind his own foot soldiers.

Except now, it was as if someone had just walked by and turned the board around. He was on the wrong side.

Why would a student training to be a field agent make herself look more average, more mediocre, in a public high school that was already packed to the brim with wholly incapable teenagers?

Because she was ahead of the curve.

It was easy to assume that high schoolers would simply follow the Quantico paradigm: get all As. Get the highest test scores in AP Chemistry, College in the Schools English, Advanced Threat Removal Techniques, International Law and Government Subjugation. Dominate a few sports to show prowess and mental toughness. Win a conference championship in trap shooting, even though you're wearing special contact lenses that slow your reaction time. Get recruited to West Point, *et cetera*.

But the kind of student destined for clandestine agencies that never appeared in Bourne books? The perfect candidate for a job with no uniform, no badge number—no life, even—but all cover and subterfuge?

That particularly skilled, one-in-a-million student would attend the school, learn every skill at a ridiculously high level, and pretend to fly under the radar by lowering her own grades. Sure, teachers might chat about this kid or that kid—"My God, did you see Nina's Krav Maga demonstration final in Phy Ed? She should be teaching the class, not taking it!"—but as long as Nina dos Santos Pandlay only put out a few brilliant performances here and there, no one would or could put the whole picture together and realize what she was preparing herself for.

Or what she was being recruited for.

"Nassir," David said, "what are they going to do with the portable nuclear weapon?"

It was Neve who spoke up. She was staring out the passenger side window from the back of the van, and when he heard her voice, David had a hard time looking away to keep his eyes on the road.

"They might use it. They might sell it. They might use the fact of its existence to get Maple Valley's training program shut down." He paused and then said what Neve must have also been thinking. "Having engaged those two, I doubt there's anyone who can stop them."

David finally took his leg off the gas and pulled over. As the van rolled to a stop, Neve did not remove her eyes from the window, and Nassir's hand stayed planted firmly on his face. David turned around.

"We need to do something," he said. "We should start by—"

"I wouldn't bother looking for the van that the weapon was in," said Neve, her eyes still glued to the window—probably waiting to see the flash that could blind her before it vaporized them all. "They've surely ditched it by now."

26 - The Second Homecoming Lesson

"Quite the day outside, isn't it?" asked Young. The strong May sun seemed to create a stillness that made it possible to be heard across the road. Young did not stop scanning the road, nor did Carter when she addressed him.

"Sure," said Carter, his face a chiseled mask.

Carter and Young stood at the parking lot entrance to Maple Valley High School, one on each curb of the turn-in. Each had two instrument cases at their feet, just like any other band teacher—or administrator chaperoning a band trip. Each scanned their respective side of the two-way suburban thoroughfare that lined the school's front entrance. By design, the back entrance to the high school could only be reached by entering the drive from the front. The rear of the school was ridged by innocuous-looking slopes that made quick access to the school by any vehicle, including a tank, impossible.

The slightest noise from the school's entryway made both of them look at once—and Young quickly looked back to the road. Carter saw them first: two ruffians sneaking out of the building an hour early.

They were non-pre-op students, so they had no reason to leave, and as soon as they saw Carter and Young posted up on the corner like a pair of overpaid sentries, they involuntarily ducked their heads and looked away. They shared some words and a nervous laugh and then darted back into the building through the same door that Dave Legnagyszerübb had been forced through after being semi-abducted after an interview nine months ago.

These two students, in white T-shirts with purple-and-pink zags on them that wouldn't be out of place in the 80s, thought that their efforts to leave the building to get stoned were somehow noteworthy. They probably believed that every adult in the building was conspiring against them, so, *of course*, they'd be busted by the two highest-chain teachers in the building. Though to these kids, every adult—cook, principal, contractor—was some version of a teacher. They had no idea, nor would they ever, how many infinitely more dangerous threats to civilization were being handled in their school on any given day.

Young, though not unaware of the gravity of the situation, seemed unable to stop her hands from coming up to her face as her smile became indistinguishable from her trademark grimace. "I sure do hope that our phy ed teachers are able to take their classes out and enjoy this warm—" her bracelets jangled as her fists went higher—"fantastic weather." She paused. "You know, it's just so unfortunate that our lower-income students don't have the access—" her hair now shook alongside her bracelets "—to the fresh air that, you know, wealthier kids have. And our low-income kids are more likely to have asthma." She stopped but couldn't stop completely. "Or they live in fear of, say, gun violence outside. So this is such an opportunity for them to experience what other kids take for granted."

"Sure," said Carter again. He straightened, trying to get a look at the large vehicle coming over the crest.

It was not a vehicle driven by a "teacher"—just a yellow school bus. Both Carter and Young reached down towards the instrument cases, almost imperceptibly, as the bus made its wide turn into the parking lot. The diesel fumes intruded on what was otherwise a beautifully fragrant spring day.

"Wow! Didn't know the brass would be here to greet me!" called out the driver, whose name neither Carter nor Young could recall at the moment. He had a great white, thick mustache and merry eyes when he lifted his sunglasses up, leaning his head out the window as the engine's pistons lurched with no discernable pattern.

Carter managed a smile. "We just have so many field trips out today, sir, that we're out here making sure that everyone gets back for finals." He paused and gestured towards the instrument cases at his feet. "And some of our band students will need to get their instruments immediately upon arrival to get in for graduation rehearsal."

"Well, I'm here to pick up the track team, but enjoy the afternoon out here in the sunshine," said the bus driver. "And thanks for taking that equipment out of my vehicle a few months back—that English teacher talked to you, huh? Or maybe that was the other school in town?"

A shadow passed over Carter's face. "Hey, any time. Good luck getting the kids to the track meet today."

The bus rumbled into gear and passed into the parking lot. Young stepped right behind the bus as it passed, standing on her tiptoes to get a good look down the aisle through the back door as it went by. Carter continued to scan the street but saw her signal that the bus was clear.

At this moment, the road was empty, the diesel fumes had dissipated slightly, and the sun seemed to squeeze the scent from the crabapple blossoms and spread them around like a wet sponge pressed onto a table.

And then, in that moment of tranquility, the white van sped over the crest in the road and accelerated towards Maple Valley High School.

Only when Young and Carter saw it did they hear its engine roar as it sped over the road's plateau, becoming slightly airborne for a moment.

Before its front two tires hit the road again, Carter was already pulling a machine gun out of a trombone case. Young kicked over the two large cases next to her and revealed what they had hidden: a metal rod with a handle on it. As the van hit the ground slightly-off center and veered into the opposite lane, Young threw the switch on the edge of the curb. The sound of a metal spring being released cut through the air, even as Carter began firing the weapon at the driver's side of the van. The spikes at the entryway to the parking lot shot up, and Carter backpedaled while firing his machine gun, puncturing the warm May air.

The van jerked to its left and hit the curb. Young, who was opening another music case for a weapon, jumped out of the way but screamed as the rear driver's side wheel came down on her femur with a crunch. Carter lowered his weapon as the van, which had flown over the curb to the right of the spikes but had lost traction when the wheel destroyed the leg of the assistant principal, skidded impossibly on two wheels for a moment before landing on its side, bouncing hard off the asphalt and then back up on four wheels almost gently.

Carter raised his weapon but allowed himself a sigh of relief, even as his assistant principal now lay on the asphalt of the Maple Valley parking lot with her leg smashed and nearly pulled apart by the spinning wheel of the van. For this clear-eyed calm, he was the principal of one of the government's clandestine training grounds for spies, agents and operatives. Young would survive, but Carter's mission was to stop that nuclear project from finding its way back into the school.

With his weapon trained on the driver's side, which was now riddled with a circular trail of bullet holes, Carter approached the van. The driver was leaning back in the driver's seat, and his or her face was still not visible.

He could see the silhouette of the driver lean forward a bit and shake his head.

"Put your hands up," Carter said in a loud voice.

The hands went up. Then another pair of hands went up from the passenger seat—Nina, Carter was sure. He heard Young groan again from behind him, and he heard the birds call and felt the lush air of May.

He lowered himself to his knees to see the ground underneath the van. Yes, some gasoline had sloshed out, but there was no constant stream. Yes, some radiator fluid was hissing from the front, but it wasn't gas.

"Ay, Mr. C—did we pass?"

Carter tightened his hold on the gun and tried to parse what he'd just heard. "Don't move or say another word."

"Oh, okay," said the driver.

Carter's face could not betray any surprise, so he stood still. The radiator coolant hissed and dripped.

"Mr. C—if I say anything, will I get points off?"

Carter was a coiled viper. "Open the door, but keep your hands where I can see them."

Evan, the driver, had a cut on his forehead but otherwise looked fine. JB, the passenger, was holding his shoulder.

Carter's heart stopped for a moment. In that instant, he went over his plans to relocate his family to one of several safe destinations every

Maple Valley admin was required to keep at all times. He had just shot a student, and all the advanced training in the world wasn't going to shield you once you'd killed a pupil in your care.

But JB removed his hand from his shoulder, and there was no spurt of blood or gnarl of exposed bone. "Ay, ah, Mr. Principal," he said, "I jacked my shoulder up, so—"

"Either of you in need of medical treatment?" he asked.

"Naw, I don't think so, Mr. C, but those blanks you fired—that was some scary realistic stuff! No cap! I saw you and Ms. Assistant Principal—"

"You mean Ms. Young."

"Yeah! Her! And I thought: This is hella real for a test! But you gotta tell us, C—did we pass?"

Carter froze. Again his face betrayed nothing, but his mind spun like a broken axle. Finally, it clicked on something and stopped.

"Did Mr. Legnagyszerübb send you back here with this van?"

"Well, *yeah*. That's the test, right? We got the test invite on our Learnstile app and figured it was a final for Acquisitions class. I mean, my sister said for that final, she just had to steal, like, a box and decode a puzzle. She didn't do the puzzle and got a C, so I figure to actually get the van back here on time and without the cargo damaged has *got* to be an A."

The cargo. He heard Young groan.

"JB, Evan, are there any buttons that Mr. Legnagyszerübb told you to hold down as you were driving? Or any keys that you had to leave in a lock? Or any levers that he asked you not to move?" Don Carter, survivor of hundreds of nearly impossible missions, now let an edge of fear creep into his throat.

They both looked at him. "Like, there's some kind of key in here, Mr. C?" asked Evan from the passenger seat.

"Oh, oh, oh—right," said JB. "Yeah, there is one, but I took the key out."

Carter fought the instinct to take a step back. Instead, he lowered his weapon and walked towards the open window of the van.

"This one. Right here."

Don Carter let out a measured puff of air.

"JB, that's the ignition."

"Yeah, yeah."

"I'm talking about any other kind of failsafe—I mean, some other part of the test that you had to do?"

The boys looked at each other. He could hear Young's muffled voice from behind him. He hoped her walkie was within reach so she could contact someone inside.

"I don't think so, Mr. C."

"Boys, keep your hands up and get out of the van right now. Lay facedown on the asphalt with your hands behind your head."

JB snickered. "Man, why, Mr. Carter? We was just—"

"So any responding agents don't immediately shoot you in the head. After all, that's what I was trying to do."

Now it was Evan's turn to snicker. "I know those are blanks, dude. We did a simulation in Weapons Survival B last year—"

Carter blinked slowly. "There are two bullet holes from my gun in the fabric behind your left ear, Evan. Get out of the van."

JB finally stepped out, and Evan followed suit with a frown. Unable to follow directions in any circumstance, they got down on their knees; JB halfheartedly put one hand behind his head. Dave, or whatever his real name was, had chosen these pawns exceedingly well.

"Tell me what happened."

Evan started. "So, like, my mom needed me to drop off her—taxes, I think? Or—"

"Not you. JB, tell me what actually occurred."

JB went to put one hand down, but Carter placed his hand over his holster.

"We were just chillin', walking down the street, when we see Mr. L leaning alongside his van. He says, 'Are you boys ready for the schoolwide CA?' I said we'd already taken that. He said we might have taken the math and reading ones, but not the standardized test for, like, pre-operatives." His chest puffed out a bit as he said it. "I said we didn't know about no pre-op standardized test. He said that was exactly the idea."

"It made sense, yo," chimed in Evan. Young let out another stifled yell as he heard an air cast being blown up and applied to her leg.

"Full of sound and fury," Carter said to himself.

"He said all we had to do was get past whatever security perimeter was set up around the school. He said it would look, like, super-realistic, but as long as we got the, ah, um—"

"Payload," added the emboldened Evan.

"Yeah, payload, in the parking lot, and said the code phrase to you, we would pass the test and get the tenth-grade pre-op requirement done."

Kelly and Julia sprinted by to attend to Young, carrying several boxes of first aid equipment each. Neither looked over at the boys.

Payload.

Instead, he scanned the dashboard and panel of the van, and when he didn't see a double-redundant key lock anywhere, he knew they'd been duped. He leaped over the center console to the back of the van.

It was empty, except for a keyboard and a dead monitor that were connected to a printer by an Ethernet and USB cable, respectively. NUCLEAR WEAPON—PLEASE REPLENISH PAPER SUPPLY BEFORE DETONATION was written on the front of the printer in tidy black marker.

He closed his eyes for a moment. After these two geniuses were convinced by "Mr. L" that they were partaking in an espionage hijacking simulation, did they even *look* at the contraption in the back? He leaped out the back doors of the van. When he landed, he paused, suddenly sure of how to proceed. He smiled, and the boys involuntarily shrank back.

"Okay then, fellas, you're halfway done!" he said in his most congratulatory tone. "So—what's the code phrase?"

"Wait, what?" asked JB, who was now distracted by the fact that Ms. Young was receiving medical attention for a broken leg. Carter wondered somewhere if JB had the cognitive capacity to connect what just happened, vehicle-wise, with Young's injury.

"What is the code?"

"Oh!" said Evan, his face lighting up. "He said that you and he were both English teachers, so you would know it was from *Pearl World Three* or some book like that about the end of the world or something."

"What is it?" He didn't ask for a follow-up about *World War Z*.

"It's—ah—'Every rich man's house has a service entrance.'"

World War Z—yes, Carter had read it. And suddenly, he realized that he and Young had made a mistake. He grabbed his radio.

27 - The Back Door

The teacher, formerly known as Dave Legnagyszerübb, got out of the beaten yellow Civic's passenger door quickly, but not in a way that looked hasty or forced. The backseat was worn yet tidy, and buckled into the three available seats were three duffle bags, sitting there like overgrown canvas children in their harnesses. He took out two of them—again, quickly, but not in a rushed way that might attract attention—and carefully put the bags' slings over his shoulders. The driver, a sixteen-year-old student named Nina dos Santos Pandlay, got out a few seconds after him. She'd been setting the parking brake, checking to see that she was in the lines of the old rear parking lot of Maple Valley High School, and readjusting the mirrors to how they were before she had gotten in the driver's seat a few minutes earlier.

To the untrained eye, she was merely going through the rigid checklists required of all new drivers before they become sloppy vehicular operators in their late teens and early twenties. But Nina was actually scanning the back lot of the building, surrounded as it was with brick additions and outgrowths clearly added as referendum money came and went. It was a secluded entry to the building, one that would have been completely rethought had it been newly designed in the age of school shootings, but it provided the perfect entryway to a late-arriving teacher and a star pupil.

The day had been wet earlier, but that had not stopped Nina, the newly minted driver, from navigating the rear entrance to the school: several softball and soccer fields strung together that approached the circle of hill-berms on the school's south and west sides. The northeast entry was where all traffic had to come in, and at the moment, it was guarded by a slightly on-edge Don Carter and a soon-to-suffer-a-catastrophic-leg-injury Ms. Young. They knew what van to look for as soon as Nassir had called the school.

During this time, Mr. Legnagyszerübb, as any patient community education driving instructor would do, was guiding Nina down 10th Avenue, ordering her to drive over the curb by the tennis courts and then down the pedestrian pathway on the south edge of the fields. She hit the gas a bit hard going over the curb, but it added to the realistic effect, in case anyone was watching, of a young lady literally getting off-track during a driver's education session.

Nina then piloted the old Civic over fields of wet, soft grass, leaving burrows in May's emerald carpets while continuing steadily toward the back of the school. Then just as Evan and JB piloted Nina and Dave's original van into the air in the front of the school, Nina plopped the car over the curb and into the rear parking lot. The sound of Nina's rear bumper roughly hitting the curb coincided with the sound of the van crushing Young's legs in front of the school.

The teacher, who'd called himself Dave, hoisted two large duffle bags over one shoulder, and Nina grabbed the third bag from the backseat after having scanned the rear parking lot, including the old loading dock and custodial area overlooking the loading dock, under the auspices of checking her parking accuracy.

He walked up the steel-edged concrete stairs—still quickly but not urgently—and set the bags down on the ground. After using his access key card, the door released with a click, and he picked up the duffle bags.

A flash of yellow appeared in his peripheral vision, and he was caught too off-guard to evade or defend the kick. His left eye had an image of a matte-black flat before it struck him in the face. Only the weight of the duffle bags on his shoulder prevented him from falling straight back over the loading dock, where he could have righted himself before the fall but still possibly broken a wrist or an arm, ending the fight.

Sarah flew through the door onto the loading dock. She unleashed another kick, this time to his midsection, but he was able to move just enough to deaden the blow and slip one of the duffle handles around her foot.

The legs underneath her trademark yellow skirt were again too fast for him as she slipped the snare and dropped her heel on his exposed back in a guillotine chop. This one landed squarely on his spine.

And then the band teacher made her mistake. Thinking he was incapacitated, she took a moment to wield her weapon. Dave realized that he didn't know if it was a flute masquerading as a weapon or a weapon masquerading as a flute.

Rather than quickly striking with the weapon, she heaved back for a knockout blow. When the two-handed strike came down, he rolled over his right shoulder, controlled both wrists holding the flute-weapon, and flipped her on her back on the loading dock. But as he tried to pick up the bag and get away, her foot launched up from the ground, and he found himself with her knee behind his head and her other shin on his throat. With one quick adjustment of her ankle, his airway and artery were immediately throttled. His concentration slipped; he noticed the small shard of concrete on the loading dock cutting into the knee that was pinned underneath his body. Sound was fading from his ears, and the world was becoming grayer.

"And I thought you *liked* me," she grunted, placing all of her considerable strength into the hold. His world narrowed like an analog television losing a signal.

Sarah raised one hip to try and tighten the vice even further. Had she not done that, the teacher who had pretended to be new, had pretended to get taken out by a bunch of kids in the bathroom during unstructured learning time, had pretended to get saved by the young band teacher in the ever-present yellow skirt, had pretended to lose a pickup game of basketball in order to give a kid a chance to steal his keys—he would have slumped over, unconscious, or she might have killed him, and then the duffle bags would have been hers to look through, and she would have realized that Nina had disappeared—and the warm May day at Maple Valley High School might have turned out very differently.

Instead, she shifted, and he wrenched his knees at a point just higher than his own face. His feet didn't strike her, but she was forced to move her head and shoulders, and she lost the grip. The world inflated with sound and color again, and the first thing he noticed was the smoothness of her leg muscle against his neck and the smell of whatever lotion Ms. Lehner had put on this morning after showering.

He shoved hard off that one knee that was against the ground and threw her off of him, taking a second gasp of air as he did so.

She hit her tailbone with a thud on the loading dock surface, but he did not pounce. He placed his hands over the duffle bags but did not stand up and sling them over his shoulder. She didn't rise to stop him. They simply sat there, panting. He looked up at her, and she held his stare.

"I do like you," he said.

"We're both too good at this to be pretending it's not work," she said. Her breathing was still slowing, but her shoulders were slumped. She was not Neve—not a cold-blooded, indefatigable assassin. The infatuation swelled in his chest.

He grinned, his chest still heaving. "When you're working, it's not always just pretending or just lying." He kept still, and his breath was now under control. "I *was* Dave Legnagyszerübb. I was a new, bumbling teacher among new, bumbling teachers. In that role, it's not a disguise— it's life. I was a lot of things that I said I was or that people assumed I was."

Sarah was not grinning. She made direct eye contact with him as one sweaty tendril of her hair, which had turned black and slick by the exertion, fell on her forehead.

"So, what are you? Why did you take the portable nuclear weapons outside the building?"

"Just one moment," he said, holding up a phone. He tapped it twice with a quick nod and put it back in his pocket.

She turned her head slightly. Sarah Lehner, band teacher and close-quarters combat instructor, heard nothing.

"Is there a trap somewhere?" she asked.

He didn't answer.

"Do you know how these—" he lifted a handle of one of the duffle bags "—came to be?" Part of him wanted to tell her he just enjoyed talking to her again: talking to her about work, just two new teachers in the long sigh that was springtime at a public high school. Just because he was not truly who he'd presented himself to be, didn't mean he didn't linger in the staff mailroom when he saw her come in and pick up her copies, didn't think desperately about how to string the conversation past "How's it going?"

"They were made by students as a project during M-VAULT time," she said. "Tiny nuclear weapons. Not the size of a car, but—" She gestured at the bags.

"Were you surprised when you found out kids made them?" he asked.

"Well, yeah, but kids can shock you sometimes with their aptitude," she said, her breathing evening out.

He said nothing.

"But, yeah, you look at those kids, and it's—surprising, sure." Then the fire came back into her eyes. "But it was the kids' work, and it wasn't right for you to take it. Especially like that."

Ah, it simply wasn't right to do what he did. Did the HRB at this school have some kind of moral high ground? Whoever said anything about being "right?"

"Sarah," he said because he still enjoyed saying it, "have you met kids? They're stupid, even when they're smart. These nukes had some pretty substantial mechanical problems, so I had to take them off-site. The best way to do that was by letting some kids get my keys, get into the vault, take the nukes out of school, and then I was able to acquire them." He'd simply taken them out of the trunk of a kid's car. The kid had stolen world-changing technology and left it in his car, along with an unreturned, waterlogged Stats textbook and a bag of lacrosse equipment.

She was shifting her hands to a more prepared position, but she froze as he finished. "So you got someone to arm them?"

"Fix them, arm them, *et cetera*," he said, his heartbeat now under control as well.

He was quite short on time. Several parties would, once they figured out what was going on, be back here. So he cut it short—even though he kind of wanted to let her know all the things he'd done to orchestrate this.

Did he still want to impress her? He was embarrassed for himself because he did want to impress her. He was like a shy ninth-grader who waits at the bus stop with a hot varsity volleyball star.

But he wouldn't explain all the intrigue. It would cut into the time that they sat across from each other, sweaty and ready to fight again in an instant but no longer needing the tether of a conversation starter like, "Hey, can you believe they're springing a surprise M-VAULT day during Spring Fling week?"

"And then bring them back here? So you can make this school ground zero for some nuclear explosion?"

Despite his attempts to stop it, he felt his entire brow and eyes droop. He was doing some great work on this job, but he felt he might be slipping a bit. "You think I'd want to annihilate this place?" he asked.

"Why else would you steal a bunch of nuclear weapons?" She leaned forward. The sun was poking into the small lot of the back entrance, and he could see the sweat on her head. But it was time to get going.

"They're going back into the school," he said.

She laughed, but it was without mirth, and he didn't enjoy it. "Ah, so you just say they belong back in there, and I let you go in? Too easy. Or you show me a well-constructed FBI badge? Dave, even our kids can do that!"

He didn't shrug or qualify. He had taught these school kids, and so he recognized that as the insult it was. "I'm not going in your building, Sarah. I don't have my keys."

She furrowed her brow—that did suit her—and stopped herself from asking the question. Then she reached out and unzipped the duffle bags; he did not move to stop her. As she bent to look in, he didn't strike her on the back of the head or silently leap off the loading dock. He just breathed in her shampoo and sweat.

"You just don't stop, do you?" she said, not looking up. "So, did you ever even take them outside the school?" She held up the harmless, non-nuclear coffee maker that had been in the large orange bag.

"I did, through several proxies, steal the kids' small nuclear weapons from you. But the nukes will end up back at your school. They'll be fully functional now, with some obvious safeguards."

He leaned to his left a bit and pulled a second coffee maker out of the bag, leaning even farther left. "This is just a distraction. I'm in the process of taking what my employer, and therefore I, truly want from Maple Valley."

The coffee maker's black plastic lid shattered as the bullet flew through it and struck the concrete wall behind them. He didn't jump on top of her. Rather, he pinned both arms against the ground with his outstretched left leg and pulled the concealed gun from her leg holster, which lay underneath that slightly voluminous, slightly curve-accentuating skirt.

It was a big Glock, and that must have been the only place she could carry it.

He immediately rolled past Sarah to the other edge of the dumpster, which provided about a foot and a half of cover for the both of them, though he suspected he was the one who needed it the most. They were prone on the ground now, one on each perpendicular edge of the dumpster.

He lay flat on the bay of the loading dock, smelling the pulverized dirt of the concrete, as well as the ozone of the flying bullets. On the concrete, a small bit of black plastic from the old coffeemaker that he'd stuffed in the duffle bag swayed back and forth in front of his eyes like a rocking horse. The bullets popped against the exterior concrete—and then stopped.

The door that he would have entered had Sarah not confronted him pinged with a glancing bullet off the exterior aluminum frame, so this one must have come from a different angle. He could hear the deeper *thack* of the bullets hitting the dumpster now and more striking the doorframe.

He pushed up on the frayed black plastic dumpster top, wagging it up and down a bit, and the sporadic gunfire became a fireworks finale. He squinted from all the concrete dust raining down but otherwise stayed right where he was, with Sarah.

He was able to peek around the dumpster's top. He immediately spotted Carter, Neve, Nassir, and the man who actually was Special Agent David Legnagyszerübb.

Carter and Neve were reloading, and David and Nassir were conferring while setting up rifles. There was very little cover out there—it was mostly the edge of the soccer fields around the school, followed by the berms that Nina had driven over before.

They must have figured they wouldn't need it.

He looked over at Sarah. She didn't move, and for good reason. Had she jumped up and said, "Hey, it's me!" they'd probably have her cooked before the words echoed off the now-pockmarked loading area.

The guns exploded again. The concrete exterior seemed to be showered in sand, and the five panes of glass that made up the entrance door exploded simultaneously.

The man who had pretended to be a new teacher for the last nine months waited calmly. Nina was inside, delivering the actual nukes back into the vaunted Vault, and so she would be hearing this deadly cacophony just beyond the walls.

Would she run back to the loading dock to help him? If so, she would fail this impromptu test—and, like many a failed operative, get herself killed.

He doubted Nina would do that. She was too good. Too good, in fact, to recruit through some kind of job fair or contact via some shadow agency in seven years. She was good enough to recruit *now*, this year.

And that's what Carter and Young and the real David Legnagyszerübb never realized. He had no interest in any physical assets from Maple Valley. He was only interested in one of the few people good enough to work for the same invisible arm of the group that employed him.

And again, Nina *was* that good—and would continue to improve, given the right learning environment.

He listened to the cadence of the fired rounds and got up into a squatting position behind the dumpster. Time to eliminate the threats, a reaction as natural as breathing—

He paused. He looked at Sarah, still lying prone on the loading dock, and wondered: teachers did not have the heart to kill. Was he an agent or a teacher?

He closed his eyes; JD, Golf, Nina, and all his students' faces swirled in the blackness.

The rounds slowed. Dave knew that, unlike the movies, a person could only fire a certain amount of shots before fatigue set in. They might still shoot at him now, but they probably would not hit him.

The popcorn of the ricochets off the concrete wall slowed, and in his head, he triangulated where they would all be standing. He had six rounds in the Glock.

He jumped out of his crouch position so that his line of sight and the barrel of the gun went over the horizon of the dumpster at the same time. The adrenaline-fueled feeling that the Creator had drawn the world—especially this particular moment—using fat, black marker outlines and bold fill colors made taking in his surroundings easier. And if he had his own gun, it would have been guaranteed to work. But this was a gamble.

His eyes and the gun were less than six inches above the dumpster's pockmarked green metal ridge when he fired his rounds in response.

Neve's gun exploded out of her hand, and she grabbed her ears instinctively from the ricochet. David Legnagyszerübb was disarmed with a second shot that nearly traveled into the barrel of his gun. The gun flew back, his hand still attached as if kicked squarely by a horse.

Then Carter missed, sending another round through the already-shattered doorway. His weapon was pointed slightly up from the recoil, and the agent shot the gun out of the hand of his former boss. This one deflected off the side of the weapon, singeing Carter's cheek.

It was a long swing of the handle across to where Nassir was shooting, but the gamble paid off as the young science teacher blasted a hole in the loading dock by Dave's right foot. Nassir's cover was poor, and Dave felt the nostalgic tang of disappointment in the man whom he had trusted to teach him basic martial arts, even as he pretended not to already have mastered several disciplines.

He blasted the standard-issue weapon out of Nassir's hand; the science teacher grabbed his hand immediately and bent over. The agent doubted that he'd shot his finger off—it was more likely that his trigger finger had just been dislocated. Maybe it would lessen the ridiculous amounts of feedback he wrote on tests.

The last report from the last shot echoed off an apartment building across the street from the high school field, and a strange silence came over the green, berm-edged grassy spot behind the building. Three men and one woman in the field behind the high school stood there, the last male still clutching his hand, though no blood came out. Sarah was also standing at Dave's three o'clock.

No one spoke as Dave put the Glock in the waistband of his pants. The bird songs were pitching ever higher since the cessation of the gunfire, and still, no one spoke. He had just shot each of their guns out of their hands. If they went for their guns in the impossibly green grass, he might relieve them of an ear or a hand.

It was David, who rarely had met an agent equal in prowess to himself, who spoke first. He tried not to sound rattled or powerless. He was both, so he stopped trying to hide it and let the indignancy take over his voice.

"Why did you take my job? If it was truly to get the weapon from the school or to use the weapon to blow up this school, then why didn't you just go in and take it?" He paused, now like a high school senior who's had some insight into why Hamlet hates himself more than he hates anyone else. His voice even went up a few semitones as if pulled upwards by the warm air, now attempting its earlier redolence by spiriting away the residual scents of gunpowder and ozone. "Because we all know now you can take it. You could have taken it, probably, whenever you want."

"You and I are good at our jobs," replied the agent who had been Dave. Neve and Nassir frowned at the lowball understatement, but both noticed that his hand remained at his hip, not too far from where Sarah's Glock was crammed.

If David did notice what Nassir and Neve had, he seemed to ignore it. He was now crossing the grass and about to walk over the broken and sloping curb toward the loading dock. Dave heard Sarah stiffen, but he did not move an inch or give anything away. David's eyebrows furrowed, visible clearly in the late spring morning light.

David crossed the threshold of the back lot and strode up the stairs. The agent who'd been posing as a rookie teacher did not move or flinch. For a moment, Dave wondered if David Legnagyszerübb had gotten a sub for today or if he'd simply disappeared from the halls and rooms of Elm Ridge High School. Right now, he was feet, and now inches, in front of him.

"I was to become a teacher and figure out who killed the man known as Larry Yearson. But you stole my cover." His forehead was a folded napkin of anger.

Dave did not smile but moved his hand farther from his hip. He narrowed his eyes almost imperceptibly as if looking over a desert landscape.

"Mission complete, then, Mr. Legnagyszerübb," he said evenly. "*I* killed Yearson. You didn't even have to do your stint over at Elm Ridge. You could have stayed in your office and completed your paperwork. Or," he added, with a hint of a smirk on his face, "you could go complete another course of work in Mexico."

"I belong in a school," said David. "I belong in this school—Maple Valley, the HRB's vocational high school. And my mission is—was—to make the school my own."

"Sorry," said the former English teacher, now standing on the loading dock. "Now I just need to go back in the building and obtain my primary objective, leave with her, and you'll be free to—do whatever it is you need to do."

Carter took a step forward. "Nina," he said. "You're recruiting Nina."

"Yes, boss," he replied. "I'm not in the business of mopping up tech projects from kids, projects that might just 'kind of' work. It's the talent that might help me spirit away such a tech project, even as an exercise, and sneak it back into the school, just as Nina's doing right now as we speak. Again—" he raised his palms in the air—"I won't wreak any more havoc on your school than I already have." He nodded in Nassir's direction. Nassir didn't flinch, but he continued to cradle his finger.

"And now you all want to run in there and get Nina and somehow convince her that to leave with me today would be some kind of moral failure or even suicide. I can assure you that it's neither. Just let my employers work with her skills. She'll get the development she needs and deserves."

"No," said Carter. "She's a student."

"Not anymore." And with that, he kicked the dumpster that had given him cover, though only Sarah could really see that his toe had made contact with an innocuous black plastic square below an angle in the green-painted iron.

The halves of the dumpster lid blew open, and showers of sodium pellets, pilfered from the chemistry lab, shot through the air, igniting randomly with flashes and whizzes that bridged the gap between a ten-dollar fireworks display and a random mortar shelling. Everyone but Carter covered their face. Sarah dove into the back corner of the loading dock next to an old rubber garbage can.

As the vaporized bits of metal and garbage floated above them, it was Sarah who first popped out of the corner of the loading dock, sprinting for the shattered door. The man with a seemingly inexhaustible array of tricks had disappeared, but the sound of footsteps on glass came from the school's back entryway. Sarah skidded briefly on the shattered glass but was soon down the hallway herself, racing to make sure the liar and the weapon did not disappear.

28 - Grad Rehearsal

Sarah was the first to leap through the starry, translucent emptiness of the shattered rear door. With that impossible deftness that had so impressed Dave earlier this year, she planted her sprinting feet directly on the cheap tile, bolting over the broken glass without slipping.

Nassir and Neve sprinted up the concrete stairway side by side, followed by David and Carter. The back loading dock was suddenly empty, with only shell casings and pulverized concrete bits left behind.

The pack of teachers hunting their former colleague knew how to approach this scenario. Normally the undercover English teacher would have a huge advantage: if he could outsprint his pursuers, any alcove or bathroom or even custodial closet that lay ajar could accommodate him long enough to evade detection. But here half the group—Carter and Nassir, who knew the building well—could fan out and check for hiding spots, while the other half—the now fully sprinting yellow skirt of Sarah and the equally collegiate-with-cheap-teacher-khaki sprint of David Legnagyszerübb, who could run fast but knew nothing of the building's layout—could try and run him down.

Despite the general low hum of lunchtime at Maple Valley, Sarah could hear his footsteps a hallway turn or two ahead of her; she thought she might even be able to detect the scrape of a piece of glass undoubtedly caught under his shoe, cutting into the linoleum floor. Right past the tech ed area, left in front of the gym, straight on past the windows that would temporarily blind them—

Was he headed toward the lunchroom area? Was that where the weapon was? Not that it mattered because if he decided to vaporize all of them, he could. Something told her that he was trained to follow through even if it cost him his life—but probably not if it cost Nina's. The focus of his whole mission here was now clear.

No, because if she was in the building, he wouldn't jeopardize her. So—why the lunchroom?

Just to her right, she could hear "the real" David Legnagyszerübb beginning to flag. Somehow, she didn't think it would matter once they got to the lunchroom.

The smell of mini corndogs hit her first as if her pumping heart could easily spread the delicious chemical around the body of anyone in a school building. But the din of the lunchroom had a different timbre to it. She had stopped right next to the garbage cans when she had a split second to see the room before the mob hit.

Half of the student body, apparently, was milling in the center of the commons in caps and gowns.

Graduation rehearsal, she realized with abject resignation as David skidded to a halt right next to her.

"Ay, it's Ms. Lehner, ask her!" came a shout about ten feet to her left, and then a choral response from the group to her right, and then—they were upon her, instantly manufacturing that same claustrophobia that any classroom teacher would recognize: the "too many questions right now" feeling.

Carter was now behind both of them, but before he could even scan the lunchroom, he was immediately neutralized by the mob.

"Principal Carter!" shouted one short girl, who was wearing lipstick and heels, both clearly for the first time. "I need to rent my cap and gown, but they say I have, like, three detentions!" Carter did not try to answer her, but she slowed him down long enough for both sides of the mob to flank him, and he was trapped. Sarah shouted out to him, but they were both now tiny neurons in the giant brain of the center of the school's nervous system—the cafeteria. And like any brain, it was uniquely ill-equipped to handle an invasion.

Ms. Lehner, Mr. Carter and the group had themselves facilitated the very defense that "Dave" required to escape with his protegé: not just a group of students in the lunchroom, but that peculiarly focused group that, after neglecting classwork, skipping labs and generally eschewing education for four straight years, was now hell-bent on the logistics of the ceremony to celebrate this achievement.

Sarah's hands were pressed with forms from two band girls who needed a signature guaranteeing that they'd returned cases and spit valves. The band girls, with pale hands adorned by deep turquoise and teal nails, did not ask Ms. Lehner why she had glass embedded in the back of her hand—embedded so acutely that almost no blood trickled out. No one questioned why she strained to look over the mob, why she would not make eye contact with anyone, why she seemed determined to push through the student mess.

That particular brand of egoism is so endemic to the high school senior that Sarah had to admire "Dave" for baiting them right into it. Who else would think to facilitate a shootout in the loading dock of a high school—and then escape so easily by running right into the middle of the school?

Carter, Sarah could see, had just given up on escaping the mob. A girl was trying to shove a battered textbook in his face, explaining that her "friend had borrowed it, for, like, some reason? In tenth grade? And just found it in her dad's car, and I was, like, hey, I have to go see Mr. Carter, I can give it to him to get my tickets for the ceremony because, like we haven't seen my aunt in a while? And—" At this point, the edge of the textbook was sinking into Carter's significant pectoral muscle.

Sarah looked up from the band girls to see someone she didn't recognize at first. He was noticeable in the din by how he wasn't stopped by the kids because he must not be a teacher here. Yet—

She sucked in a breath as David Legnagyszerübb easily sliced through the throng of kids, none of whom knew him. He made his way down the custodial hallway towards the loading dock and was out of sight as Sarah was handed a folder of makeup work from the previous quarter.

29 - Final Exam

David Legnagyszerübb's rear wheel skidded a few inches on the loose asphalt that was the staple of high school parking lots around the world, but he still twisted the throttle as far as it would go. The back of the building's loading dock was a mess of glass and concrete bits blown off the building by bullets, but he spotted the Civic immediately. He did not imagine that with the wealth of evidence in that vehicle—hair, sweat, probably more than a few false IDs with their faces on them—that they would be able to simply leave the car there. He pulled both brakes and slid next to the Civic, ready to wrest control of this situation back from… Dave. He called himself "Dave." David clenched his teeth.

The mysterious agent who had stolen David's job was now about to slip into the afternoon with the new face of superspydom, a talent to be developed and molded into an unstoppable young agent: a tenth-grader named Nina dos Santos Pandlay.

The ache he felt at this was physical, deep in his chest, extending all the way down to his lower intestine. People like David weren't subject to the same whims of career and fate that most people were. Had he ever run across a system he was unable to manipulate and crack?

In second grade, he had run out of lunch money. Asking his father for more was out of the question—not because they couldn't afford it, but because Roland Legnagyszerübb answered questions, requests, inquiries and requisitions exactly once. Anything else was met with stony silence and the slightest twitch of the blond, bushy mustache that David saw, unconsciously, as a shield.

But all it took was one glance into the lunchroom at the right time. Dolores, the lunch lady who wrote their names down in the book each day, punched the checks in the computer as kids brought them in and immediately asked for a single revision if necessary. "Sweet child," she would say, "can you please write your student ID number in the part that says 'Memo'?" The greeting—"sweet pea," "sweet potato," "sweet lamb"—changed, but the request did not.

Young David only missed lunch one day before digging through enough of his fellow second graders' bags. Almost everyone kept the lunch check folded in the small part of the backpack, and the second check he found did not have a student ID written in the memo. He added his own number to Owen Markee's check, and by the time Owen was addressed as "sweet thing" and told that he didn't have any money in his account the next day, young David was finding each of his illicitly acquired French toast sticks to be just a bit crispier, the syrup blanketing them to be just a bit sweeter.

From then on, the world seemed an open book. He was making a brisk trade buying and selling art class assignments in college—his bustling art gallery was stocked with the strangest pieces from the strangest misanthropes on campus—when a recruiter noticed his handiwork and offered him training with the Agency. When he packed all his possessions to leave home, he walked out the front door and told Roland Legnagyszerübb, who he would never see nor inquire as to the well-being of ever again, that he would be back in five minutes.

It was that mastery that made the bitter taste of being thwarted that much more acidic. It was that feeling—this was what *others* felt like when *he* had outmaneuvered *them*—that made his stomach hurt. Had his classmate's parents felt like this when they had to send another check? Had the guys at the warehouse in Durango felt it when they saw the muzzle flash and realized they had let the wrong guy in? It was this that caused him to creep towards the old yellow Civic, figuring how he would get the jump on "Dave" and Nina—how he would make them feel what he felt.

He heard a boot crunch in the glass, and he became motionless.

"David, you were able to slip out of the lunchroom because the kids didn't know you," he said with a laugh. "We're impressed."

Both Nina and her teacher stood there on the loading dock. But as soon as David stepped off the motorcycle towards the old Civic, "Dave's" face fell almost imperceptibly.

David took a slow-motion step forward and was surprised to hear an edge of panic in the super-agent's voice.

"David, you don't—"

Everything in his guts told him that he had to get to that Civic before the agent or Nina did. It was the only non-manufactured word David had heard him say. So David did not hesitate—he took off out of the blocks, at a dead sprint towards the car.

"Dave" and Nina didn't look at each other, but as they leaped through the air off the dock, David could see the realization on his usurper's face that he would be beaten in the foot race to the car. He did not slow himself in the last two feet, and through the pane, he spotted what he thought was the source of the agent's worry: a single file in the backseat. In that vivid moment, he even supposed he could see thumbprints on the slim beige folder. And he thought he understood the ill-concealed panic in the voice of his opponent—exposure. The envelope would unmask this usurper.

He beat them to the car with about five sprinting steps remaining, grabbed the door handle, and—

David Legnagyszerübb felt his fingers contract around the metal handle so hard as his shoulder and arm twisted, as if in sudden, spasmodic prayer. The next moment, he was on his back.

It seemed that all he could do was blink ferociously, with his entire eyebrow and lids, up at the sky from the ground. A hand came into frame above his head. It clicked something between its fingers, and David heard the unmistakable sound of a car window being rolled down.

An arm reached across the sky, through the car door window, and came back into view holding a folder silhouetted against the blue-white sky of late May. The first sensation returning to David was that of his right arm hurting, all the way from the shoulder to the fingertips. His body remembered every muscle contracting at once in full force as soon as the amperage from the electrified car handle had surged through that particular limb. But he still could not get up. A particularly sharp bit of gravel was eating into the back of his skull.

He closed his eyes and willed the shard to penetrate his skin, willed the pain to inflame his nerves, to make him alive. It—felt—no, he still couldn't move. The sun was a seamless candle melt of whites and yellows. *Move, dammit!*

He concentrated everything on that patch of his head, willing the gravel onto his nerves, into his nervous system. It worked, and he turned his head, his eyes moving slowly.

Nina and the agent were barrelling down the rear entry road of the building on David's heavy, black motorcycle.

"Dave" had taken his job, taken Nina, and now, the motorcycle.

She was driving, and even as they navigated the steel drainage covers buried in the asphalt, "Dave" leaned forward to speak to her, though David couldn't make out his words over the engine's roar.

He was still teaching her.

That lean—that teacher's lean, not self-conscious about proximity, not worried that he wouldn't be listened to—ignited David Legnagyszerübb's soul. The gravel piece had kept his mind somewhat based in reality, but the indignant anger that compressed his diaphragm right now—that got him, with an audible groan, on his side and with his head up.

He had taken David's place. But he would not take the student.

David stood up, his jaw still slack and arms at his sides: a poor-but-committed Frankenstein's monster impression. The nearest vehicle was the old yellow Civic, which had recently electrocuted him. But around the corner of the building, by the dock, a second-shift custodian had clearly just parked his big Suzuki bike there.

He eyed the motorcycle. Was it possible—?

Yes. The keys were in the ignition.

David thought this could very easily be another trap. But what more of a snare did he need? His "partners" were all stuck in the cafeteria, inundated by a wall of seniors asking grad questions. It was just him. And the sound of their escape bike's high, throaty roar was already beginning to dim in the distance. There would be no finding "Dave" if the two got out of earshot, and that Civic—well, who knew what other traps it might hold?

He hobbled closer. It was black with silver trim, an older behemoth with a giant four-cylinder engine, the pipes gleaming with midday sun as only motorcycle chrome can do. David took a sidestep, vomited to the side of the asphalt, and wiped his chin on his shoulder. He paused for half a beat, curled his fingers back, and touched the painted black frame with the back of his hand—no zap.

It took every neuron firing at full capacity for him to swing his leg over the seat of the bike, and he had to pull himself forward with his fingers. He turned the key in the ignition, and it roared to life.

He leaned to the side of the bike to retch again, but this time very little came out. Shouts from custodians beyond the shattered door of the loading dock demanded to know what could have possibly caused this god-awful mess.

Then, one of the custodians yelled at him, in school-inappropriate and certain terms, to dismount his motorcycle. So the bike was not a setup.

He pulled the throttle enough to lighten the front wheel, and roared out of the back parking lot over the grassy field where his imposter twin had, earlier, shot the gun out of his hand and then taken off with the student as his own.

David arrived at the corner and rocketed through the intersection. No way to track the characteristic whine of Nina and "Dave's" bike. But a hope popped into his brain: was this the time that "Dave" would teach her to ride the bike? She was gifted at learning new skills, but would he let his student do it?

He looked around the intersection—a typical suburban stoplight, with several coffee chains, a newer stucco pharmacy, a—

Two men were out of their cars in the pharmacy parking lot. One made a fishtail motion with his hand over the other hand's flat palm: the universal sign for describing a drunk or novice driver, especially a motorcyclist.

As soon as the man choreographed the motion of the bike taking off and indicating the direction, David gunned the engine, slipping into a turn lane before a giant black SUV and eating up the asphalt down the two-lane suburban thoroughfare.

The SUV faded behind him, and a median appeared between the lanes, planted with stick-straight trees. He accelerated past 80, cutting from lane to lane to increase his turning angle; as the engine pushed past 5000 rpm, he couldn't hope to hear anything. Yet he willed the bike forward, burned by the mad hate that can only come from being repeatedly beaten at the top of your game. He had to slide into the oncoming lane, past the trees, which made it appear as a moving picture—

There they were. She was in front, still a bit wobbly but clearly gaining control of the bike. He was still teaching.

Still stealing David's job.

He stayed in the opposite lane. A Jeep whizzed by in a near miss. Here he could get on the other side of the pair, down the bike, kill the imposter, and return the prodigy to her rightful school. She was smart. She'd understand how she'd been manipulated.

He once again bottomed the throttle cable out and could almost feel the gas pour into the engine. Every sensory input flooded his brain, and he could feel the tenacious nature of flying across the blacktop on two wheels: the sting of the air on his face, the insistent scream of the engine, the scattershot images that he unconsciously pieced together to determine a way—some safe-ish way—to go even faster.

He moved up, still in the wrong lane, with the trees still shielding him from their bike. Every intersection provided both a danger of being killed instantly and the opportunity to see where they were, to pierce together their pace and direction.

Another rearview mirror punctured the air five feet to his left. David saw them again through his squinting, teary eyes: they were closer, again. Another break, still closer; he could hear her downshift, and they were closer again—

Downshift? He barely had time to register this one final mistake.

She was two feet away from him, crossing into the opposite lane, and the man who had pretended to be a hapless new teacher was in the air and then he was putting one foot directly behind David and jamming the other leg into the foot peg behind him. David, helpless, somehow felt the bike right itself. And then he heard his enemy shout over the engines at the student.

"So that's key, Nina! See how I shove my *bottom* foot lower than the center of gravity to counteract me landing on *top* of the bike?"

Nina's helmet nodded.

"And now—"

David tried to reach for a weapon, a hand, or something, but could not move any of his four limbs.

"I'm not letting him brake by pushing that foot into the frame or the engine," he shouted. Just like any shop teacher, showing a kid how to use a miter saw safely or a track coach shouting instructions to a hurdler. "I can hold his wrist on the throttle because his hand's in the weaker position. And I can let him squeeze the clutch with his left hand. It'll make him feel like he's got some control, but I'm still driving."

Nina nodded. They'd both moved back into the right lanes. A conversion van passed on the left with barely a glance.

David jerked the handles, but "Dave" easily corrected them. The agent threw his head back in an attempted skull smash, missing so hard that the front suspension loosened nearly all the way.

"Dave" shouted again. "See how he tried the reverse header on me? That's why my head is always left or right, never behind."

Nina nodded again.

"Even on the bike! Or in a plane!"

She nodded again.

David was trying to pull the handlebars any which way since he couldn't brake or shift. But the agent behind him, locked as he was in this strange embrace, seemed to anticipate every swerve. The prairie grasses of the suburbs flew by as the teacher seemed to be finishing up his lesson.

"And now, Nina," he shouted, "you're done. And that means—"

David felt like he knew what was next. How would they finish? Probably head-on into a tree. He could roll out of that, maybe if he could—

"I'm done, too." She nodded again and gave a salute, her face safely shielded behind the helmet.

All at once she accelerated. "Dave" released David's throttle hand, and the bike grabbed back down to fourth gear as the engine roar died down. As soon as he had the handlebars in his grip, David heard a pop from the engine. The agent had popped the tank cover off. A roiling, brassy pool of liquid shimmered about a foot in front of his waist.

"No—" he said. He went to cover the open gas tank with his hand, but the nameless agent easily parried his wrist. The front tire of the bike locked up sideways, and they began to slide.

"Hey," said "Dave," over the squeal. "Remember that when two doppelgangers touch, the world ends."

And as the bike tipped, David saw the bright blue tip of the ignitor pushed into the tank before he heard the *whoosh* of air pulled into the explosion.

Epilogue

Nikita Udomratchaniwet spied a parking spot between two equally harmless sedans in the twelfth row of the parking lot, two rows behind the shiny blue plastic sign that read "Pineview Hills High School: Home of the Tapirs." The sign had no scuffs or dents in it, and the clean white lines of the parking lot indicated the same newness she'd seen as she drove by development after development on her way out to the suburbs that day. New navy-blue siding. New, squeaky playground equipment. New smooth asphalt. New lives in the new suburbs, the farm fields giving way to dusty excavation piles and, just as quickly, to new very-much-inside-the-box homes.

And new opportunities for Nikki as well. These developments needed teachers, and here she was, holding a shiny red folder in her hand as she strode across the parking lot. (She'd caught a look at herself in the mirror on the way out this morning, and the business-power leather bag had just been too much for a fresh young public-school science teacher, so she'd ditched it). The smart, perfectly in-time clicks of her heels seemed to be a result of a particular crispness of the asphalt on this, a particularly crisp—some might call it "chilly," but that was a word that would never come from Nikita Udomratchaniwet's mouth, as it implied a sort of silly weakness—Wednesday morning in July.

The clicks slowed only as she looked at her own face in a Civic's rearview mirror, packing anything else about her tightly down into that sleeping sack of memory, reminding herself what she was doing here. Whereas most nervous job interviewees might re-adjust eyebrows or makeup at this point, Nikki simply stared into her own eyes for a two-second count as if to remind herself who she was—that she was a force, a wall of poured concrete among a heap of soft slag.

And there was plenty of slag in here today. As she entered the glare-white entryway of the brand-new school, she saw plenty of hopeful teachers here: plenty of sweaty palms wiped on pants, plenty of tucked-in shirts about to free themselves, plenty of deep breaths and self-reminders that yes, you were made to teach.

Nikki did not cut in the line that was in front of the fold-out table. She simply stood ramrod straight, with her folder in front of her waist, almost like an afterthought, and suddenly she was at the table. It was as if all the mutts at the humane society were all waiting around for a bowl of food when suddenly the toughest dog was standing there, and the other pups just stared at the floor. Several minutes later, she's eaten all she wants, and then the other mutts fight each other for what's left.

Soon, the dog in front of her was looking around awkwardly through the foyer as if for a friend, and she was in front. She blasted the table and its occupants with a 6,000-watt smile. "I'm Nikita Udomratchaniwet, and I'm here for the science teacher interview." Others might phrase it as a question. She did not.

"Hi Nikita, I'm Ellen." She smiled. "I've got you down for a ten-thirty, looks like." Ellen, with ageless blond hair in a bob framing a round face, could have been twenty-four or fifty-two. Based on the way she was handing folders around the table and welcoming interviewees on this busy summer day, Ellen probably didn't have time to age.

"Thank you."

Nikita Udomratchaniwet moved over to the side of the brightly lit blue and white hallway. She held the folder in front of her and made it look as if she was going over interview questions in her head, tapping her toes in a brief staccato and perusing the list of All-Time Tapir State Qualifiers. The school, of course, was only a few years old but had already produced a few good hurdlers and a swimming relay or two. Again she tried to play the nervous interviewee the best she could—though if anyone could have gotten close enough to notice, there was no elevated heart or breathing rate.

Ellen came to get her and another interviewee, too—a Spanish teacher, it sounded like. "What a great opportunity for you young teachers to get your feet wet in a growing district like this!" said Ellen. She was carrying what appeared to be hot tea in one hand, and though that arm and hand also managed two folders and one clipboard, her other hand balanced a single two-foot stack of printed pages, not so much as a ripple crossed the surface of the tea.

Nikita Udomratchaniwet thought she knew why and nearly smiled as the Spanish interviewee prattled on that, yes, it was so exciting in a district willing to take a chance on young teachers. The Spanish teacher hunched into her interview room, like an eager kid going into a student council interview in the principal's office, and then shook hands with two women. One had a yellow skirt on, and—did she look past the Spanish interview, out at Nikki? Nikki's heart raced for a moment, but then she was back on track.

Ellen stood to the side of the well-lit hallway and gestured into the room, smiling. Nikki's interview room smelled of fresh paint and carpet, and the interview team looked hot out of the oven as well. She shook her concern over what she'd just seen out of her mind as the head of the table rose to meet her.

"Nikki, I'm Charles Nitti, AP here at Pineview High," said the captain of the interview. Nikki liked how he didn't try to smile too much. He looked to be about twenty-nine years old, with a single gray hair above his left ear, as if it were added to make him look believably old enough to be an administrator.

Mr. Nitti went around and introduced everyone. Soon they were lobbing questions, and she was sending the answers so far over the fence that—well, it was easy. She made a comment about peer review among students that was funny for anyone who'd ever tried to get students to evaluate each other's work, but it wasn't mean or degrading to the practice. She felt herself sharpen as they went through the stock questions, and before she knew it, she was the one lobbing the questions in the softball do-you-have-any-questions-for-us part of the show.

Her interviewers, too, hit it out of the park, and soon she was shaking hands and trying to convey how utterly excited she was to hear from you, thank you for the opportunity, thank you so much. Charles Nitti, who seemed unflappable, also let a hint of a genuine smile on his face—really, truly, nice job, and thank you for coming in, and expect a call from us.

Then it was back to Ellen, who managed to double-check her contact information while handing packets of interview questions to Mr. Nitti and directing two more interviewees who had come in. In fact, there seemed to be a pile of new recruits in front of the foldout table right now—and out of nowhere was Ellen, directing her exit.

"You can get out to the parking lot, Ms. Udomratchaniwet, a lot easier by following that set of stairs right there, and then the exit sign's just there, across from the locker rooms," she said, one of her Shiva arms pointing the way.

"Thank you so much," she responded. It did not matter how little you needed the advice—when the Ellen of your school pointed your way out, that's the way you went.

And so Nikki Udomratchaniwet strode briskly down the clean, beige floor to a slightly worse-lit small set of stairs. The natural light was a bit more prevalent here than the bright fluorescents of the main area, and her guard went up slightly. Rather than holding the folder in front of her, she now gripped it in her hanging left hand, like a butcher holding a knife.

The stairs did indicate an exit, but it was down another hallway. Only natural light here now, as all the other lights, normally motion-activated, were probably set to off for the summer. The din of the entryway faded behind her. Now, her guard was fully up, but despite her rigorous training, she still tensed a bit when she heard her name:

"Nina."

She turned too quickly, and a flash of a leg from a yellow skirt hit her shoulder. By the time she had rebalanced to counterstrike, that skirt was up in the air close to her face, and the leg was levered in between her back and her arm. She dropped to one knee. With her arm pinned behind her, it was done.

Ms. Lehner's voice had not changed. It still had that edge that she remembered from a hallway encounter or two in high school.

"Did you recognize me in the hallway before your interview, Nina?"

She paused. There was no point in lying. "Yes, Ms. Lehner."

Sarah, too, seemed to realize the futility of holding her there, so she bent her knee and hopped backward. They faced each other.

"Are you trying to get a job here for the same reason he did? To take over the program? Take our best student? Screw everything up and not tell us anything?"

Nina paused. Again, no reason to lie.

"He actually hasn't, like, told me—" She stopped herself. "He hasn't shared the main objective first, with me or the rest of the team. Getting the job was the first step."

Sarah didn't hesitate. "'He'?"

"Yes. And yes, he's alive." Now, it was her turn to give a knowing smile. "And he says 'hi.'"

Nina dos Santos Pandlay, now Nikki Udomratchaniwet, threw the folder like a playing-card trickster, end over end. It glanced off the ducking head of Sarah Lehner, music teacher. Now it was Nina's turn to jump and control Sarah's arm with the leg wedge—but when Sarah bent towards the floor, Nina threw her over her shoulder. The air flew out of Sarah's lungs with a *whoomp*, and her eyes fluttered in her head.

Nina bent down and picked up her red folder. "I look forward to working with you here at Pineview," she said as she turned down the hallway. "Together, we're going to give kids the transformative education they deserve."

She pushed the long metal handle of the door, stepping out into a chilly July day.

Acknowledgements

Thank you to Emilio deGrazia; his wholesale removal of semicolons (and parenthetical asides), as well as commas, made this a better book. In all seriousness, any narrative efficiency or clarity you encountered in this book is thanks to Emilio.

Thank you to Ian Graham Leask for taking a chance on a new author and a new book.

Thank you to all the educators and friends at Shakopee High School, especially my fellow English teachers—please never miss an opportunity for a "You are pulling down Heaven!" reference. And thanks to Jim Murphy and Barb McNulty, who took a chance on a young Language Arts applicant all those years ago.

Thank you to Mom and Dad for the love, support, lotto tickets, and soup every step of the way. Momasan, I miss you every day. I think you'd be proud of this (I mean, there's almost no swearing!)

Thanks to Theo Katzmann, Woody Goss, Joe Dart, Zack Stratton, Antwuan Stanley, Joey Dosik and Cory Wong for their instrumental support.

The biggest thanks go to Dib, Sweet Pea, C-Buddy and Book the Book. I love you. Thanks for being a reading family, thanks for going to bed early, and thanks for every bit of encouragement from that Saturday at Sever's Corn Festival to right now. This is for you. Mwah!

About the Author

Wade Laughlin grew up in the Midway neighborhood of St. Paul, MN. In fourth grade, he wrote a story about a pumpkin who made mysterious phone calls to neighborhood kids around Halloween. He read it aloud to Mrs. Portland's class at Hancock Elementary, and criticism from his classmates was copious and rather pointed: they didn't "get it."

Thirty years later, he was working as an English teacher at Shakopee High School when he decided to become an author by writing 500 words a day. The idea came to him while he was reading Harry Potter with his son: wouldn't it be interesting if any of the Hogwarts instructors didn't realize they'd been hired at a magic school? Two years after he'd started the novel, Calumet Editions said they "got it", and one of Wade Laughlin's life goals was achieved.